THE RIVER OF FIRE

THE RIVERS OF HELL 1

LIANA VALERIAN

Cover art and design by Shaunie Anne Schoonejans.

CIP - Kataložni zapis o publikaciji

Narodna in univerzitetna knjižnica, Ljubljana

821.163.6-312.9

821.111-312.9

VALERIAN, Liana

The river of fire : the rivers of hell 1 / Liana Valerian ; [illustrations by Dana
Kodermac and Shaunie Anne Schoonejans]. - Brežice : self-published L. Valerian,
2024. - (The Rivers of Hell ; 1)

978-961-07-2422-3

COBISS.SI-ID 215032835

*To those who choose their own destiny
despite the expectations of others.*

*May you always keep your humor pinned to
your courage for all the challenges you face.*

CONTENT INFORMATION

The River of Fire is full of action and spice. Not to be confused with each other. I mean, swords swing but there's also swinging swords... you know what, just read the trigger warnings on my website www.lianavalerian.com.

CONTENTS

GLOSSARY

Abaddon: Fortress in Purgatory.

Aim: Demon lord; Ashtaroth's general, spy, and assassin.

Akira: Member of the Elioud academy.

Angel: A winged being created by God and residing in Heaven. Most often tasked with relaying messages between God and humans, or acting as spiritual guides.

Archangel: The strongest of the angels, presiding at the top of the celestial hierarchy.

Archdemon: The strongest of the demons. They are at the top of the demonic hierarchy and have their own courts within the realms of Hell.

Ashtaroth: An archdemon known for his wisdom and command over legions.

Asmodai/Asmodeus: A powerful archdemon, often associated with lust and wrath.

Belial: An archdemon representing corruption and lawlessness.

Belias: Demon lord, Ashtaroth's war general.

Cambion: Humans with demonic ancestry.

Celestials: Generalized term referring to beings God created in the Heavens.

Corson: Fallen angel residing in Abaddon.

Daniel: Fallen angel residing in Abaddon.

Demon: Malevolent, evil beings that reside within the realms of Hell. Many are the offspring of fallen angels who embraced evil and have devolved into myriad iterations over the centuries.

Elioud: Generalized term for all beings with half-human/half-Celestial ancestry.

Fallen angel/the Fallen: Overarching term for all angels who have fallen from grace and reside in the realms of Hell.

Heaven: Home of God, angels, and the spirits of the dead who were pious and pure. Located above the earth.

Hell: The realms below the earth where souls of the dead who were wicked in life are sent to be eternally punished by the Devil and demons. Composed of multiple territories.

The Lethe: One of the rivers that flow through Hell. Drinking from it erases all memories.

Maalik: Fallen angel residing in Abaddon.

Naamah: Niece of Ashtaroth and daughter of Asmodai. A Lust demon, also called a succubus.

Nephilim: Humans with angelic ancestry.

Nephalem: Humans with both angelic and demonic ancestry.

The Phlegethon: A flaming river that flows through the territories of Hell.

Purgatory: A borderland between Heaven and Hell. Also known as Limbo. Souls can seek redemption for their sins and ascend to Heaven, or embrace their sins and descend to Hell.

Ramel: Fallen angel residing in Abaddon.

Saraqael: Archangel.

Sariel: Fallen angel who embraced evil. Adopted son of Ashtaroth.

PRONUNCIATION

Abaddon: ah-BAH-don

Aim: AYM

Armaros: AR-mah-ros

Ashtaroth: ASH-ta-roth

Asmodeus: az-MOH-dee-us **/ Asmodai:** AZ-mo-dye

Azeal: AH-zeel

Belial: BEE-lee-al

Belias: BEE-lee-as

Cambion: KAM-bee-on

Corson: KOR-sun

Elioud: EL-ee-oud

The Lethe: LEE-thee

Maalik: MAH-lik

Naamah: NAH-ah-mah

Nephilim: NEF-i-lim

Nephalem: NEF-ah-lem

The Phlegethon: FLEH-geh-thon

Puck: PUHK

Purgatory: PUR-guh-tor-ee

Ramel: RAH-mel

Saraqael: sah-RAH-kay-el

Liana Valerian

Sariel: SAH-ree-el

PLAYLIST

Eurielle – *City of the Dead*

April Jai – *Morally Grey*

Tommee Profit, Fleurie – *Soldier*

SVRCINA – *Who Are You*

In This Moment – *The In-Between*

ZHU, BANKS, bludnymph – *Praise*

Epica – *The Quantum Enigma*

Cloudy June – *FU In My Head*

Dark Tranquillity – *Her Silent Language*

Stevie Howie – *stalker*

Madalen Duke – *How Villains Are Made*

Chloe Adams – *Dirty Thoughts*

Sleep Token – *Sugar*

Nightwish – *The Phantom Of The Opera*

Nine Inch Nails – *Closer*

Enigma – *Voyageur*

In This Moment feat. Rob Halford – *Black Wedding*

Bryce Savage – *Demons*

Kerli – *Savages*

Bryce Savage – *Easy to Love*

Dark Sarah, JP Leppäluoto – *Dance With the Dragon*

Soap&Skin – *Me and the Devil*

Diggy Graves – *Straightjackets & Roses*

Bad Omens, Poppy – *V.A.N.*

Florence + The Machine – *Seven Devils*

Siddharta – *Rave*

bludnymph – *Lights Out*

Anette Olzon – *Rapture*

Ghost – *Year Zero*

System of a Down – *Aerials*

Epica – *Twilight Reverie*

In This Moment – *Into Dust*

In Flames – *End of Transmission*

Kiki Rockwell – *Cup Runneth Over*

Therion – *Litany Of The Fallen*

Billie Eilish – *you should see me in a crown*

MAP

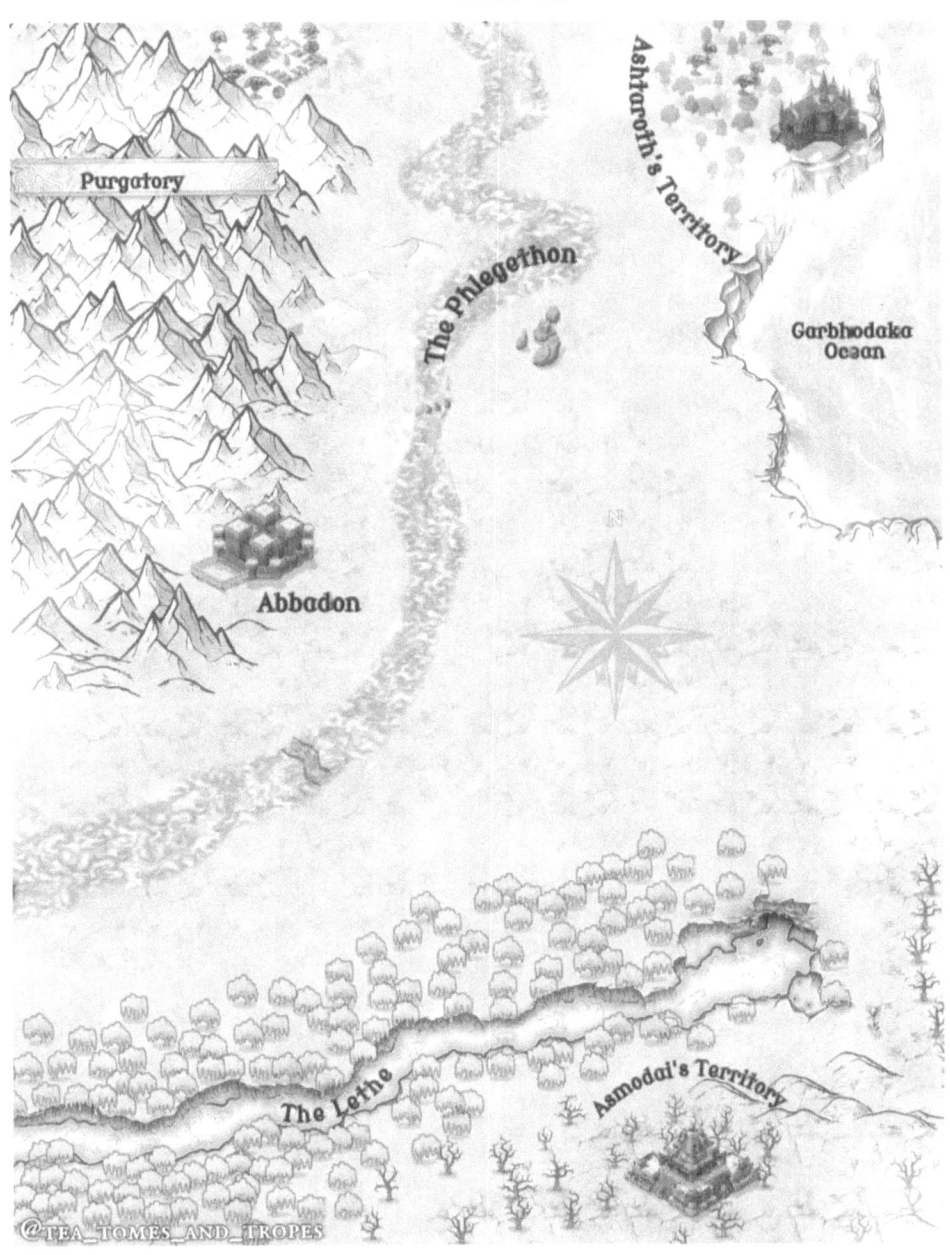

LIANA VALERIAN

PROLOGUE – ASHTAROTH

We have discussed this several times, Belial." If the disinterested tone of my voice does not convey my boredom, the way I lounge in my seat, head resting on a fist, surely must. The archdemon in question faces me and his expression becomes pinched, lips thinned. While we have had no major conflicts these last millennia, Belial is well aware that the pool which is my tolerance is shallow indeed. His ingratiating manner depletes it quickly.

Belial lifts his arms in question, an ancient dramatic peacock. "I have been warning this Council for decades. What has to happen for us to act? A total loss of control over the human realm?" He tilts his head as if waiting for me to dig myself into a hole. Imbecile.

I release my breath in a sigh, lifting my head to have a better view of my fellow councilors. We meet on neutral ground, a cavernous space deep in the mountains of Purgatory. Naturally, Heaven and Hell are seated on opposing sides of the underground amphitheater-like structure. Only a few on the demonic side show some interest in Belial's plight. Asmodai winks at me, eyes twinkling. I look at Heaven's delegation next. Angels are harder to read, their expressions perpetually blank, but I imagine the news of manifested damned souls killing humans vexes them somewhat.

"What is Hell doing to prevent rifts remaining open between Hell and the human lands? If there are no rifts, there are no avenues for damned souls to escape through." The archangel Saraqael's powerful voice rumbles through the cavern. A contemporary of mine, Saraqael has a legendary stick up his tightly clenched asshole.

Belial shakes his head and the blonde ringlets of his mortal form bounce like released jack-in-the-boxes. "We all know rifts are notoriously hard to find. That isn't the solution here. We need to diminish the number of these manifestations so Hell isn't bursting at the seams."

Asmodai snorts, drawing all our gazes. "Perhaps we should implore the Transcendent and our Lord and Savior to finally increase the size of Hell? It's been the same size since humans plowed their first fields." My adopted brother's lips stretch into a wicked grin. "And we plowed our first humans."

Predictably, laughter erupts on our side and even I crack a smile. I have always preferred not to dally with humans, even before I was confined in the Underworld. They are too... fragile.

The other side, however, is less amused.

"Blasphemy!"

I am not certain which angel made their displeasure known, as the outcry only fueled the demons' hilarity.

"Be quiet!" Belial's anger at our insouciance shows in the way he loses control over his form. Horns now poke out of the mop of angelic curls and his eyes are no longer cornflower blue, but instead glowing a fiery orange. He never was very contained, though he tries hard to hide his demonic traits from the angels. "This is no time for jokes. If humans witness escaped denizens of Hell, they will destroy each other in the resulting chaos. Do you want to experience starvation, Asmodai?"

While Belial does have a flair for the dramatic, he is not lying. The majority of us seated on this side of the demarcation between Heaven and Hell once gained nourishment from Elysium. No longer welcome to partake there, we now feed on the power generated by sins. Humans, now numerous enough that the shedding of their mortal forms chokes Hell with overpopulation, are also its best source of food.

I lift my chin at Belial, resuming the pertinent conversation. "You wish to bring half-mortal offspring to Hell to assist with the numbers? They would be eaten within hours."

"Not Hell." Belial points at the ceiling.

"Purgatory?" Saraqael sounds almost intrigued. As intrigued as an emotionless mannequin can be.

"The Fallen of Abaddon have been culling the numbers alone for decades now. They would welcome assistance."

"That's debatable," Asmodai murmurs, then raises his voice enough to be heard throughout the amphitheater. "Who would train them? The Elioud in the human realm are as powerless as any other mortal. Heaven made sure of that."

"Maalik of the Fallen spent time in my army. He is a capable warrior and leader. Since the offspring of Celestials aren't welcome in Heaven, Purgatory is as close to a neutral party in the Underworld as we can conceive of."

Belial's reply is quick and succinct. It is almost as if he had the answer ready, like a loaded cannonball waiting to be unleashed. He has been prattling about the dangers of Hell's overpopulation for years now, but it is obvious he had every step of what he sees as a solution planned.

"How many would you bring?" The angel inquiring is young – too young for me to have known him in Heaven and too insignificant to have bothered to learn his name since.

Belial still has munitions at the ready. "There are a few dozen physically appropriate Elioud with very few social attachments alive now."

The angel ponders for a moment. "And how will taking dozens of mortals risk exposure less than these sporadic attacks from Hell?"

"There are enough fallen angels in Abaddon to observe the suitable Elioud, then prepare and execute a simultaneous, stealthy extraction."

I scoff, making the archdemon turn towards me, jaw tight.

"And you think these mortals will want to help after being abducted into Hell?"

"Ashtaroth is correct, Belial." Saraqael shakes his head. "They may not have many attachments in the human realm, but their lives there are surely preferable to venturing into Hell, culling the ranks of mortal souls given form, and any ravenous demonic minions they meet while doing so."

Belial's expression turns bashful and I wonder if I am the only one who is repulsed by his artificial countenance. We did not rebel all those eons ago to pretend we are something we are not when Heaven observes.

"Unfortunately, they won't have a choice. We'll have to impart the importance of their mission. Make them see it as their purpose."

The air buzzes with noise as the assembled members each start voicing their conflicting opinions, but my attention is on Asmodai, who leans in with a mischievous smirk. "Mortals in Hell. It's been so long since I got to play with any." He pouts, and though he is thousands of years old, he now looks like the young Celestial I took under my wing when Lilith and Samael proved to have not a single parental bone between them. "No one summons me out of here anymore."

I huff and raise my brows in warning. "Be careful. Your cock gets you in trouble enough without mortals loose in Hell."

My brother waves a hand in dismissal. "Eh. What's Heaven going to do to me if I stoke the lust of an Elioud or two?"

I shake my head and focus on the discussion again. It looks like Belial will finally fulfill his desire to be the initiator of a momentous decision within the Council.

CHAPTER 1 – LANA

Beer foam tickles my lips as I drink. My best friend, Mike, prattles on, and I catch about a third of his words. The ambient lighting is low, there's acoustic music playing, but instead of paying attention to what my friend is telling me, my gaze is drawn to the neighboring table, more specifically to the toupee gracing the head of the middle-aged man sitting at it. He's talking animatedly to the younger woman at the table across from him and with each wild gesture, said toupee bobs up and down, shifting his clearly non-existent hairline. By the look of barely concealed disgust on the woman's attractive face, this is a first date and Tim/Bob/Chad used old pictures on his Tinder profile. It probably also claimed that he's thirty.

"Are you even listening to me?" Mike drums his fingers on the table and his nails make rhythmic clacking sounds loud enough to hear over the music. He's used to my fickle attention span and the fact that I'd rather be doing pretty much anything than sitting in the crowded bars he drags me to. He tracks my gaze and laughs under his breath. "You clearly need another hobby, Lana. You're too easily amused."

"What? I read and I know things. And my taekwondo class is the most I'm willing to subject myself to people outside of my job; you know this. And yet, you insist on dragging me to happy hour, which inevitably always leads to an unhappy hour sometime around midnight."

"You need to go out." Mike levels a stern look at me and my stomach clenches. I know I'm being a shut-in. "You're a late-twenties single woman unwilling to socialize, you teach history, of all the possible boring subjects, and you live alone in a one-bedroom apartment." His expression changes to a comical look of fear and I exhale. He hasn't given up on me yet. "You're a walking crazy cat lady starter pack."

I let out a relieved chuckle as the last of the tension leaves my body. "Don't you, I don't know, need at least one cat to be labeled that? And I'm already a walking cliché, having a gay best friend; I don't need cat fur on my clothes."

"Semantics," he replies with a smile on that dear, dear face. If he didn't love dick more than I did, we'd be married by now and he wouldn't be concerned. Alas, I'm probably going to worry him until we're old and gray. According to Mike, he's had some good dick. All the dick I've had was the disappointing kind, and I'm tired of even trying.

"Let's get out of here," I say and drain the last dregs of my beer. "I have a lecture to prepare for and I've been putting it off by reading a book series that has me by the metaphorical balls."

"Vampires?" he asks, side-eyeing me with narrowed eyes. He knows of my love for anything lore and mythology.

"Dragon shifters," I reply, waggling my eyebrows.

He snorts, the sound way too cute for an adult male, and looks up at the heavens. Or, I guess, the ceiling. Following his gaze, I see that it could actually use a fresh coat of paint.

"You're hopeless," he says once his gaze meets mine again, "but I love you anyway."

He settles the tab – feeding a book addiction is an expensive business – and we walk out of the stuffy bar. I drag in a deep breath of fresh air.

"See you tomorrow for our movie night?" I ask Mike and he nods. I met Mike a few months after I moved into this city. He was signing up for a self-defense class at the studio where I chose to continue my taekwondo training. We've had a standing movie night date since.

22

"Are you sure you're okay walking home?"

"You ask me the same thing every time and every time I give the same answer: I live a couple of blocks away. I have a martial arts black belt. I'm probably safer than you are, twinkypoo." I wink at him and try to keep the smile from sliding off my face. In truth, I've been a bit spooked lately.

Sometimes I feel like I'm being watched. At school, when I stay late grading papers, or when I'm walking towards the bus station early in the morning. It's not that I see or hear anything, I just get the sense that I'm not alone. "I'll be fine," I add, both to reassure Mike and myself.

"Famous last words," he says with a pinched expression.

"Shut up and let me go home, worrywart."

I give him a quick hug and turn in the direction of my building. It's late and the streets are empty – I can see why he was worried. Heck, maybe I should have escorted him home and kept *him* safe. He's the only person who bothers to drag me out of my shell. Without him, I'd just be working and reading. I give the night a sad sigh. I need to stop going down this spiral or I'll start crying. I must not think of the pathetic contribution I have made to this world so far. Maybe I *should* get a cat?

A flicker in the corner of my vision makes me turn my head toward the alleyway I'm passing by. Standing at the end is a tall man – judging by the build, at least – in a long gray cloak. The hood is up and there's a white mask on his face. That's all I can see from this distance and I don't want to see more. Masked stalkers are hot in a romance novel, not in real life.

I turn my face back toward home and speed up my steps.

Next thing I know, my nose is slamming painfully into a hard surface and I'm surrounded by the smell of... fire? I look up to see the cloaked stranger.

"How —" escapes my mouth before the man slides behind me with a speed my logical mind cannot comprehend. How was he in the alley one moment and in front of me the next?

I start screaming, but too late — a gloved hand covers my mouth as the stranger walks back into the alley, pulling me along.

I'm pretty sure it's curtain time for me. I wish I'd gone home with the skinny accountant who flirted with me at the bar the other week; at least then I wouldn't have died with cobwebs clinging to my privates.

Yes, my priorities are certainly out of whack.

On the brick walls on each side of us, red flickers of light are reflected from something behind the brute still dragging my struggling body. It's the same flickers that captured my attention in the first place. I now wish I was colorblind and just kept my nose pointing forward. Maybe then I'd be just a minute away from the dubious safety of my too-thin apartment door.

The red light gets brighter but at the same time the world around me darkens. What in the unholy fuck is going on right now? I'm still screaming into the masked stranger's hand, trying to bite through the leather glove and hurt him enough to let my mouth go. Only muffled sounds come through and my teeth are ineffective. There's pressure in my head and my ears feel like I'm on a rapidly descending plane, as if I need to yawn and let my ears pop. Fear twists a knife in my belly and tears leak out of my eyes.

A moment later the pressure disappears, but my head still feels like he reached in and stuffed cotton swabs where my brain once was.

The blackness dissipates and I see stone walls. Not brick, but giant blocks of dusty stone, the kind Mike and I saw in that abandoned medieval village we visited last summer. It's dark, lit up only by the torch that is now somehow in my abductor's hand. He pushes me forward and in my shock, I take two steps down the hallway.

"Welcome to Purgatory, half-blood," the giant says, his voice so deep it's made for Barry White songs.

Half what, though? And where?

"Purgatory?" I ask, still stunned, snippets from the theology-centered parts of my history studies coming back to me. He has to be kidding. This is probably some underground goth nightclub hidden in the alleyway near my home, and my attention made him think I was interested in a night with women in corsets and men with black nail polish. Oh, and can't forget the guyliner.

"Think of it as the anteroom to Hell," he says, pushing the cloak back and revealing his head. I know he's grinning because I can hear it in his deep raspy voice, and the next moment he takes his mask off, revealing a handsome dark-skinned face. A face with glowing eyes of a golden yellow. Eyes with slit pupils. "Or you can think of it as home," my abductor adds.

No. I don't think I'm in Kansas anymore.

LIANA VALERIAN

CHAPTER 2 – LANA

I walk in front of the stranger who cheerfully introduced himself as Maalik, like he didn't just kidnap me, feeling numb and spacey. Am I having a psychotic break? Was there a gas leak? Is this a bad trip?

We walk past heavy wooden doors, but he keeps herding me forward. I can hear voices, scared and confused. The hallway finally opens into a large atrium. The area is full of frightened people, their arms wrapped around themselves in comfort and their eyes wide, their ages ranging from late teens to mid-forties. Next, I notice the sky. Its strangeness does a better job of convincing me I'm not exactly somewhere... normal. Its color is a deep indigo and there are swirls of red coiling slowly, like a fucked up evil Aurora.

"I want to go home," I say numbly, the embodiment of every horror movie cliché. I know my demand will be ignored even before Maalik walks ahead of me to the group of people staring at him.

There are dozens of confused individuals giving him a doe-in-headlights look. A girl is puking her guts out, the people nearby giving her a wide berth. The sour smell of bile reaches me and my stomach protests. An older man on the other side is practically incoherent with panic and a woman with similar features tries desperately to calm him down so he stops attracting attention. Despite feeling like I may start bawling or throwing up at any moment as well, I feel an urge to comfort him myself.

"Let me repeat what you've been told as you were brought here today," Maalik speaks in a voice that easily carries in the wide space. "You're in the fortress of Abaddon," he begins, leisurely walking among the gathered. "This realm is also known as Purgatory." An

Asian boy with pink streaks in his white hair tries to dart toward one of the archways and Maalik easily grabs him by the neck of his hoodie. "No, I am not human," he continues, with a shit-eating grin on his face, clearly enjoying the gasps his statement evoked. He releases the boy, who is now frozen with fear. "No, I won't kill you, though I cannot say the same for most of the occupants of this realm." This elicits whimpers from the crowd he's now meandering among like a lazy lion. "And my name is Maalik." He stops in the middle and raises his hands like a benevolent saint. "But you can call me 'yes, sir'," he finishes and looks around with malice in those snake-like eyes and a predatory grin still plastered in its place.

I notice then that more men in cloaks and armor are standing by the arches around the atrium. I have a feeling they've been there the entire time and I just haven't registered them until now. Some look bored, some look curious, and some look like we're the dog shit they stepped in with their new Ferragamo shoes.

"You are here," Maalik continues, "as a last attempt to save your pathetic, sin-riddled world from," he shrugs, "well, yourselves. You see, with how humans are multiplying like rabbits in your mortal realm, so does sin. And where do sinners go?" he asks, looking around as if in search of an answer to his rhetorical question.

"To Hell?" a serious young man who can't be much over twenty asks.

"To Hell," Maalik confirms. "Which is now bursting at the seams like your Thanksgiving turkeys."

I guess they must have cable TV here. His speech is an odd mix of modern phrases with the stuffy vocabulary of old lords. Or priests, ironically enough.

"Why are we here?" a hard looking, red-haired woman asks.

"Why, to cull the ranks, of course." He once again grins as if delighted.

"How are we meant to do something you can't?" I ask, surprising myself with my bravery.

"Excellent question. While you would not have noticed in the mortal realm, you have Celestial blood in your veins. Meaning you can, when properly trained, take on these manifestations of the sin your kind begot."

Celestial blood? What does that even mean? Is that why he called me a half-blood?

I don't have to inquire further because Maalik continues with his evil villain speech. "Your mommies or daddies or more likely great-grandparents had demonic or angelic blood."

"What?" I ask numbly.

He looks at me with a suddenly serious expression. "You, specifically, had an angelic grandmother and demonic grandfather on your mother's side. A highly unlikely combination you are, offspring of Nephalem."

"Nephilim?" I ask, confused. Isn't that the offspring of angels and humans? How surreal is it that I'm even thinking about these terms as an actual possibility?

"No, not a Nephilim or Cambion. The word for your particular combination is Nephalem. The common word is Elioud."

"Elioud?" I sound like a parrot, but in all of my studies of lore, I've never heard that word.

"All iterations of Celestial-human descendants."

Everyone is looking at the faces around them, not knowing how to voice their denials. The men standing near the entrances to the atrium still haven't spoken a word. And my curiosity might have been the end of me – If the end wasn't already looming so obviously.

"And you?" I ask, "What are you? Why aren't you taking care of this threat from your realm, if it's out of control?"

"We are The Fallen," says a blond, slimmer... Fallen? He steps forward and I register him as one of the few newcomers that were curious about us gathered here. "We fell from grace but repented and did not give into evil. We are free to walk among Purgatory and

Hell, and even the mortal realm, but we are denied Elysium," he continues, his head downcast. "And there are not enough of us to corral the manifestations made from corrupt human souls. They are breaching into the human realm. The archdemons and demon lords do not much care for the mortal world."

Great, more myths come to life.

"Do we have a choice?" the solem-faced young man who spoke earlier asks.

"No," says one of the disinterested Fallen with finality. "You do not."

"We will teach you to fight the manifestations," Maalik picks up again, "and also the demonic creatures you will encounter while carrying out your duty. You will be given quarters, train, and live here. This is your final destination, after all."

"What do you mean?" the angry red-headed woman asks.

"There is no Heaven for Nephilim, nor for Cambion or other combinations of Elioud, of course," Maalik says the latter to me.

"Regardless of how we live our life?" I ask. Surely that has to mean something?

"Regardless. We all share the same fate, some by action, and some as a birthright."

I sit down on one of the two steps encompassing the atrium. I lean my head onto my hands and try to come to terms with this new reality, a part of me stubbornly hoping that this is all just a bad dream. A consequence of too much cheap beer.

A few of the humans are now shouting their refusal, making a couple of the Fallen sneer at them.

"My name is Daniel," the blond says to me and the few others who are calm enough to listen. "You will be shown to your quarters. Then we will meet here once you rest and come to terms with your fate. There is no sunlight here; you will all have to abide by the same sleeping schedules while in training. We will divide you into teams based on your aptitude with close-quarter weapons, ranged weapons, and skills with the ether."

"The ether?" I mumble into my hands, feeling too overwhelmed to lift my head. I want to cry and scream like some of the rest, but this feels too goddamn final.

"The power you wield over matter, which will manifest itself now that you are in this realm," he answers, not unkindly. He seems to be more capable of empathy and takes less enjoyment in our despair than Maalik.

"I expect a couple of years of training will be needed for these sad lumps of clay," one of the more savage-looking Fallen mocks.

Daniel gives him a reproachful look. "The Council chose you as one of the trainers, Ramel. If it takes years or not will be up to you."

"What's this council?" I ask Daniel, trying to gather some useful information and keep myself busy before I have a public emotional breakdown.

"The Celestials, both angels and demons, agree upon one thing, if nothing else. The mortal realm must remain in blissful ignorance of the fact that we can walk among them." He's looking down at my seated form with compassion.

"But why do the demons care? I get that angels are protecting the *children of God*," I say, putting dramatic emphasis on the last part, "but I can't see the demons giving a damn either way if they're anything like mythology claims."

"There are mindless demons, who live only to rip into the flesh of mortals, not having the capacity to even think of the consequences of decimating their food source. Hell, however, is led by ancient archdemons; fallen angels from eons ago, as Sataniel was himself, or their progeny."

A hysterical male voice sounds in the crowd. "This s just a nightmare. I'm going to wake up. Wake up. Wake up. Wake up!"

I shiver as the man's scream turns into whimpers and think of the blonde angel's words, of the mind-altering fact that the information I poured over during sleepless nights is not just a myth. There are creatures of fathomless age walking the realm just beyond this one, and I will be sharing air with them sooner or later. Is there air in Hell? I hope there is.

"Will they kill us?" I ask, and Daniel hesitates. I don't like that hesitation one bit. The absence of sound echoed like a death knell.

"Some are on the Celestial council and agreed to this measure. Some are so old, that they do not even deign to acknowledge the world beyond the areas they govern. They should have been apprised of your presence and understand the need for it. Unfortunately, no one can vouch that they will place any measure of value on your lives."

He's honest and straightforward, though clearly choosing his words carefully. I'm sure the translation is: 'They'll squash you like bugs for a second of entertainment'.

"How do we fight them then?" I ask, intuiting the answer before he even raises his brows to reply: "You do not."

Great. I rub my forehead and eyes, feeling like my head is too full of life-altering information, but still plagued by curiosity. Knowledge is a weapon, and I'm going to need every weapon I can get my hands on.

Seeing this, Daniel says softly, "You should rest. There will be time enough to ask questions. We do not plan on pushing you out the door into Hell tomorrow, unprepared."

Did I ruminate over my life not having purpose less than an hour ago? Be careful what you wish for. Mike clearly jinxed me with his 'famous last words' thing.

Mike... I may never see him again. Anguish gathers under my ribcage, the weight of a semi smothering my breath, my heart writhing under the merciless pressure.

I look around at the dejected faces and those of angry denial. Most of these people likely have loved ones: parents, children, partners. Jobs they are good at, hobbies they enjoy. If what these men said is true, we will all need to come to terms with an unpleasant fact. By staying here, we can help keep the people we love safe from a threat they don't even know about.

LIANA VALERIAN

CHAPTER 3 – LANA

As certain as I was that I wouldn't sleep at all, the insanity of last night left me feeling exhausted and heavy. I fell asleep as soon as I lay on the bed in the room Daniel brought me to, and dreamt of the fiery pits of doom.

The room I'm in is Spartan, with only a sturdy bed and dresser – no windows. My bladder leads me to the small bathroom, which has a toilet and a bathtub, though neither are the modern appliances I'm used to. There is plumbing, though. I'm taken aback for a moment until I consider the fact that Ancient Rome had plumbing. I'm not going to even try to riddle out the answer as to where the water comes from.

Once I finish using the toilet, I splash water on my face, then brush my teeth with the toothbrush and toothpaste that was provided. In fact, the plain wooden shelves hold an assortment of modern hygiene products, which look completely out of place in the bare-bones bathroom.

I walk back into the bedroom and open the dresser. Dark gray leathers hang inside, like something an archer or assassin would wear in a fantasy movie, complete with knee-high boots. On the shelf above lie socks, plain cotton underwear, pants, and shirts. Everything looks like it's in my size. Like they knew what my size was before stocking the dresser.

Having nothing left to explore here, I tentatively step out of my quarters and see the door across the hallway was left ajar. Through it is a kitchen, and it's as plain as everything else I've seen so far. A square table with four chairs is set in the middle. Counters and cupboards line one wall, and a stone hearth is built into the wall across from it. A cauldron hangs inside, like something out of a video game tavern. Cue the bawdy music. No, really, the silence is oppressive.

I wonder where they get food from. Nothing can grow in the gray sand that covered the floor of the atrium, and which I suspect covers the rest of this ante-realm to Hell. Not to mention the things like the razors and bottles of shampoo and conditioner I saw in my bathroom. There must be an easy way to reach home.

Just as I'm done taking in my surroundings, Daniel walks through the door, wearing a gentle smile. I feel like I instantly got a bead on this man... male? What do I call the Fallen? Do they have a gender? It would feel rude to ask.

"Good morning, Lana," he says, appraising me as if he can see whether I got any sleep or not.

"Morning," I return the greeting, then stand there wondering what I'm meant to do next.

"I prepared some oatmeal for breakfast, sit anywhere you would like." He saves me from indecisiveness and I sit at the table he gestured toward. Daniel serves me porridge from the cauldron in a ceramic bowl and provides a matching ceramic spoon. He then sits down across from me with no food placed before him.

"Don't you need to eat?" I question, and test the warmth of my food. Don't need a burned tongue on top of everything, now do I?

"I could eat," he replies, his smile growing slightly, some twinkle in his calm blue eyes. "I can also choose not to and avoid the needs of the physical body that follow."

"Hah. Must be nice," I mutter and swallow a spoonful. The food is plain but feels comforting. "Where does this food come from? And everything else?" I ask.

"We take regular trips to the mortal realm for provisions. Maalik goes most often."

His answer confirms my suspicions and I ask, hopefully, "Will we be able to visit home?"

He observes me for a moment before replying. "Perhaps some of you. In time."

The hope I feel is almost painful; I want to see Mike again, to explain why I won't be there at the movie theater for our regularly scheduled date. Though he probably already sent me twenty memes that went unread, seeing as my phone is somewhere on the floor of that alley. He may have even already called the police. Would they call my parents? Duh, Lana, of course they would. We're not the closest of families, but I still don't want them to think I'm dead. I sigh at the unrelenting wrenching pain in my stomach and grasp for something else to think about.

"Where is everyone else?" This small kitchen slash dining room can't be where they expect us all to eat.

"There is a larger dining area. This is the kitchen Maalik and I use." Daniel thoughtfully taps a finger on his lips. "Being apart from the Nephilim and Cambion in the sense that you are both, we were not quite sure which wing of the fortress to put you in. So we chose a room close to us."

I shake my head as a shiver runs down the back of my neck. "I see. And how did Maalik know my ancestry?"

"He met your grandfather at an archdemon's court before he left Hell to be with his angel in the human world. From what I know, his brethren tracked him down and slaughtered both of them," he continues, his voice still kind, but now also sounding sad. He sighs and then adds, "Offspring that are equal parts angelic and demonic are rare. What is rarer yet is when they are not conceived with... force."

I know I'm just gaping at him. This is all too much. My brain feels like it's short-circuiting. I decide I don't want to talk about me or why I'm here anymore. Dropping the subject, I nibble on my food until curiosity wins over my cautiousness. "Why are you here, Daniel? You're a fallen angel, right? But you don't seem… evil."

Thankfully, my question doesn't offend him and his voice is still warm when he replies. "Breaking Heavenly rules has consequences."

The rules, but not sinning? I straighten as his name finally registers and tickles a memory bank somewhere in my brain. I think I know who he is, but I don't want to be rude. "Your name is Daniel. Were you one of the Watchers?"

Daniel is still smiling in a very Mona Lisa way, so I oh-so-cleverly deduce I'm right. I've read about the Watchers. They were sent to observe humankind, but many couldn't resist and interacted with them. Some even fell in love – or lust.

I must have zoned out dissecting this poor guy's situation – while studiously ignoring my own – because Daniel softly clears his throat. "If you are done eating, I would gladly show you around. There were a few escape attempts last night, so we are not quite ready to begin your assessments. In fact..." Daniel tilts his head in curiosity. "You adjusted remarkably fast."

I arch a brow. "Is there a way to escape?"

Daniel takes my empty bowl to the sink and answers without turning. "No."

"There you go." I push away from the table and stand up. "Though I would call this numb, and not well-adjusted."

✳✳✳

It takes a couple of days before everyone is calm enough – or resigned enough – for us to gather together again. We're outside of the fortress walls in the training field Daniel showed me the other day. I spent most of the time waiting for this assessment talking with him. He told me a lot about Heaven and the fallen angels living in Purgatory; about their neutrality in the Heavenly conflict. But he avoided talking about Hell or what my life is going to be like –

probably to avoid the possibility of me going into hysterics like some of the others.

The faces I saw in that atrium are once again a sea of communal apprehension in the gray dust. And, yes, as I thought, all I see is sand and dunes in the distance. The sky is still breathtakingly beautiful though, if creepy.

"We're going to test your fighting skills now, your attunement with the ether." Maalik grins – he seems to like doing that, probably realizing how intimidating it looks to us. The motherfucker. "And your natural dominance, let's say, the hierarchy among you. After all, you will work best in small teams. We don't want any infighting," he warns.

I think I know where he lands in their hierarchy of dominance and I roll my eyes. Maalik snaps his gaze to me and gives me a feral smile, like he knows what I was thinking and wants me to know that, yes, he has the biggest dick. I huff a smile. He's creepy as fuck, but I have a feeling I would have enjoyed his wicked sense of humor – if I wasn't still reeling from being kidnapped by him.

Several hours later we're sweaty and groaning as Maalik, Daniel, and the rest of the realm's living residents stand to the side discussing who to place together for training. Their group includes the two Fallen I remember speaking in the atrium – Corson and Ramel, I now know.

None of them seemed surprised when we couldn't even move a dust mote with our willpower. If they hadn't shown us how it's meant to look, I would have thought they were playing a joke on us. But Maalik summoned a ball of flames which he promptly threw at Corson, the latter flipping him off lazily after easily dodging the projectile.

At least I got a nod from Maalik after demonstrating my knowledge and skill with martial arts. I'm very glad that I've been training since before I hit double digits in age. I kept up with my taekwondo lessons in adulthood – I'm a physical person, so reading couldn't be the only form of escapism in my arsenal. Maybe it'll help me stay alive as I face this threat they brought us here for. It sure as fuck didn't help me enough when Maalik grabbed me.

The younger guy from the other night, Kevin, also has some fighting skills. After talking to him between whatever exercises the Fallen wanted us to do, I saw why he would have had to learn to defend himself – he was living on the streets when the Fallen picked him up.

There are too many of us here, and I couldn't pay attention to everyone's appraisal, but it seems to me like we're not fit to fight off an army of rats, let alone demons or whatever.

The Fallen finally finish their debate and come closer. "Step into a line in front of us as we call you," Maalik says.

Ramel snaps out the name of the angry woman who also spoke up when we were brought here. I shudder and pray to whoever can hear me down here not to be placed under his tender care. He seems to be picking out the brawlers, the ones that stand out with their muscles and the grim and angry looks on their faces.

I can't get a bead on Corson's choices. They're average-looking, but I don't see much identifiable emotion reflected on their faces. Perhaps some antisocial tendencies are the criteria then.

When it's Maalik who calls my name and then Kevin's, I don't know whether to feel relieved or worried.

As the rest of the Fallen – some with slit eyes, like Maalik, and some that could pass as gorgeous humans, like Daniel – finish their roll call, Kevin and I are joined by Jessica, Ethan, Liam, and Simone. Such normal names in such an abnormal place. Ethan and Simone are Cambion, like Kevin, while Jessica and Liam are Nephilim. From what I saw, Maalik chose to teach a group that showed at least some technical skill in fighting.

The absolutely enormous sword he has sheathed down his back makes me think blades are going to be a part of our curriculum. I'm a history teacher; I can walk down aisles at the museum and tell you what each blade is called and the historical period they hail from. Have I ever held them in my hands? No. This will be interesting.

Strangely enough, for the first time since I landed here ass over teakettle, I feel a sense of excitement. I try not to think of what learning to fight will lead to. Probably best to come to terms with things in increments.

LIANA VALERIAN

CHAPTER 4 – LANA

"This is impossible!"

Ethan's whining doesn't help me concentrate on healing this tiny self-inflicted nick on my hand.

I've gotten to know my new team members a bit and Ethan is definitely the most vocal. My other teammates fall onto the other side of the spectrum: Kevin and Simone are withdrawn, Liam seems to be the quiet type, and Jessica is the shy one. We've been training together on the field every day, but we're in the keep's meeting room with Daniel now, and he's teaching us how to heal wounds. In theory, at least.

I take a break from squinting hard at my hand and look around. Another team is clustered on the other side of the long table and they seem to be having about as much success as we are – basically, none at all.

I only know the name of one of that team's members, a short-haired and stocky girl named Darla. Though I can see the boys on the team are trying to familiarize themselves with Simone, with the way they're staring.

I can't blame them, though. She has to be the prettiest girl I've ever seen outside of a billboard ad. Her hair is a gleaming chocolate brown waterfall, offsetting her pale skin and bright gray eyes. There's something elfin about her features, in the shape of her mouth and eyes which draws the gaze. But if those arresting eyes happen to meet yours, it's always only for a second before she looks away. Everything about her screams 'Leave me alone'.

Daniel makes another round on our side of the improvised classroom, so I drop my gaze back to the drying drops of blood cupped by my palm. Any longer and this wound will heal all by itself.

We've been told that the traits our heritage afforded us will manifest themselves now that we're no longer in the human realm. One of them is faster healing. Another is veritable immortality. While we're living in the Underworld, we won't age, as if we were as dead as the majority of its residents. So long as we're here, we'll be preserved at our prime, perfect pawns for the council that ordered us to be here.

But to purposefully heal this wound, we're meant to use the ether – the intangible life force that's in and around every object and creature – to kind of nudge our blood cells to promote wound closure. It's not magic in the sense that it creates something out of nothing. We can only manipulate that which is already there.

"Hah!" Simone's exclamation interrupts my meandering thoughts and everyone turns to see why she's so excited.

"Well done, Simone." Daniel is inspecting her palm where, under a smear of blood, the wound is clearly healed. The wide smile of accomplishment on Simone's face shows off most of her pearly white teeth. It's a display that makes a guy at the other side of the table whistle loudly. Simone's smile immediately drops. Judging by the sway of her body, Darla then kicks the leering man beneath the table, making him yelp. "Bitch!"

I frown at him. That was the first time we'd seen Simone smile, at least in public, and he made her regret it.

"Arsehole." That was Ethan again and this time his outburst makes me huff out a laugh. His slight accent at least makes his grousing marginally less annoying.

We're all pretty protective of Simone – she has that wounded little bird thing going on and it makes me curious about her past. An awakening darkness within makes me want to ask her who hurt her, so I can kick the shit out of them.

"Is alienating the people who will have your back in Hell a new training method Ramel's using, Nick?"

Judging by the way his deep voice freezes the room, no one else heard Maalik enter, either. We look like a bunch of kids who got caught pilfering from the cookie jar.

I clear my throat. "Look, Maalik, Simone healed her wound." The Fallen gives me a knowing look. Drat, he's onto my deflection tactics.

"I'll be impressed when you can all summon more than just a puff of smoke. Or at the very least not trip over your own damned feet on the field." After that dry remark, Maalik turns towards Daniel, who is, as always, unruffled and vaguely amused. "Talk to you for a moment?"

As they leave the room, the whistler boy, aka Nick, immediately rounds on Darla. "Touch me again and you'll regret it."

The juvenile threat makes me roll my eyes. What is this, kindergarten? "Why?" I drawl. "Do you have scabies?"

Okay, maybe I'm not all that mature myself.

A couple of chuckles make Nick's face turn purple. "Shut up, teacher's pet. We all know why you're sleeping in the same hallway as them."

Now a couple of guys on his team laugh at my expense while the rest avoid looking at me. I can't help but blush a bit myself, though I try to stay calm. I never considered how it would look that I'm separate from everyone else, and maybe I should have. "Oh, yeah," I mutter. "Daniel's big on orgies. Schedules them right between morning and noon prayers."

Thankfully the room laughs at the image I've painted and the lingering awkwardness is dispelled. I'm clearly going to need to keep an eye on this guy.

Over the next weeks, I learn to feel comfortable in my new leathers. We've moved from hand-to-hand combat to using dull practice weapons. We still manage to get bumps and scrapes though, giving us ample opportunity to practice our healing.

I've grown close to Kevin, pairing up with him for practice whenever possible. I feel a kinship with him; neither of us has much to return to in the human realm. Of course, that doesn't mean we'd choose to be here. We practice together outside of our lessons, too, as both of us chose to learn to wield two light swords. Though using a bo staff comes naturally to me due to my life-long interest in martial arts, I perhaps chose to master a different weapon type to keep myself distracted from feeling trapped down here.

As time passes, the escape attempts become fewer. One idiot on Corson's team actually ran out of Purgatory into Hell. Not sure what he saw, but when the Fallen brought him back, he was pale and shaking.

While Daniel's lessons moved from healing to defensive uses of ether, Maalik tries to coach some destructive ether out of us, gathering the warmth from the air into fire, using wind to slice through objects — whatever we're capable of. That's how Jess discovered she can pull minerals out of the ground. One day she could possibly even make weapons. The tiny blonde doesn't exactly look like a blacksmith, but what do I know?

I managed to heal and shield, even manipulate wind, but fire's proving to be a bitch.

"Stop trying to think it into happening," Maalik chides, then taps my stomach with the back of his gloved hand. "Pull from here."

I raise an eyebrow. "My pancreas?"

Maalik grunts. One of these days I *will* make him laugh. "Your being, your core. Your soul, if you want to put it that way."

I purse my lips and place my hands in front of me like I'm waiting to catch a basketball. I think of the warm wind and try to get a feel for the pancreas essence that is me. A spark ignites too close to my fingers and I drop my hands with a gasp.

"Good," is all that Maalik says before walking over to a sweating Liam.

To my left, Kevin is practically playing catch with a golf ball sized flame. "Showoff," I mutter, then bring my hands back up. I have a feeling I'll be more motivated to learn once push comes to shove and we're facing those amorphous manifestations of evil human souls and the demonic minions salivating to take a bite out of us.

Corson has been teaching us about the topography of Hell and the many dangers we'll face in the realm. The living residents of Hell are sorted into hierarchies, a sort of demonarchy. Their leaders, kings, barons, and dukes are archdemons, and some of their names are familiar to me from reading about myth and lore in theology; there's Ba'al, Samael, Azeal, Belial, Ashtaroth, Asmodeus, and even Lilith is real. Above them, of course, the Devil, to whom our Fallen refer to as Sataniel, as he was once known in Heaven — Lucifer or Light Bringer being a *nom de guerre* chosen by the ancient peoples. We spend more time on the anatomy of lower demons, as they're the ones we're more likely to face and survive.

Soon we'll venture into Hell, like baby birds kicked out of the nest, and we'll need to be armed with as much information and fighting skill as we can muster.

Fire flutters to life between my hands, like a tiny butterfly emerging from a chrysalis to test its wings for the first time. It's beautiful, and I can't imagine using it against someone as a force of destruction.

"Congratulations," Kevin says dramatically. "You're a wizard, Lana!"

I snort and the fire extinguishes, leaving no trace of it behind. "You think I could get away with setting a fire under Nick's bed?"

"That would mean getting close to his bed."

My eyes widen and I reel back in horror. "Eww, you're right."

Kevin chuckles, then scratches the back of his head, looking around to see if anyone's within earshot. "Is he still following Simone around like a puppy?"

"He's making her uncomfortable, but she doesn't want anything said to the Fallen, to make a thing out of it." I look at the brunette who's trying (and failing) to use ether in any way that might be remotely considered offensive.

She's a very unlikely Cambion, having worked at the NICU before being brought here and mastering nothing but healing since. Kevin and I display at least some personality traits that may be attributed to our hereditary predispositions – shorter tempers and angrier reactions.

I asked Maalik about my grandfather, the demon who left Hell to be with an angel. According to him, it was a union of love and they both got killed by assassins from Hell before they got much of a happily ever after in the human realm. Would that mean I'm more prone to good than evil, or is it just a technicality, and demon blood is demon blood? It's something that's kept me up at night, wondering if I am who I'm meant to be, or just an imposter trying to conform to society's norms of right and wrong.

"We'll keep her safe," I murmur, and the vow at least feels right, like protecting anyone weaker might come naturally to me.

"Less chatting, more practicing, grandmas!" Maalik yells at us from Liam's side.

To my amusement, Kevin salutes him and shouts back, "Yes, sir!"

I giggle and lift my hands up to cradle an imaginary fireball again. Maybe I'm a bad influence. He is almost a decade younger than me and still impressionable.

When I turn my head to look at him, I see that his warm brown eyes are twinkling. He looks nothing like the solemn boy I saw in that atrium our first night here.

I decide then and there that, whether it's good or bad, I'm the right kind of company for him.

CHAPTER 5 – ASHTAROTH

"Well, not all of them suck."

Sariel is looking at the Elioud from our vantage point on a hill overlooking the fortress of Abaddon, his eyes nearly manic with glee. All my adoptive son needs to complete the image is the snack humans unimaginatively call popcorn.

"Perhaps I should send you on tasks to the human realm more often if you are so easily amused by mortals."

"Aw, come on, Father. Even you must find it interesting that there are Elioud in the Underworld."

"Must I?"

I sweep my gaze over the training mortals. There are a few dozen of them and a handful of Fallen overseeing them. They look like swarming ants.

"Look at that redhead, she totally owned that guy!"

I sniff in disdain. "Is there a dictionary I can use to translate your words, or am I meant to infer the meaning from the tone of your voice?"

My son snorts. "Yeah, it's called The Urban –"

"It was a rhetorical question," I interrupt him. I find the Elioud he was referring to, a tall and shapely woman with pale skin. It is as much individuality as I can discern from this distance. "Mortals die easily. You starve them – they die. You cut their heads off – they die. You stab them in the heart – they die. Utterly useless."

Sariel turns to me and cocks an eyebrow. "I thought we're not meant to impale them, with swords or otherwise. Speaking of impaling mortals, they've been here a while now, how are you keeping Uncle from them?"

I press my lips together at the reminder. "Hmm. I convinced Asmodai entering Abaddon is not worth the backlash from the Council. Once the offspring venture into Hell, however, it will be out of our hands."

Sariel scoffs and turns his attention back to the field outside Abaddon. "Here's to hoping he doesn't leave cum-soaked bodies in his wake. I bet the angels wouldn't find that amusing." Suddenly, he straightens and points towards the left side of Purgatory's training field. "Whoa! Look at the size of that guy! Definitely has a behemoth for a father."

Thankfully, I concealed us from both sight and hearing, or everyone would have heard his shout. I look at the man he described and have to agree. That kind of stature suggests an ancestor among Hell's brawlers, the oversized brutes we call behemoths, who feed on violence. Demons predominately share similar physical attributes, but there are a few exceptions. Very small demons are universally known as imps. Those that gain sustenance from sex, with features similar to those of humans, belong to the family of succubi and incubi.

But my gaze quickly returns to the redhead, now using her staff to sweep a smaller blonde off her feet. While they're both wearing tight leather armor, it is not the blonde's backside I eye.

Perhaps Sariel senses my hunger, as he smirks suggestively. "So, are you going to wet your sword with any Elioud?"

I frown and turn away from Abaddon. "No. And if any enter my domain, I will know, and I will oust them."

"Right," Sariel drawls. "Is playtime over then?"

I unleash my wings, the susurration of feathers answering his question as I launch myself into the dark sky.

There is nothing to see here. And it is time for me to feed.

CHAPTER 6 – LANA

The gates in front of us look creepy as fuck. Gargoyles are perched on wide stone columns, and the dark, misshapen ironwork is topped with spikes. Not to mention that this area of Hell is so foggy, you could cut it with a knife.

"Is that blood?" Liam asks, a note of apprehension in his voice. He unsheathes his sword with a soft rasp of metal over leather.

I step closer and eye the oozing liquid. "Yep. Definitely blood." Not all that shocking seeing we're looking at the gates to a graveyard in Hell. I use a booted foot to nudge at one leaf, opening it just wide enough for us to enter. Jess bounces on her feet nervously. It's not that I'm immune to the creep factor myself, but we were told there are soul manifestations here, so in we must go.

Simone sidles up to me quietly and continues with the conversation our arrival at the gates stopped. "Can you talk to him again, please?"

By 'him', she means Maalik. And I'm the one she's asking because the brute in question chose me to lead our group, a decision that baffled me. I don't want to be responsible for the deaths of five people with whom I bonded in training. Apparently, that's exactly the reason why I'm the best woman for the job — words delivered with that sadistic grin of his we've all come to loathe. The bastard. I can't say we don't respect him though; everything he does is to ensure we have the best fighting chances possible.

This is the last mission we're doing together as a team before he sends us all out on a solo patrol, to see if we can handle it both physically and mentally. It's not the same when you don't have anyone watching your back or diverting you from wondering if you're about to be shredded by demons.

"I really did try, honey." I eye the tall tombstones and the bones scattered before them. Were the bodies just not buried in the first place, or did something dig them up? "We all have to do the solo patrol."

Simone's fighting skills have definitely improved, but she's not quite as confident as everyone else. "I don't know why they want me out here. I'm better at healing, anyway," she pouts.

I throw her a sympathetic look which turns into a cringe as the sound of bones snapping under my foot echoes among the tombs. Soul manifestations won't run from us, seeing as they don't have a brain to think with, but we encounter demonic minions as often as those ethereal forms.

"I know. And I'm going to fight to have you stay at the keep and help Daniel with post-patrol injuries."

Simone sighs and nods with resignation. "Okay."

"Oh, Great Leader."

I glare at Ethan. "Don't call me that, fuckwit."

Ethan gives me a shark's smile, then points to the right with his sword. Damn it, I didn't even notice the amalgamation of souls hovering by a dilapidated tomb. At least I think I would have noticed if there were demons around. Now that we know what to look for, it seems my internal Spidey sense is sharper than anyone else's.

"Do the honors, then." I bow and sweep my arms in a grand gesture. Ethan bounces on his feet, then withdraws a throwing knife. He takes a second to aim and the knife sails towards the manifestation, flying straight through it.

That's enough, though, as all that's needed is Celestial metal interrupting the bonds holding the blob together. The souls given form dissipate. Since souls can't be killed, being eternal and all, no one's quite sure what happens to them. Maybe they end up in the Fiery Pits with Lucifer. Maybe they're reincarnated in the mortal realm and given a second chance. My guess is as good as anyone's. Except, you know, God and the big D's.

I snicker, wondering if the Devil has a big dick. Bet he does. Liam looks at me like I've lost my mind. Little does he know, it's not lost – I purposefully misplaced it years ago.

I whistle to myself as I lead my friends deeper into the demonic burial grounds. We rarely encounter more than one target in an outing. This should be an easy, if morbid stroll, and we're not so far from Purgatory that we can't walk home and be there in time for dinner.

I freeze between one step and another. Clearly, I haven't learned my lesson when it comes to jinxing myself.

"What is it?" Kevin asks, looking around and trying to discern any shapes that don't belong through the fog. Good luck with that, with all the creepy statues.

"Demons," I whisper, and take a step back.

Liam's serious voice sounds to my left. "I feel them, too."

"So, we fight them," Ethan shrugs, unconcerned.

"Don't be so blasé," Jess hisses.

"All of you shut up and run," I command through gritted teeth. This isn't good. "They're not weak and there's too many of them."

Ethan frowns, but to his credit, he doesn't argue. Just as we clear the gates, a high-pitched shriek chills our bones, and we dumbly stop.

"W-what do you think it is?" Simone stutters.

"Too damned close, that's what it is." Ethan's words spur us back into movement.

I sense it before I see it, a figure running parallel to us in the fog, darting between the skeletal trees. Before I can decide what to do, it changes its trajectory, now on a course straight toward us.

"Jess, duck!" I shout and she immediately drops, leaving room for Liam's sword to slash through the air at hip height. The creature dodges the blow and cocks its head as it reassesses us.

It's taller than us and has four arms, two on each side. Or it has some sort of arm-like appendages, at least, seeing as they don't end with a hand, but instead curve into a giant hook-like claw. The rest of its features are what we've come to expect from demons: slimy and scaly black skin, super bendy joints, and a teardrop-shaped head sporting a gaping mouth full of razor-sharp teeth and black voids where eyes should be. From Corson's lessons on Hell and demonology, I know they call demons like this one raptors.

Jess rolls closer to the rest of the group and pops up, face set in grim determination.

"Declaw it, then we go for the neck," I order, and we position ourselves into a flanking formation, hours of training having honed our muscle memory to perfection.

As soon as the creature charges, Ethan lifts his weapon into an undercut, aiming for the lowest of the demon's arms on his side. The angelic steel slices through the limb like a knife through butter. As the raptor shrieks in outrage and pain, Simone throws a shuriken at its open maw. It lodges in the back of its mouth – and now it's really mad. Flailing wildly, it runs at us, its hooks audibly slicing the air. We're forced onto the defensive, ducking and dodging, Liam even parrying once or twice, but the claw seems to be made of strong chitin, thick enough to deflect weapons of angelic make.

Finally, Jess drops to her knees and takes off one of the demon's legs, rolling once again before the off-balance demon can collapse onto her. Liam lifts his sword and decapitates the wailing creature, the severed head landing on the ground a second before the rest of its body follows.

"That's one way to do it," I sniff, and run a hand over my sweaty face. "We better go before the rest of them come; it's a miracle they haven't heard this one's screams."

Sweeping my gaze over my crew, I check for visible injuries. I then sheath my swords before we take off towards Abaddon with a story to tell.

***

My first solo patrol went well. In fact, I didn't encounter anything scarier than an imp. I was looking forward to hearing how it went for the rest of my team, but one never made it home.

"It's your fault!"

Everyone is gathered in the atrium, and I'm sitting on a step gripping my hair in a nightmare case of déjà vu. Only this time, we're not having our realities shattered by the truth of our existence. We're here because Simone isn't.

Nick is yelling at me and practically foaming at the mouth with fervor. Like I don't feel guilty enough already. If only I'd tried harder to tell the Fallen that Simone was not ready to be out there alone.

"Please," Kevin sneers at him. "You're only upset we can't find her because she's not here for you to perv over."

We all went out looking for her, even the Fallen. Akira, Corson's team leader and the best of his sleuths, tracked her a couple of hours west, towards the direction of Acheron, miles away from where she was meant to go. Her tracks then disappeared, as if she had simply vanished. No one here is strong enough to use the ether for travel like that, and there were no signs of anyone else being with her.

We've been awake for over a day, and our nerves are frayed, the uncertainty mocking us.

"A few months as team leader and you already manage to lose a member – what does that say about you?" Nick's ignoring the glares everyone is throwing at him, which includes his team leader, Darla. Everyone knows he's salty about the fact a woman got the nod from Ramel, their Fallen instructor. Only a couple of his gorilla-shaped friends are standing with him, arms crossed and looking like they're a hair's breadth away from violence.

"Simone was as prepared for this patrol as the rest of you," Ramel snaps. "Whatever she encountered is something none of you would have been able to overcome."

"So, what now?" I croak, my voice rough from tension and from shouting Simone's name all night.

"We will ask the Council for aid." Daniel's voice is soothing, and I nod like I don't realize it's pointless. What will they do, these mysterious angels and demons who set laws which Hell is only half pretending to follow? If a higher-tier demon killed her, we'll never know.

My team clusters around me, their faces drawn with exhaustion and worry. Jess is silently crying, her face unmoving with grief. She looks like she's too exhausted to sob, but the pain doesn't care – it finds a way out.

Maalik looks at us and sighs. "Try to get some rest."

Despite his alien eyes, it's obvious to me he feels heavy with remorse. Maybe he's thinking he should have listened to me as well. At least I hope he's thinking that and feels guiltier than I do.

"No more solo patrols for a while," Corson tells us, the other fallen angels agreeing with nods. "Pairs at the least."

With the gathering finished, I stand up and turn toward the hallway which leads to my bedroom. I don't blame Maalik in the end. Ramel was right. Simone was capable of handling herself. Logically, I know I shouldn't be blaming myself, either. What ifs and should haves are a bitch, though. Maybe Nick is right. Maybe Maalik made a mistake by picking me to lead this team.

Once in my room, I wash the dust off in a perfunctory way and crawl into my bed naked, too mentally and physically exhausted to bother with dressing. My last thought is that perhaps I should be a bit more optimistic. Maybe the Council can do something and Simone will come back, shaken but unharmed. Maybe tomorrow, maybe the day after.

I was never very good at lying to myself, though.

CHAPTER 7 – ASHTAROTH

"One last thing." Belial's postponing of this meeting's end is met with groans from our side.

"Some of us have places to be, Belial." My brother sounds every bit the playboy that he is, his *laissez-faire* attitude making Belial's jaw tic.

"The Fallen of Purgatory are asking if there is any news about the missing Elioud." Belial addresses Heaven, though he is clearly speaking to us. Sowing discord once more, is he?

"Still?" Azeal growls. "Why do they give a fuck? It's not the only dead mortal."

"She," Belial corrects, "is the only one whose body hasn't been recovered."

I snort in disbelief. "Shall we name all the demons who do not leave a trace of flesh and blood to be found after they have fed?"

Belial ignores me and addresses Asmodai. "Would you happen to know anything about it, *King of Seduction*?"

My brother rolls his eyes. "My answer is the same as it was months ago when you first asked, Belial. No, I did not fuck the girl to death."

My brow twitches at Asmodai's words. Or, more accurately, at the words he did not say. It is strange that he has never bragged about any conquests among the Elioud in Hell. He has always been the opposite of modest when pertaining to his exploits.

"If there are no more important matters to discuss..." Belphegor's lazy drawl stops my musings. He is correct; none of this is of importance.

"Inquire among your courts about the female again." Saraqael's request borders on being a command, and Azeal snarls. His pride is wounded, I feel, but he makes no further signs of aggression towards Heaven.

In truth, Saraqael is one of the few archangels that occasionally bless these meetings with their presence, the majority unable to share space with their fallen brethren.

I stand to leave, signaling my unwillingness to continue this conversation. Perhaps my brother did kill the woman, or perhaps another demon devoured her. Regardless, it is of no significance to me, and certainly not worth coming to blows over.

Asmodai jumps to his feet and straightens his suit jacket. He is nothing if not a cliché. "Do visit, Brother – the children have been asking about you."

I click my tongue. "How would you know? You have too many to keep count of."

My brother smirks lasciviously. "I can't help it if I'm potent, now can I?"

"You best hope they never band together in a coup. They would prevail by attrition, pecking at you like carrion."

"Naamah will be most disappointed in hearing you think of her as a vulture, Ashtaroth. You are her favorite, you know."

I huff and spirit myself out of Purgatory into my own domain, welcoming the tempestuous skies after being enclosed in a cavern under the mountains for hours.

CHAPTER 8 – LANA

"I'm pretty sure she wants me."

"Uh-huh." I smile at Kevin. He's really lightened up over the years, as if he found his footing in this place, more than he ever had in the human realm. A home. I don't see the angry young man I met that first night in Purgatory's large atrium anymore. He's one of the most relaxed Elioud here now.

And, with the deluded vanity that comes hand in hand with a twenty-something's testosterone supply, he thinks he's God's gift to women. Even down here where God certainly isn't present.

"I'm telling you, I'm gonna come back and she'll be waiting for me in my room." He grins, unashamed. Deluded he may be, but his gorgeous face indeed ensures he doesn't sleep alone very often. Hell, he even has the older women blushing at his flirty grins. It's a good thing I'm immune to him.

"At this rate, you're going to plow through the available female population before the year's out," I tease him.

"By then I'll forget about the first ones and start all over again," Kev winks at me. I scoff and shake my head. It's not like he's leaving broken hearts behind. At least not yet. As his team leader and self-appointed (still young and beautiful) auntie, I worry about him getting entangled in what I like to refer to as 'camp drama'. While we spend a lot of time patrolling the regions of Hell closest to Abaddon, it's still our home base. Our war camp. "You're just grumpy because you don't get dicked down often enough," he says with mock solemnity.

I snort and punch his arm. "I'm not judging you, asshat." While I certainly show more restraint than him, it's not like I'm an innocent maiden. I just realized pretty early on that being a female team leader brings out the worst in the guys who rank below me. Most just want to prove that they out-man me, fail spectacularly, and thus leave me dissatisfied.

Kevin and I are walking the eastern bank of The Phlegethon – The River of Fire. Over the sounds of our crackling steps on the charcoal ground and the bubbling of lava, I take the opportunity of him shutting the fuck up about his skill in wielding his sword – and I don't mean either of the ones sheathed in his crisscross harness – to listen for any danger. I gaze over the horizon while we catch our breaths and feel a tug northward.

"Demons," I say to Kevin, "More than one."

"I feel it too," he replies, now looking more like that serious young man I met three years ago. When the going gets real, Kev leaves the humor behind. Unlike me. I'll probably have 'made fun of a demon lord's tiny tail' written on my gravestone.

"Actually, golems, I think," I correct my earlier assessment. The fiery constructs created by more powerful demons in a fit of strong emotion are not typical creatures of flesh and blood.

"I'm forever envious of your senses." Kev shakes his head. While he can sense demonic presence, he's not as precise at pinpointing the number or strength of demons present.

"Aren't you lucky you're with me?" Jess, Ethan, and Liam veered down the opposite side of the river's flow today.

"Yes, I feel incredibly lucky we ran into more than one golem, Lana. What a gift!" he rolls his eyes at me.

I get it; a golem isn't a thing lightly taken up by just two of us, especially if there are more of them.

"Well, we can strategically retreat now and regroup with the others," I nod sagely, and Kev scoffs at me.

"You mean run away, oh Great Leader?" he mocks.

"Precisely." I nod decisively.

We turn back to head to the area where we split from the others, but before we can take more than a couple of steps, I hear the sounds of the lava's bubbling pick up like it's about to boil over. *Fuck.*

"Uh, why didn't we feel this one, Lana?" Kevin stammers in apprehension.

"The lava must have muddled our senses somehow," I say as we turn towards The Phlegethon.

Indeed, a golem is clambering to his feet, rising to his full height of over fifteen feet. How did something that enormous hide in the river without us noticing it? Well, we stopped bothering to wonder about illogicalities years ago. When you're constantly peppered by them, you take them in stride or you have constant headaches. The golem's head is lit up like a match, and lava drips from his stony body, matching the orange glow of it. The pungent smell of brimstone pushes itself into my nose.

"Are we running?" Kevin asks.

"I think it's pointless," I retort, "a fight's going to happen. But we can try. Split up."

He follows without hesitating, the compulsion to obey me ingrained in his muscles. I run north, following the bank, while Kevin runs back the way we came. The golem decides to follow him, faster than I thought it would be, and I curse, switching directions. No way he can handle it alone.

"Kev, fight!" I yell as I unstrap my bo staff. Can't slash at stones. Kevin turns around and moves his arm in a slicing motion in front of him. The air he commands smashes into the golem's massive body, but instead of pushing it away, the golem merely staggers. This bastard is too heavy for us to move with our fledgling ether.

Kevin gapes at it, then pulls out his swords, knowing they'll be as little use against something so massive and well-armored, just as his wind was. The golem charges once again and Kevin dodges its gigantic fist, which smashes right where he stood a moment ago, sending plumes of black charcoal dust in the air.

I finally reach them and wedge the tip of my staff into the space between two of the giant rocks that make up its body on its leg. Joints, if you will. Thankfully, my staff was made by angels, and doesn't disintegrate in the heat. The action distracts the golem, though it probably feels like a bee sting, and it stomps, the force of the crash throwing me backward. I slide across the ground, so very thankful I'm wearing my leathers, despite the heat in this area of Hell. Once I stop, I groan and try to get my feet under me.

Kev recovered faster and is still dodging the golem's blows, slicing at it with his swords, as ineffective as it may be. He knows better than to panic over me while still in danger.

I run back, thinking that maybe I could use ether to slice wind between some of those joints, toppling it over and hobbling it long enough for us to run away. Hopefully, it would get bored with the chase eventually, and stop trying to turn us into red pesto.

Just as I get in range, the golem finally manages to catch Kevin with its next blow. I hear the crack of bone as the hit to his side hurls him backward, and then the thud of his head touching down on the ground too hard for him to keep conscious.

"No!" I scream, and do the first thing I think of — I grab a large rock from the ground in both hands, and then hurl it directly at the golem's undersized head. It turns towards me, abandoning its downed quarry, and starts stomping in my direction.

"Okay," I say to myself as I whip around and start running north again. Adrenaline pricks at my muscles and my breath saws in and out of my lungs as I sprint towards the river. I need to lead it away from Kev. Maybe it'll forget about him while chasing me. That's as far as I have time to plan before I see that the river turns to an outward bend, exactly where I'm rushing to.

"Shit!"

Turning would waste precious time – the lumbering fucker behind me is too fast for its size.

By some stroke of serendipitous luck, the river narrows and stones poke out from the lava, large enough and spaced close enough apart that I can conceivably cross there.

Hoping I'm not about to give a painful new definition to walking on coals, I jump and hurtle through the air, landing on stone after stone, then jump across the last of the distance to the other side of the bank. I land on my hands and knees, and take a quick look heavenward in gratitude that my steps were sure and fast enough, and that I wasn't deep-fried or grilled. As the golem is still approaching, I scramble up to my feet and start running again. The burst of speed cost me too much energy and I can feel myself slowing down.

I glance behind me just in time to see the golem cross the river and smash one of the stones under its heavy weight, landing on one knee, and trampling another of the boulders I crossed on. There's now no way for me to get back.

Well, I'll cross that bridge when I get to it. Or not, I guess.

I seize the opportunity to take stock of the area I have found myself in. On this side of the river, the ground feels like earth compressed by centuries of pressure into a hard, dusty surface. There's a stack of boulders twenty or more feet tall to my right.

"Work smarter, not harder," I mutter to myself, and run towards it just as the golem finds his footing and crosses the river. I climb up and don't stop to think of the many, many ways that this could go wrong. I stand on a precarious ledge facing The Phlegethon, and wait for my foe.

The construct charges at me, smashing into the boulders. I get thrown back as the golem gets buried under the rocks. The plan almost worked, surprisingly enough, but then I didn't account for the force of the crash sending the smaller stones in the same direction as I fell, which, *duh*.

One of said stones rolls right onto my right leg and I scream in surprise and pain. I don't think anything is broken, but it hurts like a motherfucker, and a sprain is inevitable. I eye the stone and wonder if I can push it off myself, and if doing so would actually crush something.

Before I gather the courage to act, the mound of boulders where the golem is buried begins to stir, and the construct itself bursts out.

I'm screwed.

CHAPTER 9 – ASHTAROTH

There's a lost sheep in my playground. The lamb is tall, with straight auburn hair pulled into a severe ponytail. She somehow manages to look both innocent and confident. I observe her struggle with the golem, the way she moves, and the choices she makes. A well-trained, strategic entity. I watch her with curiosity, which is more than I have bothered to feel in... centuries? Eons?

There is something familiar about her. She is clearly one of the 'soldiers' the Council acquired to assist with our little problem. So, she's a halfling of some sort, and I wonder whether it's the angelic or demonic kind. There's that curiosity. It is surprising and intriguing, and I'm not yet ready to part with this newfound reemergence of emotion.

As the golem approaches the little lamb pinned under the rocks, it does so with as much relish as such a creature can feel. She must have given it quite the chase. The slight wrenching feeling I get in my gut – clearly the unwillingness to have this curiosity disposed of so quickly – decides my next move for me. I swipe out my arm and unleash a burst of hellfire, which disintegrates the stone pinning the auburn-haired lamb. More importantly, it disintegrates the bonds holding the creature together and, as it flies back into The Phlegethon, it disassembles into inert stones.

The lost sheep recovers from the surprising turn of events quickly and her head snaps in my direction as if drawn by a magnet. I wonder if she would have sensed me, had she not been distracted. My gaze follows a drop of perspiration which lovingly slides down her neck. I wonder how the sweat of her exertion smells. More curiosity.

I grin and disappear into the ether. It's time to show my intriguing, fiery curiosity, who the shepherd is in this area of Hell.

CHAPTER 10 – LANA

I'm pretty sure a demon lord just saved me from a golem. Nothing I have yet encountered while down here has had this astonishing amount of power, the sheer oppressive and suffocating presence that makes you want to bow to your betters. Seeing as I'm still splayed out on my back, I went a step further than bowing. I laugh to myself in disbelief. What the fuck.

I roll to my stomach, then climb up to my knees and plant my good foot down. I brace my hands on my knee to stand up and test how much weight my abused leg can hold. I mean, I'm not going to be running another sprint today, that's for sure, but I can, surprisingly enough, hobble a step forward.

I look around and try to sense anyone still lingering in the vicinity. There's nothing at all. He vanished into thin air, and his aura of malice with him.

I need to get back to Kevin before some lucky imp makes a meal out of him. I'm not losing him like we lost Simone. I don't think I could handle something happening to him.

As I limp past the now more scattered stack of boulders, I gasp from the electricity I suddenly feel, thousands of pinpricks over every inch of my skin. A gloved hand wraps around my throat and pushes me against the boulders. I recover from the surprising sensations and look up (and further up) at the demon standing there.

"Holy fuck…" I gasp, my eyes widening and my mouth falling open.

The side of the demon's lip twitches into an almost-smile. "Not quite," he whispers patronizingly, both words carefully enunciated.

The whisper is laced with arrogance and I have no doubt he believes himself superior. Despite feeling that he's condescending to me, his voice hooks itself into my lower stomach and tugs the insides towards him. It's like my womb and ovaries want to escape my body and worship their new owner. I must be ovulating or something, because there's no way I'm getting a daddy demon breeding kink right now.

"Perhaps an unholy fuck?" The demon finishes, and this time he does curl his lips into an arrogant smile, his eyes narrowing imperceptibly. The way he holds his chin tilted upwards makes me feel like I'm a subject kneeling in front of the throne he's sat on.

His eyes begin to follow a path down my body, audaciously exploring me with his gaze. He deliberately stops at the apex of my thighs, then leisurely continues his survey back up to my face, his smug smile widening once our eyes meet, as if he's relishing the upper hand. Plumes of fire now glow in his amber irises.

I really hope he has no idea that what I'm experiencing right now isn't just fear. That his dominant perusal flicked a neglected switch inside me. What the fuck, Lana, no. No. *Bad girl.*

But his smell is all around me, like marshmallows and wood smoke, and fuck, they should bottle it for posterity.

I can't help but catalog the being holding me captive against the boulder by my throat, his hand splayed in dominance. Raven-wing black hair caresses his face in a careless way that's probably unintentional, but men everywhere would spend hours of their lives trying to achieve the same. There's a crown on his head, resting over a slight widow's peak and an expressive brow. The material is like nothing I've encountered before; it seems to suck the light out of its surroundings and glow with darkness.

He watches me admiring him as my gaze moves down over straight, slashing black brows, past those glowing, calculating eyes and a strong blade of a nose, to the *piece de resistance* – that mouth. Sweet baby Jesus, I have never seen a more attractive mouth on a male, with a strong and defined bow, and a lower lip full enough to nibble on for hours. That mouth twitches under my gaze and I tear my eyes away from it, over his defined cheekbones and strong jaw, past his strong neck, to the collarbone I can see peeking out of his armor. His skin is a golden tan and the size of his body matches his towering height – he's muscled. Not like some of the brawlers in Ramel's group, but with functional lean cords of muscle, down from his wide shoulders to the long, strong legs. A body that's meant for the battlefields of Hell.

I bite my lower lip and he chuckles, just two expelled breaths of air that hit my cheeks with incredible warmth. With a shake of my head, I snap out of my reverie and my eyes refocus. I need to mentally slap myself back into the land of sanity – I'm ogling a demon strong enough to snap my neck with as much effort as it took to expel that breathy laugh, and a part of me thinks I would appreciate it because the death would come from his hands. This absolutely magnetic, beautiful creature was created to be perfection, and my brain is short-circuiting. I meet his burning gaze and try to speak. "What..." I choke on air and clear my throat, then try again. "What do you want?"

The regal god in front tilts his head indulgently, and looks at me like he's feeling magnanimous enough to grace me with an answer. "Gratitude," he says.

"T-thank you?" I stutter. That evil grin returns to the mouth of all wet dreams combined, so beautifully sculpted but still sensual, lips both elegant and symmetrical. Anything with a pulse would instantly imagine it between their legs.

"Master." He enunciates the word clearly so there could be no confusion, and I bristle, despite the obvious danger I'm in. Pride is definitely one of my sins.

"Excuse me?" I say, a bit louder than I spoke before.

In answer, he presses me tighter against the boulder with the hand that was lazily resting on my neck and collarbone, and takes a step forward, bathing me in his electric warmth. His fingers tighten and my mouth opens again in fear.

Yes, um, *definitely* fear.

The flames in his eyes intensify as his expression becomes serious, and I kick my pride to the curb with a belated healthy dose of self-preservation.

"Thank you, Master," I breathe quietly, his palm still suppressing the flow of air to my lungs, his fingers and thumb pressing against the sides of my neck, slowing the rush of the blood meant for my brain to a crawl.

He closes his eyes and leans towards my neck, dragging the tip of his nose from my collarbone to my ear, where he murmurs, "I expended energy to save you, little lamb. I think it only fair that you be the one to replenish it."

I unsuccessfully try to ignore the borderline orgasmic sensation the touch of his skin invokes. Holy Hell, I had actual cocks give me less pleasure than this devil achieved with two seconds of his nose on my neck. Heck, my once-favorite vibrator needs to step down from the pedestal of Best Thing Ever. I can't help it; I moan an embarrassing sound of need.

He pulls his head back from the crook of my shoulder and grins widely. "Do not fret, you will enjoy it," he says, while the look in his eyes tells me he fully knows that wasn't a moan of terror. Such smugness shouldn't be attractive.

I think of all the ways demons find nourishment. There's flesh, of course – I witness that too often. There's blood, full of juicy ether, the life force of all creatures. There are acts of corruption, carnage, and sadism. Or sucking down a human's soul like it's a slushie. I'd enjoy neither of these options. That leaves sex. Lust and passion. The *soupe du jour* of incubi.

I open my mouth to protest – I didn't ask for his help after all – but at that moment, he lowers his head back to the junction between my neck and shoulder, licking once. And then biting down.

A scream originating from the core of my very being tears out of my throat. I kick my head back into the boulder with a thuc, my eyes tightly shut as a supernova explodes in my head, a solar system annihilated behind my closed lids. My body flushes from head to toe as I'm suffused with a delicious warmth.

I can vaguely hear him grunt once in surprise, because dominating my hearing is the embarrassing sound of me panting out needy moans, like my soul is being separated from my body, and I'm helpless to hold on to it. There's a direct line between his bite and my pussy and, oh God, I need to be filled, I need him to touch me, I need to touch myself and relieve this painful pressure. It's all I can think about.

He's nibbling on my flesh, definitely drawing blood, but I don't get the sense that's what he's after. Licking the wound that he made, he moves a couple of inches lower and strikes again.

I don't resist this time and move one hand up my torso towards my breasts and the other between my legs. I don't get very far before he releases my neck, lifts both of my hands above my head, and holds them against the boulder with one of his. The other grabs my jaw, angling me and holding me still at the same time. I feel like I'm being used, though I have no idea just how he's making use of me.

Through the haze in my mind, I feel a hot pressure spread my legs and I automatically start moving my hips, humping the air.

No, it's not the air I'm humping, but his hard thigh. I'm humping his leg like a dog, rubbing against him with a need I can't suppress, and tears of embarrassment are leaking from my tightly shut eyes.

He ceases his ministrations to my neck and licks my tears away slowly, capturing the salty drops on his tongue, and then dragging it up the path the tears took over my cheeks.

As he moves back I manage to open my eyes. He's looking down his nose at me to admire the anguished pleasure and humiliation he created, his chin lifted, his mouth slightly parted in a smile of sadistic pleasure.

I'm wound so tightly that it only takes a couple of seconds of writhing against his hard body before pleasure coils in my center, and then shoots out to my extremities in a blaze of fire. I scream like I'm being torn apart, my body contracting and arching through the spasms, all while he looks down at me proprietarily. A master who threw his favorite pet a treat.

"Delicious," he purrs as my breaths still come in pants, his thigh the only thing keeping me from collapsing. I'm made of putty, like every last bit of tension in my body was expelled in the explosion of pleasure. "A Nephalem," he says with some wonder, moving his head closer and inhaling deeply. "And you came for me so prettily," he whispers against my lips.

My tears are still flowing and I'm not sure whether I want him to kiss me, to soothe the raw and vulnerable hurt I feel inside me with tenderness, or if I want to sink to the ground and bury myself in my shame. I just orgasmed all over this soulless creature's leg, and it felt like being reborn into a higher state of consciousness.

Before either of us can make a move, he snaps his gaze to the river, as if he can see through the boulders. He suddenly looks pissed as... well, Hell.

"Lana!"

It's Kevin. He's alive, he's okay. I exhale in relief, the worry I didn't know was gnawing inside me throughout this ordeal dissipating, and more tears join the ones that the demon still holding me captive didn't lick away while I writhed against him.

His eyes return to mine, a firestorm of anger churning within them, but his expression softens upon meeting my gaze, which I'm sure reflects a mix of shock and relief. He gives me a fond little half-smile, like one would give to a darling kitten, and says, "Until we meet again, little lamb."

The hand still on my face squishes my cheeks in a degrading and domineering show of ownership. His mouth tightens, and he disappears, leaving me to slide down the boulder, landing in a heap and shivering. It's like True North stopped existing; I'm no longer linked to the ground by gravity, and all the warmth has been leached from my body.

His disappearance hurts more than his bite did.

CHAPTER 11 – LANA

"A demon lord?" Kevin gapes at me while helping me limp toward home – as much as he can with one arm hanging uselessly by his side.

"Archdemon, I'm pretty sure," I reply, hobbling across the river using the conveniently placed remains of the golem that started all of this.

"And he didn't hurt you?" He's incredulous, lips parted in disbelief, eyes as big as dinner plates.

"Beyond what you see on my neck and the fact that he made me hump his leg until I came on it like a bitch in heat – no." 'm bitter and I don't hide it. Better to feel anger than humiliation.

Kevin is still staring at me, wide-eyed. "Was... was it good?" he finally asks, all but vibrating with curiosity.

I sigh dramatically. "He ruined me for all other men, with just his mouth on my neck and his thigh between my legs, Kevin." There's a lot of that bitterness in my voice and a frantic edge of hysteria mixed in as well. I'm as ashamed of myself for enjoying it as I am angry at the archdemon for influencing me like that. But I'm not lying or exaggerating.

"Holy shit!" Kevin's smiling at me like I just told him the last three years were a dream and we're going to Disneyland tomorrow.

"What?" I grump and shoot him a glare.

"Well, the entire team was thinking you need a good lay, you were honestly becoming intolerable. I just don't think any of us imagined in our wildest dreams that the endorphin provider would be one of the big evils," he laughs, jostling me because my arm is slung over his shoulder.

"First of all, fuck you," I say. "And second of all, fuck all of you."

***

"Which archdemon?" Daniel asks while cleaning up my neck, having already wrapped my ankle. We're in the dining room and I'm sitting on one of the chairs by the table.

I flush a deep crimson and mumble, "I don't know."

Talking with Daniel about this is highly embarrassing. He's a thousands-of-years-old virgin and the most self-contained person I've ever met. I feel both like I'm corrupting him with my demon-humping ways and worried that he would think less of me. Hell, I think less of me.

"Perhaps Asmodai as he is the father of the incubi and succubi," Daniel suggests.

"Asmodeus?"

"That is one of his names, yes, more commonly used by mortals. The Duke of Lust." He's still calmly dabbing at my neck. For some reason, I feel like throwing up.

"What would he look like?" Maybe I can rule him out. Though why it would matter in the grand scheme of things, I don't know.

"I am not certain," Daniel replies while smearing an ointment over the bruised punctures. "He was born in Hell of Lilith and Samael. I have never laid eyes upon him."

Lilith was the first wife of Adam, who refused to obey him (you go, girl), and who became the first female demon (less inspiring as a role model).

"However," Daniel continues, "the peak of the demonic hierarchy can all feed through a multitude of ways. Some can procure nourishment just by willing it, and some like a more engaged approach."

That was definitely a hands-on approach – though I wish he put those hands elsewhere, too, and not just on my wrists, face, and neck. Again, *what the fuck*, Lana?

"In any case, no matter who it was, you are blameless in this."

I choke on my inhale. "Blameless? I practically gave an archdemon a lap dance and it wasn't even his happy ending!"

Daniel flushes at my shouted words. Good, I'm not the only one that looks more tomato than 'human' right now.

"He could have made you eviscerate yourself or walk on all fours, howling like a wolf." He makes his point while finishing treating the marks the demon in question had left behind. "The wounds are clean and even," Daniel says. "There was no tearing of skin. This was not done to hurt you."

"No, I don't think so," I mumble again. "Just my dignity." I roll my eyes and sigh.

"Did he not present himself to you in an attractive form then?" His brows are up, and is that mischief in his eyes?

It occurs to me that I didn't even think of the fact that he could have taken on a… less humanoid form. I shudder, thinking about being pinned down by something with scales or a tail. However, what girl would mind a forked tongue? I slap my hand against my face as if I'm trying to beat the intrusive thoughts away.

Daniel chuckles and I realize my saintly friend is relieved that I got off instead of getting offed. Before I manage to voice my outrage, he sobers and says, "I only hope he will not care to repeat the encounter."

I look at the floor, staying quiet. The demon's parting words didn't seem like a final goodbye to me. And I don't give voice to the conflict I feel – I'm not sure that I want it to be a permanent goodbye. Being wanted by such a godly being would be incredible. I could never feel insecure about myself with the most beautiful individual I have ever seen worshiping my body. The shame returns immediately and my shoulders slump. This is not a giving, benevolent creature. Untold horrors happen at his command.

I stand up too fast and wince at the pain in my ankle. "I'm going to take a shower." I need to feel clean again. Then I need to check up on Kevin.

"But I just wrapped down the swelling!" Daniel has his arms out in the closest way of saying 'what the fuck' as he will ever express.

"I'll wrap it up again after." I wave as I shut the door and limp to my room.

I hobble toward the bathroom, strip, and wince in chagrin at my still-wet panties.

"What a clusterfuck."

CHAPTER 12 – KEVIN

With my arm secured in a sling, I hurry to the training fields outside of Abaddon. Spotting my friends, people closer to me than anyone else has ever been (except for Lana), I feel a definite spring in my step.

They are gonna *looooove* this.

"Kevin!" Jess shouts and runs towards me with furrowed brows. "What happened to your arm?"

"A golem. But never mind that –"

"That's brilliant!" Ethan interjects, while Jess leans in to examine my arm behind the fabric.

"What's important is that... wait, 'brilliant'?" I shoot Ethan a glare. What I really want to do is punch his stupid mouth shut.

"Not that you got hurt, of course." Ethan placates me with what I can see is little sincerity, clearly evidenced by his awestruck smile. "We've just never encountered a construct before."

"Who do you think made it?" Liam asks. He's at least thinking about important things. The wrong important things, but still.

"Guys, who cares about golems and who made them and why they were there! Guess what happened?" I make eye contact with each of them, enjoying the suspense.

"Your balls finally dropped?" Ethan's voice is as dry as the sand around us.

"Fuck you, asshole!" I swear if my arm wasn't in a sling, I'd jump into the Fiery Pits for the guy – but he pisses me off daily.

"Tell us what happened, Kevin." Jessica's always there to make sure we don't kill each other in a fistfight gone too far.

"Right. Our illustrious leader, our great commander, the stalwart presence leading us to victory in every fight —" Everyone groans on cue and my grin spreads further, "— got to third base with an archdemon. Or was it second base? Regardless! There was dry humping."

Jess' mouth falls open, Liam frowns, and Ethan goes bug-eyed.

"What?"

"How did that happen?"

"Was there spanking?"

CHAPTER 13 – LANA

After bathing and sleeping off the lingering shame and arousal, I limp out to the training area where my teammates, and the rest of the Elioud as well, train daily to maintain optimal physical readiness. While we heal faster than we did in the mortal realm, it's still going to take Kevin and me a couple of days to recover from the sprain and broken humerus.

Jess, Liam, and Ethan are stretching while giving Kevin, arm in sling, their rapt attention.

Oh no...

"Lana!" Ethan yells once he sees me, his chocolate eyes sparkling with mischief. Ethan is tall, lithe, and always obviously Cambion. Most of us don't really know where in our family trees the Celestial blood mixed in, me being an exception thanks to Maalik. But Ethan's grandmother swore up until her last days at a mental asylum that his grandfather was a demon that stole her virtue and left her bred and unwed. His family was sure it was the desperate ramblings of a mentally unstable woman, trying to save her reputation in a strict society. I mean, it worked for Mary, right?

"Yes, Ethan?" I ask warily as I finish approaching my little group.

"I heard you got a dose of demon di–"

The blast of wind I send his way knocks him on his ass and interrupts the very obvious thing he was about to say.

"Really, Kevin?" I say to the culprit between gritted teeth.

Kev raises his functional arm in a gesture of surrender, his bound one making it look like he's about to swear in for presidency over a bible.

"I didn't know I wasn't supposed to say!"

To his credit, he looks regretful, with his eyebrows furrowed and bottom lip pouting out, and I can't really stay mad at him when he's technically right.

"I thought it was implied." I glare at him.

"Hey, everyone knows Evander bangs every succubus he encounters on patrols," Jessica says in a soothing voice, her eyes somewhat giving away the mirth she feels at my situation. Evander's a team leader and a bit of a himbo.

"I don't care if every winged creature in the realm took a turn riding Evander's pogo stick," I reply grumpily. I know it's too late to stop the rumor mill – curious glances were already being thrown my way from every corner of the field since I stepped out of the fortress. "This was different and we all know it."

I groan when I see everyone within earshot now obviously struggling to catch my words and perhaps a salacious little nugget of information that distracts from the humdrum of daily life in Purgatory and Hell.

"Twenty laps around the field," I say to my team in my best 'I Am Your Commander' voice. "You guys are going to make up for two of us being benched." Whines and pitiful looks are the reactions I expected and got, but I have no mercy on them – even on Liam, who minded his own business like he usually does. He's a goody-two-shoes. Cracking the proverbial whip works on lightening my mood, and I drop unceremoniously onto my ass in the dirt, Kev joining me.

"I really am sorry, Lan," he says quietly. "Figured you'd know I'd blab to them ASAP."

I sigh and pat his good shoulder, "It's okay, the chances of keeping this under wraps were slim anyway."

"Why are you this upset though? Jess was right about Evander and, uh... I may or may not have dallied with a succubus or two on solo patrols," he says, blushing at my stunned expression. He can't take the eye contact and looks at our teammates ribbing each other while jogging around the field, clearly wishing he was there and not under my scrutiny.

"I'm not judging, Kev," I hurry to say. "I'm just surprised. And it is different. Succubi and incubi, while far from innocent, normally leave humans alive. Weak and sex-addled but alive," I add with a twist of my lips.

I grab a dried out husk of a stick and start drawing squiggles in the sand, needing to occupy myself so I feel… less.

"He's likely thousands of years old, party to countless atrocities, and probably picks his teeth with the bones of innocent babies in his free time," I mutter into the ground, far more embarrassed than Kev was about his demonic horizontal tangos. Despite not initiating the encounter and knowing I was unlikely to break free, it's not like I didn't enjoy it. I enjoyed it more than the demon did, and I'm sure that was a purposeful move made to compound my guilt further. Speaking of baby bones, I quickly drop the hollow stick.

I look up at my squad, Liam now laughing as Jessica tries to trip Ethan up so she can take the lead. The normality makes me smile and gives me the courage to look at Kevin. He gulps, shakes his head, and says, "I'm not sure what to say, Lan."

"It's okay," I repeat, even though it's not, but it's obviously the motto of the day.

***

I'm sparring hard-to-hand with Jess, finally back in fighting shape after what feels like an eternity. Her long blonde hair's up in a ponytail that keeps slapping me in the face as she turns.

I sputter and say, "Do you have a weapon permit for that whip?" making her stop mid-move and laugh.

I take advantage of her distraction, drop to my hands, and swipe my leg out low, tripping her. Standing up, I give her a smirk. "Don't get distracted, girly-girl." She flips me off, still lying on her back, and now we're both laughing.

Long hair *is* a distraction in a fight. In the last few years, I managed to singe the ends of mine, and also slice off a significant amount of the ponytail it was in at the time with my own damned sword. We're still clinging to the dredges of normality, though.

Also, demons and manifestations of evil souls – being amorphous – don't exactly resort to hair-pulling in a fight. The former usually come equipped with claws and razor-sharp teeth, the latter burn like acid if you happen to graze against them.

I just finish helping Jess stand when a blanket of oppression covers us. It's like storm clouds descended all at once, and static electricity sparks over organic matter. I know this feeling, though this is a hundred times more powerful, and not at all pleasurable.

All at once, two dozen cloaked figures materialize at the outer edge of our training field. The corner closest to my team, naturally. Our Fallen mentors burst out into the field and stop a step in front of us, their pupils automatically positioning themselves behind them, team leaders first.

Akira, Corson's team leader, intones quietly, but loud enough for the front row to hear him. "Hell is empty and all the devils are here." He's quoting Shakespeare.

He's right, because it's obvious that a good amount of Hell's top demonarchy is here, and not in their own regions.

I can't help but look over the powerful beings standing in front of us and wonder which one of them is my demon. *Not that he's mine*, I remind myself. But have I stopped thinking of him these last couple of weeks? No. Am I admitting that to anyone else? Also no.

It's bad enough that everyone knows about the nature of the encounter. In the first week following my... attack, Nick, the asshole, crashed into me while running and snarled, "Don't touch me, demon cockslut." Suffice it to say his attitude towards me hasn't improved through the years. I just flipped him off, trying to keep my face impassive, but his team leader, Darla, slapped him across the head and nodded at me. Girls supporting girls, gotta love it

Suddenly, I feel a sting at the now-healed junction of my neck. I press my hand against it automatically and my gaze snaps to one of the cloaked figures. Nothing really distinguishes him from the rest of the pack – he's taller than some, and less brutally brawny than others, but they're all imposing and menacing in their own way.

I know without a doubt it's him, just as I know that my unthinking reaction pleased him. Like he's letting me know that, while not visible anymore, his marks remain on my skin, in my flesh.

I drop my hand just as Kevin sidles up to me. "Are you okay?" he asks, brushing against me to speak near my ear. A massive lightning bolt splits the sky, the thunderous boom instantaneous.

While the majority of the soldiers around me are ducking, flinching, or yelping, I instinctively step in front of Kevin and look at the figure that displayed his displeasure. I don't know what to make of the pulse of emotion I feel in my belly at his reaction to Kevin's touch. It's not something I've felt before, a mix of protectiveness but also smugness. I divert my gaze just in time to notice that Daniel followed it and is now frowning. That's an expression I haven't seen on his beautiful face before.

"May I inquire as to why you *gentlemen* are out *en force* in Purgatory?" Maalik's voice is always loud enough to echo, despite not shouting.

"We couldn't decide who to send," a honeyed voice replies. "It seems that we, ah, don't trust each other not to take advantage of a... rather delicate situation."

This demon's voice makes me think of the snake that ured Eve to the Forbidden Apple.

"What is the situation and what does it have to do with us?" Ramel sneers, tact never a part of his arsenal.

"Well, it seems that there is an ungoverned rift, through which demons are escaping to the mortal realm."

This proclamation has us all stirring from our enraptured states and looking at our mentors, trying to gauge their reactions. Surely this is a task for us, right? Will we get to visit the human realm? While Maalik has been bringing us some essentials like razors and novels (that is essential to me, okay?), we haven't seen a bright blue sky in three years. I'm not sure what would be worse – visiting and then returning once our mission is done, or not visiting at all.

"You need us to find the tear?" Corson, our proverbial master of intelligence on all things Hell asks, his brow furrowed.

The snake-tongued demon laughs condescendingly. "No, of course not. We know the tear is in Asmodai's realm. And before you ask another imbecilic question, he appears to be missing. Or at least not returning communiques."

This time there are murmurs in our ranks, all of us wondering how an archdemon goes missing.

"Quiet," Maalik says to us, and then louder, "and your *Dark Prince*," the title uttered with much sarcasm, "doesn't know where one of his minions is?"

A monstrously brawny demon bristles at Maalik's irreverence and grunts, "You are free to go ask our Lord yourself; see how many pieces are returned to your *brothers*."

"Why are you here?" Daniel repeats the pertinent question, likely stopping the two males from coming to blows. He normally lets others do the talking, but it seems like he's had enough of the tension between our two groups.

"If we go, we will be sensed immediately. Our presence will be considered an attempt to conquer an unprotected region."

The shock of hearing that voice freezes every cell in my body. My face warms. My ears are ringing. I feel light-headed and realize I stopped breathing. Cognizant of Kevin and Daniel's attention, I try to control my expression.

"The Elioud, however, won't be as easily sensed, and they're insignificant enough not to be considered a threat," Forked-Tongue finishes.

"And they're also expendable pawns to send to the slaughter, correct?" Maalik grits out.

"You said that, not us," the demon retorts. "The fact of the matter is, your soldiers are the only ones who can get in and out without detection to tell us whether he's interred in his domain and not giving a damn that we're at risk of being exposed beyond containment, or… if we have a bigger problem to contend with."

Maalik growls, gnashing his teeth and looking at his fellow Fallen. They nod, some with more reluctance than others.

"There is an elaborate system of tunnels throughout Asmodai's ziggurat," Corson supplies. "It could be for ventilation or lighting; their use is unknown to us. Regardless, it is possible for a lithe individual to crawl through them to the interior. Two, at most, could plausibly avoid detection."

Everyone takes his words in in silence, letting Maalik strategize. "Lana?" he asks, not looking at me.

I think about it objectively. I'm not the strongest, fastest, or most powerful among the soldiers. But I know why he asked me first. I purse my lips and nod. Thunder echoes in cracks as the sky fills with a webbing of lightning.

"Lana, perhaps due to being Nephalem," Daniel starts to explain, and I swear he's looking at my assailant while doing so, "has a uniquely strong sense of detection. She can not only sense when demons are present, but also their numbers and strength. Certainly strong enough to sense the presence of a being as old and powerful as Asmodai."

After a beat, Maalik asks me, "And? You're not going alone."

I don't need to think it over. "Akira." I pick my teammate for the unusual mission. Maalik and Corson nod at my choice; Akira is Corson's stealthiest Cambion. He's careful and calculating. He's also too proud to just leave me behind in a tight spot, like some of his other soldiers might.

Kevin however lets out a low, closed-mouthed noise, unhappy, but ultimately he must know my choice was the only correct one.

"Weapons?" Maalik asks next.

I shake my head. "Just a couple of knives. If it comes to a fight, we'll be overwhelmed by sheer numbers anyway, and there's no point in dragging large weapons through small tunnels."

"That's what she said," Nick snickers, and Darla smacks him. Her hand must hurt all the time.

"Read the room!" she hisses at him.

"Your ankle is fine?" Maalik checks with me, ignoring the idiot behind us.

"Yup," I reply. "Perfectly capable of running like a scared little girl when being chased by a hundred imps determined to make Lana kabobs," I finish while mock-saluting him.

Maalik, more than used to my antics by now, just scoffs.

The demon who had the most to say is now suspiciously quiet. I look at the figure whose burning gaze I feel on my cheek. Lightning is still crackling angrily above us, showing his displeasure over my choices. Well, tough luck. I'm a soldier and if nothing else, the last few years have indoctrinated me into believing that it's my duty to shield innocent people. Like Mike.

Just because the demon lord got his teeth in me – both literally and figuratively once – doesn't mean he has a say in the decisions of Abaddon.

"Go get ready." Maalik nods at Akira and me. "This will take a couple of days," he says to the figures still choking us with their oppressive aura.

I turn in the direction of the armory, Kevin and Daniel leaving with me.

"Lana..." Kevin says plaintively.

"I'll be fine," I tell him. And myself. And perhaps even the demon glaring at my back.

"Which one?" I quietly ask Daniel as we move across the field.

He knows what I'm asking and replies even quieter, "Ashtaroth."

"Ashtaroth," I repeat, and feel every hair on my body stand at attention. As if he heard me invoke his name, despite my quiet voice, despite the distance now between us.

As I step into the fortress, I glance behind one last time. Some of the cloaked figures are still conversing with the mentors who remain on the field. Some of them have turned and vanished. But one figure stands still, the darkness under the hood of his cloak turned in my direction.

LIANA VALERIAN

CHAPTER 14 – ASHTAROTH

I push the heavy reinforced double doors to my throne room with both hands and with force, making each panel slam into the walls. I march inside, my steel-plated boots echoing with each step that pounds against the mosaic leading toward my throne. The depictions of human souls burning in the Pits of Hell flicker in the light cast by the standing black candelabra.

Sariel looks up at my noisy entrance and stops mid-sentence in his conversation with his friend Armaros. His black-feathered wings are out and they twitch as he meets me halfway, then follows me to my seat.

"How'd it go?" he asks.

Though his charming words have melted uncountable numbers of females and males into puddles of lust, the abbreviated manner in which he speaks vexes me even more than usual today.

"It is done," I clip, and sit back, my heavy armor now feeling like it's compressing my lungs.

"Then why're you ticked off?" my son asks, quirking a black eyebrow, confusion clear on his face.

"You know, brother," Armaros says, a depraved smile firmly in place, "he came home smelling of pussy the other day. Mostly human pussy," he finishes, his grin now looking unnaturally large on his narrow face. "Maybe he accidentally decapitated her before he got off."

Sariel uncharacteristically ignores the gruesome and lewd suggestion and turns his face back towards me, his charcoal black eyes wide in surprise.

"One of the soldiers?" he asks and then adds, as if this new information added up with today's events to draw a clear picture of the situation, "I see."

"Leave," I growl at them.

They turn at once. Not even Armaros is idiot enough to test me in this mood.

They're halfway down the aisle when I decide that their impertinence should not go unpunished.

I wave a hand and the mosaic they're walking on dissolves, square by square. A gratifying canon of surprised yelps soothes the inexplicable fire burning inside me as they fall into nothing, landing in the dungeons so conveniently placed under my throne room.

I pinch the bridge of my nose. She will get herself killed, and I have yet to have my fill.

CHAPTER 15 – LANA

"The courtyard is suspiciously empty," I tell Akira.

We're perched like buzzards atop a cliff overlooking Asmodeus' fortress. Corson was right when he called it a ziggurat; it looks like something the Mayans built. Other than the fact that it's made of what looks like pure onyx.

Akira just grunts, still observing our destination, looking for movement.

"I expected imps dancing around fire pits, worshiping their demonic overlords."

This time he says nothing at all. As a successful banker from a wealthy Japanese family, he was probably used to speaking only when necessary, even before he came under Corson's tutelage.

"Have you ever been so close to an archdemon's stronghold?" I try again.

This time I get a reaction. "You talk too much."

I grin. "I know. You're blessed to be in my presence." His slightly angled eyes narrow further and I swear he's holding back a smile. I'll get there eventually. If we don't die screaming first.

It took us over a day of trekking through Hell, crossing from one domain to another, from lands covered in charcoal and ash, to barren deserts and through dead forests of gnarled trees. We didn't encounter a single denizen before we got to our destination. We must have gotten diplomatic immunity. I snort at my own internal joke. Akira ignores me.

"I sense a lot of demons inside, but I need to get closer to be able to separate what I'm feeling into numbers and hierarchies." I get to the task at hand, not willing to spend many more nights out in the open. While the majority of Hell isn't completely inhospitable – save the Burning Pits, from what we're told – the presence of soul manifestations and hungry demons make it impossible to rest without one of us keeping watch. It doesn't make for restful nights.

Akira nods and points his chin to the back of the structure. "That side is closest to cover. We should descend there."

"Agreed."

We carefully move around the structure, still staying out of line of sight, stopping to check for movement intermittently. Once we get to the closest approach, we use the skinny nascent pine trees as handholds, and their roots as steps. Halfway down, we spot one of the tunnel openings Corson described.

I sigh. "We're going to have to climb." Getting in unnoticed is just the first step in a sequence of doozies.

Once we're at the building, I crouch and give Akira a foothold up the first block. The shorter man then reaches down to pull me up. We carefully repeat the process, not speaking, until we get to the opening and I gulp. It's narrow and I can't see a light at the end. Claustrophobia tightens my ribcage.

Akira grabs my hand in solidarity and nods for me to go first. Once I get a feeling whether Asmodeus is here or not, we can return to Abaddon. It's possible we're going to have to crawl backward.

Fuck. Here goes nothing.

I, surprisingly, get used to the rhythm of my movements after a while, and avoid thinking about being trapped in the narrow darkness. I still can't get a feeling for our quarry, though.

I don't know how much time passes in silence before we hear it: screams, laughter, shouting. Pretty much what one would expect from ungoverned demonic minions. We've reached a balcony and I peek out over the railing, Akira joining me.

The scene before us is utter chaos. Demons are tearing each other apart. There are imps and raptors, like the one we faced near that graveyard years ago. The odd incubus is standing out – they're usually more lovers than fighters. A demon with fists wreathed in flames grabs hold of a hellhound and bites its head off, ichor spraying all over his face and the surrounding imps that are vying for a taste. A muscular demon, practically a behemoth, suddenly lunges towards one of the imps and rips it in half, throwing both pieces of dead demon away from him – one of them right in our direction. I quickly duck closer to the ground. The imp's lower half splatters against the wall behind me with a grotesque sound and I'm overwhelmed by an acidic smell.

I swallow down my nausea and close my eyes, trying to focus on our objective and not the overpowering sounds and smells. The more powerful demons are farther below us. I catch Akira's gaze and point down. His lips tighten but he nods.

We don't know the layout of the giant building. If the archdemon's contemporaries knew it, they did not share it with us. We crabwalk the perimeter of the balcony that's encircling the chaos below until we find another tunnel with a downward inclination. I eye the depthless dark and wince, imagining myself sliding down on my ass, straight into a behemoth's waiting maw.

No way but forward, I guess. I dangle my legs into the hole and, with a final smile of bravado at Akira, push off. A damp wind stirs the hair that escaped my braid as I keep sliding, the tunnel feeling slick as if covered by algae. God, I hope it's algae.

With a splash, I hit the water and quickly move to avoid being crushed by Akira when he lands. Taking stock of my surroundings, I realize that what I landed in can be more adequately described as sewage. I gag and almost press my hand against my mouth, before noticing it's covered in green slime.

Shit, I really am going to hurl. I feel the tell-tale tingling sensations, the saliva gathering in my mouth. Just before I upchuck, Akira lands behind me with his own splash. A splash that sends a wave of sewage over me. Suddenly I'm so glad my mouth was closed that I momentarily forget my nausea.

Seeing as we haven't been overrun by demons, I figure we're alone, and scramble toward the nearest ledge. It's not easy hoisting myself onto dry land while being covered in goo. While I slip and slide like a demented slug, Akira snickers and pulls himself out effortlessly and elegantly. Fucker.

When we're both out, we use bursts of wind to blow most of the slime, algae, and water off ourselves. We're still looking kind of green and there are scrapes from the tunnels wherever leather doesn't cover us. Shuddering over the thought of infection, I use the ether to encourage our blood cells into clotting the wounds. The ability now comes easier to me than most. Of course, Daniel is far better at it... and so was Simone. It only takes a thought to send thrombocytes to the sites of our scrapes, coaxing them to plug the ruptures.

Once I'm done, I turn in a circle and stop when I'm facing the direction with the strongest pulse of demonic presence. I point in the direction with my chin. Akira unsheathes his twin daggers and I follow suit, though I still feel like they'd be pretty ineffectual if we get surrounded by several upper-level demons.

As we exit the demonic version of aqueducts and walk down the corridor I chose, the temperature suddenly increases. While moments ago I felt a damp chill, a dry heat is now permeating the air, drying my skin and leaving behind a gritty residue. Along with the heat come angry sounds; first at a murmur, but as we creep closer, I hear growls of rage.

A red and orange glow suffuses the end of the dark hallway, light flickering on the walls, the hot wind stirring dust. We approach warily, not knowing what exactly we're getting ourselves into. The demonic presence is definitely strongest here, though, so approach it we must.

I can now sense that a couple of dozen upper-level demons are congregated in the area beyond the next turn. What I don't sense is the presence of an archdemon or anything that would be strong enough in power to be a demon lord. I stop Akira and shake my head, then shrug – now what? He looks at me, then towards the source of the flickering light, and I can understand what he's thinking – we've gotten this far.

Once we've taken the turn, we can see that the corridor is in shambles – black brick lays everywhere as if a battering ram hit it from the outside. The heat and light are coming from the hole in the wall and we can hear high-pitched wailing now, joining the growls of anger.

We try to stay out of sight of the demons we sense below as we peek outside. I see the demons I felt and in the numbers I felt. There are succubi and incubi, demons known for seduction and trickery, and something I'd expect in numbers in the court of the Duke of Lust. While these breeds look similar enough to humans, many have wings and hooves, tails and horns. They also come in varying colors, besides the spectrum found with humans: from lavender to rose, and with hair of green, blue, or white. What they all have in common, though, is an ethereal sort of beauty and allure, making them the perfect predators to feed on the body's carnal responses.

It's the presence of physically stronger demons, ones likely in positions of army commanders, however, that make me think we chanced upon some of Asmodeus' upper court. These demons are farther from human appearance; they're grotesque and alien, some much larger, all much stronger. Asmodeus' generals, demon lords, are likely in their own dwellings, and not present.

While I expected to see these demons, I didn't expect them in the state of imprisonment they're in. All of them are in suspended steel cages, futilely rattling the bars, unleashing occasional growls of rage. The sex demons look a bit peaky, like whoever imprisoned them didn't think about their... dietary requirements. I wonder how long they can feed off each other.

The captive demons aren't the strangest part of the scene before us, though. Under the cages is an opening in the ground itself, like a meteor had hurtled through all the lower levels of the citadel and stopped so far below that we can't even see where that is. The depthless crater glows. Suffocating brimstone mist fouls the air beyond what we're already used to, and the wailing seems to be coming from it as well. My mouth opens in a gasp of shock.

If I'm not mistaken, and I don't think I am since I still spend all of my free time reading what is now various grimoires (there's only so much cliterature Maalik can bring me from topside), that hole leads to the Burning Pits. The very inner sanctum of Hell, Satan's domain. A domain said to be mostly molten rock and spewing lava.

I give Akira an unmistakable 'what the fuck is going on here?' look and he returns his own that says 'fuck if I know'.

Okay, he would never really say that, but it's implied.

Taking one more look at the caged commanders and courtiers, trying to memorize as much as I can so that I can describe it to the Fallen, I gesture to Akira that we're done here.

This is super confusing. We haven't seen or felt any indicators that there's a rift to the human realm here, and to top it off, the archdemon's court somehow got collectively imprisoned, leaving the lesser demons completely unchecked.

The presence of the crater leading deeper into the Underworld gives me a clue to Asmodeus' location, however. I think he's in Lucifer's inner sanctum with the vilest of demons and souls. Since it doesn't appear that he's gone of his own free will, I wonder what provoked the Devil into bringing him there.

CHAPTER 16 – LANA

Adrenaline makes my muscles burn. The levels above us are full of demons, most less lethal than the lieutenants caged below, but far too numerous for us to contend with. Trying to hear past the beating of my heart, I'm belatedly hit with fear over the gravity of our situation. We're playing hide and seek in the enemy's territory, outmanned and outgunned. I hadn't thought this far ahead when I jumped into the slimy chute earlier.

We were trained to banish manifestations of sin and the odd demonic minion – that golem was the toughest opponent I've faced in my years below the human realm. Especially without my full team. I definitely wasn't adequately prepared to skulk around archdemons' houses. Akira, however, seems to be in his element. Either that or his icy exterior hides any fear and doubt. Though, I guess, anyone trained by Corson would be familiar with espionage and subterfuge.

We're back at the sewers and round a corner, sliding over slimy algae, just as a nestful of water imps drop down from the dripping grates above us. I've encountered the creatures before in a foul swamp I was clearing with my team. Their spindly limbs are covered in pale skin tinged sickly blue. It's fitting that they'd be at home here in this pungent sewer water.

Akira and I unsheathe our daggers in unison as the imps chitter with excitement, probably thinking that prey conveniently landed in their laps like a pizza delivery. The creatures start forming balls of fetid water to throw at us.

While having water thrown at you may sound innocuous enough, I know from experience that these imps pack a punch that's disproportionate to their size. Besides, there's a lot of them. I quickly use the ether to throw up a shield of hard-packed air, Akira following my lead.

I take the first few punches of water head-on as I throw myself at the nearest imp, daggers poised to stab into its little neck, one at each side. The imp gurgles and rancid water dribbles out of its mouth. I pull my daggers out just in time for an imp to land on my back, arms wrapped around my neck in a violent imitation of a piggyback ride. I land face-first onto the slain imp beneath me, my mouth filling with noxious liquid. I gag and buck up with enough force to flip us over, the imp now crushed beneath my weight under my back. The snapping of his bones and the sloshing sounds of his perforated innards, combined with the foul taste in my mouth finally push me over the edge of my tolerance. I tip to the side and burning stomach acid expels from between my lips, my stomach contracting in painful spasms. The smell of my vomit hardly registers through the offensive bouquet of odors already permeating the room.

"Whenever you're done resting, I could use a hand with the other dozen," Akira grits through clenched teeth as he uses his bare hands to rip an imp's head off. I manage to suppress the urge to throw up again and flip him off before scrambling up to my feet.

An imp charges towards me and I kick it, punting it into the wall. It slides down and lands in a heap. I almost feel bad for a second, like a giant bully, but then another latches onto my leg, biting me in the calf. While it doesn't manage to pierce the thicker leather of my boots, it's still applying enough pressure to hurt.

"Motherfucker!" I growl and hop on one foot, shaking the other like a dog when its owner finds the funny spot to scratch. Finally, it detaches. And sails straight into Akira. The soldier turns and glares at me before snapping the imp's neck.

"Sowwy," I pout. He shakes his head with a look of utter disgust and turns towards the next cluster of demons. I flip my daggers over into a reverse grip and punch one through the nearest imp's temple. I face the next demon.

Minutes later, I'm bent over, hands propped on my legs, trying to catch my breath. "That's it," I tell Akira. "That's the last time I'm going on a road trip with you."

He gives me an incredulous look.

***

We manage to find our way out of the sewers and climb into a circular room. The walls are tall, reaching all the way to the top of the ziggurat, where faded light filters in through high, narrow openings. The majority of the space is occupied by a turret staircase in the middle. Looking up, I see bridged pathways branching out of it. I think we're at the heart of the building.

There are corridors spaced throughout the area, some of which clearly lead to occupied halls. I frantically search for a smaller opening like the tunnel we entered through. Before we can make our choice, low growls stop us in place. I feel three hellhounds, now far too close to us for my liking. Clearly they're onto our scent and stalking us.

We dart into the nearest dark corridor just as a hunting howl splits the air. They've found us.

"Run," I pant, not daring a glance behind as I pump my arms and push myself into a sprint. The hellhounds are faster than us, naturally, and it's not long before Akira whirls around and swipes his daggers, one after the other, at the hellhound crashing into him.

Instinct takes over and I push them with a gust of air, then pull out my throwing knives, allowing myself just a breath before I throw them at the hounds. My aim is decent; I hit one of our attackers in the eye, while the other turns, and the knife's tip embeds into its flank. Green blood oozes from their leathery black skin, but neither my targets nor the hound Akira sliced at slow down.

One of the hellhounds, knife still lodged in its eye, snaps his shark-like serrated teeth at me, and I scream as the skin on my arm is sliced into ribbons. Akira bathes them with fire manifested from ether and they yelp and dart back.

While the creatures observe us, caution in their many rows of eyes, I expend precious energy to stop my wounds from bleeding. These foes are too much for us.

"I see a tunnel ahead." Akira's words are terse, and he pushes me ahead of him, turning to scorch our pursuers one more time. "I'm out," he snaps, clearly irritated by his own limitations.

Ignoring the pain from the bite and the many scrapes and bumps from the tunnels, I sprint towards our exit, my lungs burning and my heartbeat drumming out an irregular tattoo. I can hear the snarls of the approaching hounds and it feels like they're right at our ankles. Once I'm close enough, I dive into the tunnel, arms extended, screaming again at the new burst of pain. I quickly scurry forward and Akira crawls in behind me.

Just as I think we're safe from the much larger creatures, Akira's wail of pain stops my heart. I turn my head to see his brown eyes spread wide open in panic, a hellhound dragging him out by the foot. The smell of rotten eggs and acid emanating from the demon burns my nostrils.

I splay my hand behind me and send one more narrow gust of air just above Akira, freeing him from the hellhound's grasp. Luckily, he recovers fast enough to scramble out of reach.

The last of the light is gone and we don't stop crawling, even though my arms are shaking, and sweat stings my eyes and the scrapes on my face. All I can hear are our heaving breaths and the slide of leathers against stone. The hounds are either too far away to hear, or they've gone around to try to intercept us.

An uncountable amount of time later, we're out of the ziggurat. Though the smell of brimstone is always present in Hell, I gulp down marginally fresher air while waiting for Akira to join me, before we slide down the building.

We're on the other side of the pyramid now and there's zero cover. Gritting my teeth, I resign myself to more running. There's no way of knowing when the hellhounds will raise the alarm, if they haven't already. At least the courtyard is still empty.

A glance at Akira shows me he's deathly pale, and though he clotted his wound enough to not leave a bloody trail, it must be pure anguish to run on the bitten leg. He catches my gaze and nods forward, refusing any aid I may be able to provide. It would only slow us down.

So we run.

LIANA VALERIAN

CHAPTER 17 – LANA

"How much of that is your blood?" Maalik snaps at me the next day when Akira and I arrive back at Purgatory. He was waiting for us at the edge of the realm – this is his way of showing he cares. And, indeed, in his snake eyes I see worry over the fact he sent us on a mission where I got so visibly injured.

Though our pace was slower, neither of us wanted to break stride for a couple of hours of sleep, so we made decent time. We're filthy, hurting, and exhausted.

"I honestly don't know anymore," I reply, my voice faint. "I just know I need ten baths and twice as many hours of sleep." I was tempted to jump into The Lethe at some point, the smell getting to my frayed nerves. Thankfully, Akira stopped me. Probably to prevent the loss of memory of everything we've seen, though.

"Tell me," Maalik demands.

"He's not there," I sigh. "What is there is an opening into The Pits."

"The Pits?" Maalik is incredulous and makes eye contact with Akira, who nods back in confirmation. Seriously? I know I look like I've been through a macerator, but I'm not hallucinating.

"All the higher-ups in his court are locked in cages above it. It looks like only one being could have been responsible for the situation and his name starts with a capital D. We didn't see the rift, though," I add.

"I see." He frowns. "I'll let Belial know." Belial must be the honey-tongued orator. I don't have enough energy to care. "Clean yourselves up and let Daniel tend to your wounds." Maalik dismisses us.

"Don't have to tell me twice," I mutter.

By now we've reached the atrium and I wave my hand once in farewell to Akira.

"Will see you later, Lana," he finally speaks, of his own free will.

I guess it took almost dying together to get his attention. Who'd have known?

***

I wake up drenched – both from sweat and arousal. Panting, I squeeze my thighs together and squirm.

I dreamt about the archdemon. He was sliding inside me, moving above me, his solid weight pressing me down in a show of dominance. My hand slides up my stomach towards my chest. I feel like I'm just a touch away from orgasm.

Thankfully, my senses return before I act on the need coursing through me. Frustrated, I throw my covers back and jump out of bed, heading straight towards the bathtub for Hell's version of a cold shower. I can't control my dreams, but I can control the choices I make with my body. At least, when his fiery eyes aren't burning me into a pliable pile of playdough.

Another thing I can't control is my curiosity. Though I'm telling myself knowledge is power and blah, blah, blah. Cooled off and dressed, I head towards the keep's library.

It doesn't take me long to find what I'm looking for, and soon I'm thumbing through a heavy leather-bound grimoire, doing what I wanted to do ever since I found out what the archdemon's name is. *Ashtaroth.* I swallow as shivers gallop across my skin.

A demon in the first hierarchy of Hell, I read. *A Great Duke of Hell. Known as Ashtaroth, Astaroth, Astarot, or Asteroth. Associated with temptations, seductions, and leading individuals astray.* Yeah, no shit. *Guiding people towards desires and indulgence.* Tell me something I don't know, book. *Connected with two deadly sins, either lust or pride.* Interesting. I wonder how this ties in with the existence of the missing Asmodeus, or Asmodai, as the Celestials call him, the Duke more commonly known for the sin of ust

I turn to the next page and find a drawing of Ashtaroth's seal.

I trace the pentagram with my fingers, then veer off to the branching curlicues.

"You will not summon him to the library, I hope?" The sound of Daniel's voice jolts me out of my fixation and I blush. I was just caught caressing a demonic seal.

"I'm just reading up," I mumble, unable to make eye contact. "How did you know which one he is, by the way?"

"The lightning." Daniel sits across from me and folds his hands in his lap. "You must not have encountered mention of it in your reading yet. There is a lot of conflicting information in these grimoires, both in those written by mortals and in our own accounts."

I make a noncommittal sound and turn the page, getting away from the seal.

"Resisting temptation is not easy, child. If it was, Hell would be a lot emptier, and you would be living the rest of your mortal life in ignorance." Daniel's voice is gentle, but I hate that he sees right through me, into what's happening inside my body, my mind.

"I think you have rested enough after your excursion. Nick is alone south of the keep as Dean has injured his wrist. You could join him." Daniel gives me an out from our uncomfortable, mostly one-sided conversation, and I take it. Even though Nick is far from my favorite person.

I snap the book closed, tell him I'll see him at dinner, and change into my leathers.

The delineation between Purgatory and Hell is invisible – at least to our eyes. If the Fallen see it differently, they haven't shared with the class. One moment I'm standing on familiar gray sand, the ever-present aurora above me, the next I smell the rotten eggs of brimstone and the sky is on fire. Even though The Phlegethon is a couple of miles away, the ground feels chalkier, the air warmer.

I don't walk more than twenty minutes in the direction of Nick's tracks when I see the blond soldier in the distance. He's sneering at me before I even get close enough to get a word out. I still try to be civil though, so I greet him politely enough. "Daniel said Dean had to return," I add to my greeting.

"So, what?" His voice is even more hostile than usual. What crawled up his ass? "He sent the mighty demon fucker to protect me?"

I can't help but flush from head to toe. "You're an asshole, Nick," I hiss back at him. I turn on my heel to leave, unwilling to put up with his venom today, when I'm suddenly pushed from behind. The unexpected force surprises me enough that I lose my balance. I barely catch myself from faceplanting into the dry ground, scraping the heels of my palms.

I don't get to assess myself before Nick is yelling. Turning, I see that he's completely unhinged, the veins in his neck standing out with tension. "Don't turn your back on me, you frigid prude!" His eyes gleam with the kind of madness only a hurt male ego can produce.

I can't help but press on the wound – he went a step too far today. "Which is it, Nick? A slut or a prude? Or is anyone who chooses to not fuck *you* both?" I raise my palms in question as if I really am curious about the answer. Then I go for the throat. "And what do you call the ones that take pity on you once, but can't stomach to do so the second time you ask, knowing you couldn't even get a succubus off?"

His face turns a mottled purple and he unsheathes his longsword. "I'm going to gut you," he says, his voice so low it's barely recognizable.

I jump a step back, completely bewildered. "What the fuck is wrong with you, Nick?" My voice is shrill from shock; I never really bothered to engage him when he hurled his many, many insults over the last few years. I really didn't expect him to pull a weapon on me.

"You!" he shouts, spittle flying. "You're what's wrong! I'm fucking tired of watching you strut around, high and mighty, the team leader who can do no wrong. Lose a team member? It's not your fault. Get railed by an archdemon? No problem, Daniel will just take care of your booboos. And when someone needs to infiltrate an archdemon's stronghold, who do they pick? You!" His breathing is heavy, shoulders heaving with the movement. "I bet you suck cock all night long just so they don't kick you out on your worthless ass."

"Nick..." I hold my hands up placatingly and try to keep the edge of fear out of my voice. If I can't calm him down, one of us might not walk back from this. "You know it's not like that. I was picked for that mission because of my senses and no other reason." He snorts, but I continue, my voice turning harder. "And you have no idea what happened with Ashtaroth." I want to add that I didn't get railed either, but I'm distracted by the bolt of lightning across the sky, the following clap of instantaneous thunder. *Oh. Shit.*

Nick doesn't seem to notice the telltale meteorological reaction that followed me saying a certain name out loud in Hell. He's too busy laughing, the sound tinged with a healthy dose of hysteria. "Fucking liar. I bet you threw yourself at him like the desperate whore you are." He raises his sword to point it at me and I don't hesitate to pull mine out, despite a part of me still hoping that he'll just calm down. "I'm going to show them how weak you are. I'm going to drag your carcass back and show them all."

"Nick, stop!" I shriek, but it's too late. He lunges toward me with a powerful overhead attack and I duck and weave instinctively. He doesn't stop pressing the attack and swipes at my midsection diagonally. I barely manage to jump back in time and use one of my swords to deflect his. I can't keep this up for too long. He's larger than me and hasn't been injured recently. "Nick, please." I try to reason with him again. "Don't do this."

Nick doesn't reply, striking at me again, and this time I don't jump back far enough. He nicks the side of my torso, just under my ribcage, the leather splitting like butter and my skin with it. Fuck. Of course it does; his sword is made of angelic steel just like mine are.

I hiss and grit my teeth. It's time I reconcile with the fact that this is a kill-or-be-killed situation. I'll deal with the consequences later.

I barely notice the now-storming sky above us as Nick tries to strike at my head from above again. I don't dodge this time and cross my blades in front of me instead. As I stop his strike I snarl in his face – it's game on, buddy. Nick tries to use his greater physical strength to push down, but anticipating it, I twist and deflect his sword away.

He might be enraged, but all the training he received over the years is guiding him into all the right moves. He immediately tries to swipe towards my middle again. I manage to evade it and get some space between us.

I need to go on the offensive. The next time he charges at me, I duck, but I also use both of my swords to slash at his legs. He staggers back, the twin tears in his leathers weeping blood.

"Fucking bitch!" His face contorted in rage, he feints and kicks me in the stomach instead. My breath punches out as I fly backward, trying to hold on to my swords through the impact with the ground. "I'm gonna fuck you with my sword before I cut open your throat." His voice is full of glee as he slowly walks toward me.

But my eyes are not on him anymore. They're on the figure that materialized beside him.

The black-haired archdemon grabs Nick's arm so fast, that he doesn't even manage to fully turn his head before I hear his bones being crushed with a nauseating sound. Nick's high-pitched screams join the clap and boom of the thunder from the storm still ravaging the skies, and he drops to his knees.

I gather the courage to stand on shaking legs as Nick sobs, clearly in shock from the realization of who just attacked him This is the third time I've been near this demon – though I only really saw him the one time. His face is absolutely expressionless and the roiling flames of his eyes are the only sign of life.

"Did I call you?" I blurt out, my voice surprisingly even. His gaze slowly moves to me, then to the cut at my side and the dark, shining wetness on the leather around it. He takes a step behind Nick and places a hand on his shoulder.

"Please, please, please," the man on the ground snivels. The crotch of his leathers turns darker as he empties his bladder from pain and fear.

I should voice protest at whatever will surely happen to Nick... but he tried to kill me. I have no doubt he would've desecrated my corpse if it came to that. I look up from Nick's wet face and meet Ashtaroth's eyes. The thunder goes silent. He must take whatever expression he sees on my face as a green light and tightens his grip on Nick's shoulder.

A wet tearing and snapping sound, the likes of which I've never heard before is far too loud in the sudden silence, and it makes a primal part of me freeze. I can't quite focus on what the archdemon is doing, staring into the distance instead, but I expect he's ripping Nick's head off.

Instead of a head, something white, red, and pink is thrown before me, startling me from my stupor. I know I shouldn't look down, and maybe that's what makes it impossible not to. The thud of Nick's body hitting the ground is muffled by the high-pitched ringing in my ears. It takes longer than it should to realize that the off-white serpentine shape lying before me, with pink smears of blood and pieces of flesh still attached, is Nick's spine.

I turn away from the macabre sight and cover my face with my hands, like the grisly scene could ever be unseen. It's burned into my retinas and I feel my gorge rising. I place a hand on my stomach and the other over my mouth as I gag, my body convulsing violently.

A scent that's both fresh and homey invades my nose, soothing my roiling stomach. As I slowly rise from my hunched position, I can see Ashtaroth lifting his hand towards my face. His red, gore-covered hand. "No!" I blurt, but he just braces the back of my neck using his other hand to keep me from flinching away and touches my forehead with his blood-streaked thumb. I can feel him leave a smear of wetness, like he's anointing me with warpaint. Like I'm a certain lion prince and my father, the king, is about to show me off to his subjects in the jungle. The subjugating action has me fuming enough that I tear out of my stupor. I clench my fists and bare my teeth in a snarl. I want to bite that infuriating smirk clean off his perfect face.

He slides his clean hand down slowly from my neck to the small of my back, then pulls me into him. I gasp as our lower bodies come into contact. I don't want to know what part of this made him hard, whether it was the violence or my anger, but I can't ignore the pulse of liquid heat I feel at the press of that hardness against me. Looking up at his face brings vivid flashbacks from the dream I had just a few hours ago and I flush. I'm a sick, sick person. My colleague just tried to kill me, who is now lying as spineless in death as he was in life just a few feet away, and I'm cozying up against the archdemon that butchered him.

I don't find out what it is he has planned for me though; the eyes roving languorously over my face halt as the hand holding me against him tightens. He growls quietly.

"Soon." His perfect lips form the promise that makes me shiver and between one blink and the next, he steps back and disappears.

I must have been leaning on him more than I realized, because I stumble back and opt to sit down. The movement stretches my wound and I send what little energy I have left to its healing. It's not much. But that's Daniel I see running towards me — and Nick's remains. Divine intervention, I snicker to myself. Yeah, I'm definitely not mentally sound these days.

"What happened?" Daniel asks, sounding less surprised than I would have been if I happened upon a spineless corpse.

"He attacked me," I answer, waiting for the third-degree. But Daniel just nods, like it makes perfect sense that his trainee is lying on the ground sans spine, his other trainee the only other person that's present.

He kneels next to me and inspects my wound. "It appears to be healing on its own. We will clean and dress it at the keep."

"How did you know?" I ask numbly.

"I was pacing outside. I felt... disquieted. I had already decided to follow you when I saw the first lightning strike. I hurried over and had barely glimpsed you standing with him in the distance before he noticed my presence."

I hang my head. He saw me pressed against the archdemon, a detached spinal column garnishing the romantic scene, bits of gore sprinkled around like rose petals. Instead of being disgusted with me, Daniel stands up and offers me his hand. "He prevented your death." Once more he's reading me like an open book.

"Again..." I mumble and let him pull me up.

"I cannot resent him in this moment," Daniel says, his voice steely.

"But, Nick?" I gesture towards the grisly remains of the vicious young man.

"Did he deserve it?" He asks pragmatically. An odd question coming from such a kind being. Deserve it? Does anyone deserve to get their spine ripped out? Though, it was a quick death. Aside from some crushed bones, he didn't suffer. I have a feeling he would have made me suffer...

"Yes," I reply, lifting my chin. "He deserved it."

CHAPTER 18 – ASHTAROTH

I stare at my viscera-covered hand and flex my fingers into a fist.

How is it possible for one person to come so close to death as frequently as my lamb does? She is a magnet for mayhem, the wolves always circling, waiting to strike.

I narrow my eyes in thought. Sheep are in danger from wolves in a field... but not when confined to a stable.

"Naamah!" I yell into the ether, my voice echoing through the empty throne room. For someone who spent eons in tight control of his emotions, I certainly am displaying a multitude of them now.

The succubus pops into existence in front of me, immediately assuming her usual alluring posture: her red-tipped fingers resting on a slim waist, curved hip cocked out, head tilted playfully, curls spilling over the generous amounts of skin on display. Her wings are out of sight today.

"Uncle, I told you already, I don't know where Father is," she pouts, her bright red lips dewy and glistening.

"I have a task for you," I say calmly.

"Oh?" she perks up immediately, her spade-tipped tail swishing animatedly behind her. "What kind of task?"

I grin, already relishing the culmination of my plan. Asmodai would enjoy the lengths I am going to in order to fuck this intriguing mortal out of my system.

My grin fades and I grit my teeth. We need to find out where my brother is and staunch this exodus from Hell into the mortal realm – our existence depends on it.

I exhale through my nose and return my attention to Naamah. My niece is used to the prolonged spells of stillness and quiet that come with being older than the dirt under my bastion – time is often of little consequence to ancients.

"When the time is right, I need you to fuck a Cambion boy to distraction. I don't want him thinking of anything but being between your legs for as long as possible. Feed until he is weak." I pause for a beat and then add, grumbling, "Do not kill him." The lamb seems to be fond of the lanky young male that's often by her side, and I can always dispose of him later should he prove a nuisance.

She cracks her tail like a whip and those luscious lips spread into a siren's call of a grin.

"It will be my pleasure, Uncle."

CHAPTER 19 – LANA

I spend the next days recovering – once again. Daniel feels so guilty for suggesting I go out to join Nick alone, that he's refusing to let me leave his sight.

I take advantage of the downtime to read up more on the creature occupying my waking and sleeping mind. I tell myself that the next old tome I devour will be the one to explain why he saved me twice now, annihilating my attackers. All I get is more myths and contradictions.

"I think I may have invoked him somehow," I murmur, not looking up from the open book in my lap.

"What do you mean?" Daniel asks from his position across the library desk. Reluctantly, I meet his gaze. He's sitting in a recliner just like me but with far more dignity.

"I mentioned him by name when Nick was insulting me. And I was looking at his seal that day."

Daniel shakes his head. "It is not that simple. There are summoning rituals, yes, ones the world has mostly forgotten. But even then the stronger demons had a choice whether to answer. Perhaps he was listening for you, but you did not willfully summon him."

I hang my head and voice the thoughts that have been plaguing my mind at night. "It's my fault. Maybe I could have subdued him somehow. Maybe he could have been... I don't know. Reformed?"

The sound of a book snapping closed makes me flinch, but Daniel's voice is soft as he replies. "From your account of the fight, you gave Nick ample opportunity to cease his madness. More than most would have given him. He would have killed you because you were unwilling to kill him instead. And I understand, child, I do. The choice, however, was taken out of your hands and I am not the only one who is glad that it was."

Tears slide down my cheeks and I quickly move the book before they can smear the ink. I did want Nick dead in those final moments. But, I don't think the archdemon would have spared him even if I had dropped my gaze in that pivotal moment. He would have probably just taken him elsewhere before he killed him.

"It was not your fault," Daniel says, probably accurately reading the play of emotions on my face again. He reaches for another book, giving me space to think.

"Will everyone see it that way though?" I've been sleeping with a dagger under my pillow, thinking of the couple of cronies Nick had had, but they haven't approached me. I haven't seen them even during Nick's funeral.

Once we got home that day, Maalik sent a few soldiers after Nick's remains. We burned his body the day after, the majority of Purgatory's residents in attendance. Daniel had already appraised them about the circumstances regarding his death and it took all my strength to keep my chin up, expecting insults – what Nick spewed at me and worse – expecting all the soldiers to give me hateful looks. What I got instead were curious glances. Darla walked up to me during the makeshift funeral, squeezing my shoulder. "I'm sorry," she said, and she meant it. I told her it's not her fault. It's not like she told him to let his anger and jealousy twist him so much that he would kill over it. Though I expect Nick was twisted before he even came here.

We're not born predestined to be evil, like Heaven likes to believe. We're shaped by our experiences and circumstances, just like normal humans are. We just have to put more effort into controlling our impulses; Cambion to take the path of least resistance and Nephilim, well... to offer too little resistance, turning the metaphorical other cheek one too many times to those predators that exploit any goodness and kindness in a person. As for me, I have to struggle with both, with a temper that's easy to rile, and a tendency to see only the best in people.

I shake myself out of my thoughts once I start worrying that I may see only the best in a certain archdemon. Daniel's just observing the play of emotions on my face in silence until I focus on him again. "Acting in fear of the opinions of others will lead you down the wrong path, Lana."

***

A couple of weeks after I last saw Ashtaroth, Daniel finds me in the library to let me know Kevin is waiting for me for a patrol. Not questioning the unscheduled activity, as it's far from the first time, I get dressed and head outside to meet him.

"Ready to kick some misty ass?" Kevin asks as I approach him, and I can't help but smile at his puppy-like behavior. A vicious and bloodthirsty puppy, but still. "Maalik says there's an unusual amount of activity north of Abaddon, around The Phlegethon."

Where we encountered the golem. I raise my eyebrow at Kev, but when he doesn't comment on it, I let it drop and we head out.

Two hours later, as we approach The Phlegethon, I'm overwhelmed by a sense of déjà vu; listening to lava bubble, our steps crunching over charcoal, and Kev regaling me with his sex life. Or, well, lack thereof.

"Not a single one! It's like they've all gone on a communal pussy strike. At this point, you're starting to look tasty."

I raise an eyebrow at him skeptically. "You wouldn't survive me."

"I know, but what a way to go, eh?" He's wiggling his eyebrows at me and I roll my eyes so thoroughly, that it's surprising one doesn't just pop out of the orbital bone it's nestled in.

"Blobs straight ahead." Kevin nudges my attention back to our surroundings.

Four manifestations of evil, the amorphous constructs created when too many evil mortal souls congregate, are hovering in the air forty paces ahead.

"Maalik wasn't kidding," I say. It's unheard of to have so many together – it's not like they're sentient enough to form packs.

We approach the targets and unsheathe our swords to engage them. Just a slice of Celestial metal disrupts the twisted bonds holding them in their semblance of a shape, making dispatching them easy – for us, at least. An unwary mortal wouldn't know to avoid coming into contact with their misty shapes and would react as if burned by acid. Or worse, immersed into it. I've been grazed by them enough times during my first excursions to Hell to know I need to avoid that.

"Do you want to continue exploring or head back home?" I ask Kevin.

"Let's just go a bit further, just in case."

Fine by me.

We climb up a dune to avoid the bend in the river I got trapped by while running from the golem. Just as we crest the hill, we both freeze, feeling a demonic presence, but also hearing sweet notes of signing – silky and inviting, like a siren's song.

"Succubus," I say. "Old one."

"Oh, well." Kevin scratches the back of his neck and looks at his feet. "Do you mind if I... you know?"

I don't know what to comment on first – his sudden shyness about sex, or the fact that he wants my blessing to go have it with a demon. Maybe the former stems from the latter? Maybe my experience opened that final door in our friendship.

"Kevin..." I sigh. "I don't know."

"Come on," he pleads with his puppy eyes, "I'll be ok."

I chew on my lip and turn in a circle. I spot a log I could use as a bench, out of line of sight of whatever raunchy acts he's about to engage in with what will undoubtedly prove to be an easy conquest

– what succubus would turn away a free snack, after all. I point at it and say, "Fine. I'll wait there. But you better not take forever and she better not damage you or I'll nail her tits to Abaddon's walls."

"Promise!" he yells, already darting down the dune.

Sighing again, I sit down and close my eyes. I'm not very good with stillness. And quiet. And boredom. Just as I'm pondering whether to find something to kill, the air around me stills. I'm craving having toasted marshmallows in a pinewood forest and that, coupled with the tingling sensations and warmth I feel on the left side of my body, tells me I'm not sitting alone anymore. And exactly who's sitting with me.

I open my eyes and turn my head to the left. I find myself face to, well, neck with… you know what, I'm not going to even think his name. The last time I said it, someone lost a vital body part.

There's a bead of sweat in the hollow of his throat, slowly descending toward his clavicle, and I wonder if it would taste like pine honey. Sweet but spicy. Woodsy.

I growl at myself and wrap my hand around the handle of the sword sheathed at my hip closest to him. I hesitate, though. Is there a point, apart from showing my pride, to do something that by all accounts from many skin-bound grimoires, would just please him?

"There is no point," he says mildly, his voice reaching to my soul and calling it home to him.

I finally look at his face. His eyes aren't burning at the moment, but those perfect lips are slightly curled into a patient smile. I'm not really religious, other than in the sense that I was born into a Christian family, but I find myself sending a prayer to the Big Man, unable to tear my eyes away from his mouth. *Lord, have mercy on my harlot's soul.*

The sides of his lips twitch under my scrutiny. That mouth probably sent millions to their doom, but he's still proud of the effect it has on me. "And no," he says, "I cannot read your mind. Your expression tells me everything. I am older than humanity and have seen every iteration of a mannerism. You, my pet, have a very expressive face." He's chatty when he's not removing spines or common sense from a body.

"Do you really have a dragon?" I blurt out, panicking because I couldn't tear my eyes away from his mouth again while he was talking. He seems taken aback at my question. *Go me*, surprising an ancient being; both his eyebrows are now up. "Never mind," I rush out. Clearly no dragon.

He recovers quickly and that self-pleased smirk is back. "If you are curious about me, I would not suggest that sixteenth-century occultist rambling be your source of information." He clearly has some knowledge of the mortal world and what he might consider to be recent history, but his manner of speaking hasn't quite caught up with the times. Maybe he has less contact with modern phrases than Maalik.

"What do you suggest then?" I ask, my voice breathy. I absolutely loathe the effect this male has on me.

His smile widens, "Why, ask me, of course." Ask him? Suddenly my head is empty of questions. Not that it was full of much else but how absolutely beautiful he is, that night-dark hair caressing his strong brow, swaying in the wind, the light stubble on his cheeks giving a roguish mien.

"What do you actually look like?" Huh. I guess I had a question after all. I managed to surprise him again, his eyes narrowing infinitesimally for a second.

He answers carefully, as if he doesn't quite understand why I'm asking. "I have been able to assume this mortal-like form since I could assume a corporeal form. So one might say this is what I truly look like when in a tangible state. Can I assume other forms? Yes. Certainly none you would find as pleasing as this one," he finishes arrogantly, a man assured of his incredibly good looks.

"Did you set this up, with the succubus, so you could talk to me?" I ask, my brain not quite eye-fucked to death yet.

"No." His smile is all 'the cat that ate the canary'. Now it's my turn to furrow my brow in confusion. That is not the answer I expected – it was all too convenient to be serendipitous. "I 'set this up'," he mocks, "so I have a small measure of time before Fallen besiege my home demanding your return."

Wait, what? I spring up and pull out my swords, the futility of it second place to the need not to be at the mercy of one of Hell's most sadistic denizens for a prolonged period of time.

He moves so fast that my eyes can't focus; one moment, he's sitting on the log, the next he's holding both of my wrists, looking down at me with the same smug smile he had while watching me writhe in pleasure against his body. "This may be unpleasant," he notes, as if remarking that it may rain tomorrow.

The oppressive pressure of his presence increases a thousandfold, gravity pulling me in like there's a black hole at the core of my body. The pain of the tremendous pressure in my skull is all-encompassing and I shriek like a banshee. Just when I think I'm either going to pass out or die – neither option unwelcome under these circumstances – a flash of light startles me into inhaling, my lungs finally expanding.

I find myself standing in an opulent room fit for a king, the red and black color scheme and the gothic furniture making me feel like I stepped into a cathedral.

Ashtaroth is scowling at me. "Your nose is bleeding," he accuses, as if it's my fault. I swipe my fingers under my nose and they indeed glisten with ruby red. The creak of leather draws my gaze to his clenched fist. "I have never transported anyone with human blood through the ether until now," he says almost sheepishly, taking off his gloves and dragging a hand across his face.

Hello Mr. Mercurial. Also, *hello* to those hands. Is it just not possible, according to any law of the universe, for something on this bastard to be unattractive? There are intricate glyphs tattooed across the tops of his hands, veins prominent just the right amount, and black rings adorning his long, elegant fingers. *Fuck my life.*

"Why did you kidnap me?" I snap at him. He focuses on me, again looking confused. I would roll my eyes, but I'm worried he'd pluck them out to adorn his next martini if I did so. "Why have you abducted me?" I try again.

He's back to his usual commanding posture, a satisfied grin on his angelic face. "Can't have you dying before I feast on your cunt."

A part of my brain wonders if he's trying to speak colloquially to please me. It's a very tiny part, because the majority of my brain descended into my pussy as soon as his words registered.

I blink at him, a doe caught in the headlights.

CHAPTER 20 – ASHTAROTH

"I'll have you know that I'm perfectly capable of taking care of myself. Trained, even!"

My little lamb is valiantly avoiding addressing my words in their entirety. No matter, her body truly does tell me everything I wish to know about her reactions.

"It's different now: my brother is missing, there are uncontrolled rifts to the mortal world, and entries to The Pits manifested." I do not know why I am trying to mimic her informal way of speaking, something that always irked me. Why should I care if she sees me as an ancient beast – I am one, after all.

"He's your brother?" she asks, surprised.

I wave my hand in negation. "Not in the physical sense. It is our relationship. It is hard to have a brother when you're created in a time before time."

Her mouth opens in an 'o' as she ponders this. Adorable. I want to stretch her lips with my cock.

At that moment her stomach rumbles and I glare at it. Having her spread-eagle on my bed with my tongue between those luscious ass cheeks will have to wait. "I will see about arranging dinner," I say, instead of throwing her face down on the mattress. I can wait a while longer. "Meanwhile, you may wash the dust away." I gesture towards the bathroom, where I had a toilet added to the plumbing just days ago.

"There are clothes in that dresser." I point toward the dresser I had built for her, carvings of grazing sheep decorating the doors. I smile at the offended look she throws the pastoral scene. Deliciously predictable.

I need to leave before I fuck her to starvation. I find that I want to show my acquisition off to my court anyway. And let it be known she is not for them. "You have an hour," I say. Surely my staff can prepare a feast for the court in that amount of time if pressed? Not wasting any time, I will myself into the kitchen.

The exact time I have been here last is unknown to me; I gain no sustenance from food and I have underlings to arrange the feasts in my honor. The kitchen staff surely did not expect me to materialize into existence amid them and they panic, fumbling with cookware, making an ungodly amount of noise as it drops out of their hands.

"My... My Lord!" the head cook stutters. I vaguely remember taking him into servitude centuries ago.

"A feast for the court, ready in an hour," I clip.

"But... but... that's not possible," the cook squeals, the sound irritating me as much as his words.

I grab him by the neck and throw him at the wall, spices hung to dry knocking off it and landing on his unconscious form. Probably not the best move, if alacrity is what I am after. "Does anyone else wish to express objections?"

No one meets my searching gaze as they scatter to their stations and begin preparing. Good.

The food being taken care of, I will myself to my throne room next, intent on sending a guard to the servant's quarters to rouse them from whatever task they are engaged in so that they can prepare the dining room.

"Is that mostly-human here?" I hear my son's voice behind me. I turn and frown at him and Armaros, who is, as always, by his side. "Naamah told me what she's up to," Sariel says sheepishly.

Gossips. I pinch the bridge of my nose. "You are utterly unbearable."

"You really need to get with the times, Ash. Who wants to feel like they're fucking someone's great-grandfather?"

"I warned you to cease with that insulting diminutive," I growl.

126

He ignores me. "First, you should know some important words. Let's start with 'creampie'."

Armaros slaps him upside the head, sparing me the effort. "I don't want to sleep in the dungeon again, dickwad," he growls at Sariel.

"Fine," my son mutters. "Can I meet her?" he then asks me, beaming.

Denying his request is on the tip of my tongue, but then I reconsider. "You may escort her to the dining hall," I say instead. "She is in my rooms."

His eyes narrow in suspicion. I did not choose an imbecile for a son. "I'm not going to fuck your... your... thing, Father," he insists coolly. "I will wait to seduce her until you're done with her."

"That would be a novel occurrence. Gather the court first," I instruct. "Armaros," I hail the other Fallen, "tell the servants to prepare the dining hall immediately."

They set out to carry out their tasks, Sariel still giving me disgruntled looks over his shoulder.

The chessboard has been set. Now to watch the pieces fall.

LIANA VALERIAN

CHAPTER 21 – LANA

Not seeing any other options at the moment, I make use of the bathroom, the water warmer than at Purgatory. Bottles are set out and when opening a few, I'm greeted by the refreshing smell of snowy mountains and pine trees. Maybe the toasted marshmallow scent is all him then? I wonder how the thousands of years old Great Duke of Hell would feel if told he smells of a dessert that's especially popular with children.

I laugh at the thought of that imperious face pinched in affront. Clearly, I've lost it if I can laugh at such a time. He's probably going to fuck me and then discard me. Hopefully not in pieces. The hell of it is that I don't know if I would mind. The fucking, obviously, not the dismembering.

I sigh and open the offending dresser. I heard him calling me a lamb and I don't appreciate it. I am a grown, strong woman, a fighter. And I sound like an affirmation tape.

The dresser is full of red and black clothes – shocker. I pick loose and silky black pants and a tight red wrap top with long sleeves. There are flats and heels at the bottom. I opt for flats; it's not like I'm trying to be sexy.

Just as I'm cinching the sides of the top closed, there's a knock on the door. I frown at it. Ashtaroth wouldn't be knocking. Then again, I guess a demon out to make a meal out of me wouldn't knock either. Since I don't answer, the person knocking opens the door cautiously, then wider once he sees me looking in his direction.

He's gorgeous: tall, wide, and muscular, the cords of his biceps straining the skin that's on display in his leather tank top. His hair is as black as Ashtaroth's but cropped, except for at the front, where it's slightly longer and styled up and forward. He has prominent cheekbones, putting the apples of his cheeks and the edges of his jaw in relief. His eyes are completely black, only the sclera white, the pupil and cornea indistinguishable from each other.

"Hi," he smiles confidently, but warmly. "I'm Sariel. I'm Ash's son."

I stumble back a step. Surely that cold-hearted demon couldn't have raised this creature with crinkles on the edges of his eyes. He laughs at my shock.

"No, no. Adoptive son. I'm a Fallen," he adds.

"Oh," I say. Then add, "Did you just say *Ash*?"

Sariel grins at me. "Only call him that if you want to piss him off."

"I see." That makes more sense than him willingly accepting a nickname. Though his name isn't the easiest to say. Like maybe in the heat of passion. *Shut up, ovaries.* I guess I should introduce myself, since he did. "I'm Lana. Nephalem," I add teasingly, mimicking his clarification as to why he doesn't have a father.

"Really?" he says, eyeing me with more interest. "You're rare."

"I know. Anyway, may I help you? Are you here to spring me out of jail?"

Sariel laughs at my joke (but not really a joke) and shakes his head. "No, I'm here to escort you to dinner." Oh. I'm not sure how I feel about that. Ashtaroth kidnapped me, and now he just foisted me onto his 'son'? I also don't bother asking the Fallen whether he approves of me being his father's prisoner.

I am hungry though, so I accept the fallen angel's outstretched arm and let him lead me out of the room. I observe the hallways as we go, noting more gothic décor: black candelabra and macabre paintings of hellish battles. "Is he subscribed to Gothic Weekly, or something?" I murmur and Sariel laughs wholeheartedly again.

"If anything, they would come here for inspiration," he says with a smile.

"Oh, right," I say. "Old."

"Very old," he agrees, and we must reach the entrance of the dining hall. I hear murmurs of a gathered crowd behind the archway guarded by menacing demons. The guards don't look at us as Sariel leads me through the doorway.

I stumble when I see that the dining room is full. There's a raised dais at the other end of the room and, naturally, Ashtaroth is sitting at the center, his eyes on me and my escort. Specifically, where my hand is still located at the crook of Sariel's elbow.

I turn my head as Sariel leads me to his father, seeing tables full of various demons, most of them human-like. It's then I realize I'm going to be sensing nothing but demons for as long as I'm here, feeling the power of the one in front of me now the most.

I briefly make eye contact with him, his face impassive, as Sariel takes me to the other side of the table, seats facing the room. The ones to Ashtaroth's left are all empty and Sariel starts leading me there, just as Ashtaroth uses his foot to push out the chair to his other side. Sariel grits his teeth but guides me there instead, pushing my chair in, and then taking the one next to me. To his other side is another fallen angel, if I'm not mistaken, and he gives me a wary but curious smile. Why did Ashtaroth want me to sit between them?

He isn't looking at me, so I look at the food on the table in front of me instead. There's roast duck, fish, boiled and diced potatoes, steamed vegetables, and a tureen of thick soup. I can't imagine eating something filling when my stomach is clenched from all the demons staring at me, or cutting meat with a steady hand as Ashtaroth's power is all but vibrating the air next to me.

Sariel must see me eyeing the tureen the longest and says, "Here," before serving me a big helping. I thank him and try the soup with a slightly trembling hand. It's unexpectedly delicious.

The silence of the room suffocates me, but thankfully, Sariel starts a conversation with the Fallen on his other side, whom he introduces as Armaros. The other fallen angel has golden-brown hair and sparkling olive-green eyes. The most remarkable thing about him, however, is how innocuous he looks. If he wasn't sitting at a feast in Hell, he wouldn't be out of place as a kindergarten teacher surrounded by toddlers. While obviously strong, he has a pleasant layer of softness over his muscles. Next to him, Sariel looks like he was sculpted out of a block of marble.

"So, Lana." Armaros leans forward as he addresses me. "What's it like being an Elioud in Hell?

I chuckle at the way he suggestively lifts his eyebrows. "Oh, you know," I say. "The sights are great, though the natives aren't the most welcoming to foreigners. I'm also not crazy about the lack of fast food and streaming services, and my job doesn't pay for shit."

Armaros' laugh is as friendly as his face, full and coming straight from the belly. Sariel almost chokes on his wine, obviously not expecting the answer I gave. He sets his goblet down and wipes his mouth with a napkin. No fasting, here; both angels are indulging in the many delicacies offered by Ashtaroth's court.

"What was it you did Above?" Sariel asks, a full goblet once again in his hand.

"I was a high school history teacher. Come to think of it, I ventured into Hell on the daily there as well – it just came with health insurance."

My proclamations are met with beautiful appreciative grins and for a moment I forget that I've just been kidnapped by an archdemon. Or that I'm surrounded by what feels like half of a demonic court. In my defense it was easy to forget, seeing as none of them are making any sounds at all. They're all staring at me with varying nuances of frightening expressions and I don't know which scare me more: the ones of hunger or those of disgust. Noticing the reason for my discomfort, Sariel gestures for the demons to begin eating.

Back straight with tension, I slowly finish my own food, then sip dark wine from a golden goblet, praying it will make this situation better. Alcohol is, after all, a solution.

LIANA VALERIAN

CHAPTER 22 – LANA

I sit stiff and uncomfortable, seeing the hungry faces of Ashtaroth's court watching me with undisguised intent; they would love to defile me. And though Ashtaroth is the reason I'm here, I know he's now also the only reason I'm safe from being used like a doll, passed around until my body is scalloped empty.

As if to reaffirm his possession over me, his hand lands on my thigh and I can't help but flinch. I was so focused on how much I don't want those gathered below the dais to touch me, and he was focused on ignoring me. Or at least, it felt that way.

Since Sariel is sitting right next to me on my other side, he felt my body twitch and his gaze is now on the reason for it – his father's hand on my leg, those long fingers caressing my inner thigh, the ring-adorned thumb rubbing gentle circles close to the bend where thigh meets pubis.

Perhaps the movement would be soothing were it coming from anyone else. But it's coming from the magnetizing creature that's been haunting my dreams and I feel every minuscule shift of his hand between my legs. It's like he's touching my sex, and the touch isn't firm enough to satisfy me.

The longer his ministrations continue, the shallower my breath gets. A flush heats my face and my mouth opens to accommodate my panting breaths. Feeling all too aware that demons are watching me and that Sariel is sitting close enough that I feel the heat emanating from his strong body, I feel exposed and take a quick glance in his direction again.

But he's not watching his father's hand anymore. He's watching me, my flushed cheeks, my suddenly dry mouth, and then the rapid motion of my chest as I breathe in air redolent with lust.

I can't look away from him. Though his handsome features don't have the same effect on me as his father's do, my body only knows that a beautiful fallen angel is watching me being petted with naked heat in his gaze.

I bite my lower lip and his eyes follow the motion, the tip of his tongue licking a trail over his own lip. Does he wish he was the one biting my lip? Do I? Would he enjoy watching me writhe with pleasure, close enough to touch?

As soon as I have the thought, Ashtaroth's hand tightens on my thigh to the point of pain. I turn my eyes towards him and see that he's breathing heavily, his eyes boring into mine. He looks conflicted for a second and then his lips press together.

Too fast for me to follow, he again uses that incredible speed and grabs me – this time by the waist. Next thing I know, my ass is on the table, right between two place settings. My thigh tips over his goblet of wine and I observe the growing red stain with dazed fascination.

He wrenches my attention back at him by growling near my throat. I shudder and slowly lift my gaze to meet his. As soon as I do, he presses his hand to my sternum and forces me to lay down on the table, dishes toppling and clanking, being pushed out of the way as first my shoulders and then my head come to a rest on the cloth-covered wooden surface.

Looking around, I see that the gathered demons paused their conversations, food still halfway to mouths in some instances, all eyes wide and waiting to see what their Lord does next.

Once he has my attention again, he tears the loose pants I'm wearing down the middle and mercilessly disposes of the remaining tatters. The lower half of my body is completely naked and as he spreads my legs wide, I feel air hitting the drenched folds of my pussy.

I whimper and look at the only other person who has a clear view of the private space at the apex of my thighs – Sariel. My tormentor's son is gazing at the wet flesh, breathing heavily and fisting his hands in his lap, as if making sure they don't reach out to touch his father's pet.

The sight sets my blood on fire, but I don't get to fantasize too long before a thud signifies Ashtaroth sitting down on my chair, my feet now resting on both armrests.

"I find the meal my chefs prepared to be unsatisfactory," he says in a mocking tone, and I realize it's the first thing he's said since I entered the hall. The crowd laughs.

He reaches between my legs, knuckles caressing the inside of my thighs, making goosebumps spread in their wake. Once he reaches his quarry, he uses his thumbs to spread my inner lips, making Sariel growl as my entrance is exposed.

My breath catches in my throat with an embarrassingly loud noise and Ashtaroth takes his eyes off my center just long enough for his imperious gaze to meet mine. Then he descends on my flesh, mouth open to encompass my pussy from clitoris to entrance. He gently drags his bottom teeth up, grazing sensitive skin until his lips close over my clit, where he sucks.

My back arches off the table and I moan, the sound echoing in the once again silent hall. Although seeing the room upside down, I can still notice his guests starting to jolt into action as if given permission, grabbing a partner – or more than one – the sounds of clothes being torn and shucked away joining the whooshing in my ears.

I look back at the gorgeous beast between my legs, the tip of his tongue now swirling around my clit, his eyes alight with depraved glee. Gaze still holding mine, he pushes one of his long fingers into my channel, pumping once, twice, before he adds another finger and spreads them inside me.

"Ah!" I yelp on an outburst of air and hear a commotion at our table.

It's Sariel. The sight of his father's fingers moving inside me must have pushed him over the edge of control, as his chair is now on the ground and he's in the process of pulling Armaros up by the front of his shirt.

The surprised look on Armaros' face is almost comical and Sariel spins and pushes him to the floor on his hands and knees. Before Armaros can make a move in reaction, his trousers are pulled down, and pulling on one of his ass cheeks to open him, Sariel enters him in one thrust.

The cruel entrance makes Armaros scream louder than the noise of wet slapping flesh and groans of ecstasy now permeating the dining hall. Sariel just growls like being inside a tight and warm hole is the salvation he desperately needs.

Ashtaroth, now leaning back in the chair and slowly fucking me with his fingers, is observing his son taking the other demon roughly and laughs in twisted triumph. I realize now that this was his plan from the start, ever since he noticed Sariel observing me, noticed me enjoying the attention. Maybe even earlier than that.

I don't know if the public spectacle was engineered to punish or pleasure either of us and all I can think is that it was me – my body and my pleasure turning the dinner into an orgy, making two gorgeous fallen angels fuck on the floor with a violence I wouldn't survive. It's a heady feeling that speaks to my darker side, and I can't help arching like a lazy cat, my arms coming up to rest near my head, lust drunk and thinking only of gratification.

I open my eyes with a needy whimper of protest as the pleasurable sensations between my legs cease, and see Ashtaroth leaning over me, one hand unclasping his trousers to free himself.

My breath is shaky for another reason now, because, of course, of course I'm not safe with him. Even when he's making me feel good, I'm always at his nonexistent mercy.

"Shh," he whispers, his thumb pushing on my trembling lower lip and then inside my mouth, making me taste myself as he depresses my tongue.

When he pushes on my stomach to hold me down with his free hand, I expect him to take me as brutally as his son did his friend, with no consideration of anything but his own pleasure.

Instead, I feel the silky head of his penis nudge against my clit, already wet with precum. He swivels his hips against me, drenching the rest of the thickness in my arousal, and releases me to rest his forearms at the sides of my head. "Did you enjoy making my son want to fuck you?" he growls, tugging on the lobe of my ear with his teeth, his warm breath tickling me.

I didn't really do anything, but I still nod, exhaling shakily as he brings his eyes back to my face. "Are you enjoying how everyone is watching, waiting for you to be fucked?" His glowing eyes flicker with flames, burning with lust and dominance, and I'm hypnotized by them as the velvet skin of his cock slides over my wet folds, making me hungry for more.

"Yes," I breathe, so quietly that there's no way he heard me.

But he saw it, and whispers against my still trembling lips, "Do you need to be filled?" His dirty words reach within me and grab hold of my insides with an iron fist.

"Yes," I groan, the sound agonized. I'm on fire, I'm hurting; I feel so empty, so alone, so incomplete.

"Beg me for it," he commands, then tugs on my lower lip with his teeth.

I want to beg him to kiss me, but I know that's not what he meant and it's not what this is about. And I want him inside me so badly I could die. "Please," I whisper against his lips.

He shakes his head slowly.

I gulp, too tense to breathe, and try again, "Please, fuck me."

He notches the tip of his cock at my entrance and just waits, looking at me patiently, seemingly unaffected. If I didn't feel him hard and leaking, I would think he has little interest in the act.

But me, I want, I *need*. I damn a piece of my soul for pleasure and say, "Please, fuck me, Master."

He groans and drops his head to the crook of my shoulder, mouthing at the flesh he likes so much. I'm braced for the pain of his entry, but he surprises me again, only pushing the plump head of his hardness into my channel. Lifting his mouth from my skin, he hisses long and loud as he starts to fuck me with just the tip of his cock.

"So warm," he grits out, then pushes in a couple of inches more. I want to slide my fingers into his silky black hair, but he grabs my wrists immediately, holding them firmly captive on the table. "So fucking tight," he growls, "choking my cock with your tight, wet cunt."

His filthy words in my ear make me dizzy, like all the oxygen has left my brain as blood travels down between my legs, where his cock is moving, still only partway inside. Ashtaroth's erotic smell of warm sugar and fresh cedarwood is all around me, making my mouth water.

I manage to lift my legs and wrap them around him, using my heels to press him down, wanting to feel him all the way inside, as far as he can go. Not denying me, he finally fills me until I feel his heavy testicles rest against my ass, below where we're joined.

It hurts and this time I'm the one hissing, and it's not in pleasure, because his girth, the stretch – it burns. Staying still inside me, he bites my shoulder like he did that day after the golem and it feels just the same, only better, because this time his weight is on top of me, his length inside me, just like in my dreams these last weeks. Stars burst behind my now-closed eyes, my mouth opens in a silent scream, and the shock of the pleasure and pain forces my muscles to unclench, and now he's moving, slowly at first, then picking up speed.

His hands release my wrists and slide down my arms, then tear my top open. He takes my breasts into his calloused palms, pinching both nipples and making me gasp.

He licks the drops of blood his teeth brought to the surface of my skin, then I feel his lips on the shell of my ear again and he's panting, the sound so incredibly hot that I could burst into flames.

"You are so... fucking... perfect," he growls, punctuating his words with hard thrusts that have me yelping. "This perfect little hole was made for me," he says then straightens, lifting one of my legs until my calf is resting on his shoulder, and he's using my thigh as leverage to pump inside me with a speed that borders on supernatural. I can just see the root of his cock and it looks as thick as it feels.

There's nothing left of the lazy smile, the arrogant twist of his lips, the mocking words. The creature fucking me now is uncontrolled, his eyes wild, his breath irregular. He presses down on my pubic bone with the heel of his free palm and my clit rubs against it every time he jars my body with his thrusts. And that's often.

"I will fuck your hole raw," he growls. "I will mark you with my seed from the inside out until every inch of you smells of it. I will breed you until your insides are so full of me that drops will slide down your legs in a stream everywhere you go, marking my territory for me. And then I will piss all over your hot cunt, because it is mine, you are mine!" He shouts the filthiest words I've ever heard.

I'm close to coming, so close, so desperate to, but also afraid of what I'll feel, that I'll explode into charred pieces of myself over this table because I have never been so turned on in my life. I'm fisting the tablecloth as my head whips side to side. Seeing the need and panicked desperation in my eyes, he moves his hand to take my clit between his thumb and forefinger and then he pinches, and it should hurt, *it does*, but it also feels so fucking good, focusing my pleasure.

At the same moment, a shout of satisfaction so raw that it borders on obscene sounds from behind him. I know Sariel filled Armaros with his come and the thought of the two gorgeous males finding pleasure together pushes me over the edge of the tallest cliff I've ever been on.

The inner muscles of my core clench so hard that Ashtaroth grunts and struggles to move. My back arches with the tension that seems like it will go on forever, and it will kill me, because I can't breathe. My mouth opens, though nothing comes out.

Finally, all at once, the tension releases, a wave of almost painful pleasure exploding from my core outwards, then again, and again, and I'm sobbing and twitching and shaking as he fucks me through the pulses of an orgasm so powerful, I didn't know my body was capable of it.

"Fuck," Ashtaroth breathes, then slides his hands under my body to lift me up against him, moving me like a toy up and down his cock, grunting with each thrust, then impaling me so hard that I scream in pain. No one hears my scream, however. The roar he releases is so loud that crumbled bits of the ceiling are raining over us. His cock is kicking against the walls of my tunnel as he releases, warm heat bathing my insides, and the feeling of it, coupled with the memory of his words, makes me moan.

While his panting breaths warm the side of my face, I see Sariel sitting casually on the floor, one arm resting on a knee, smiling at me. Armaros looks completely disheveled behind him, like every inch of him was grabbed, bit, squeezed, and licked.

Sounds from the rest of the guests still enjoying each other filter in. Reality smacks me like a rogue baseball bat and I bury my face in Ashtaroth's neck. The arousal I still felt even after my orgasm now withers. I'm crashing from the high of my release so fast that my limbs are trembling uncontrollably.

Feeling the change, he squeezes me with the arms that are still wrapped around my body. Holding me aloft, he takes a step back, then turns on his heel towards the servant's entrance on the side of the dais and exits the dining hall without a word to anyone, his dick still mostly hard inside me.

CHAPTER 23 – ASHTAROTH

The little lamb is worrying herself into exhaustion as I carry her to my rooms.

I don't see the problem – I believe I showed remarkable restraint when taking her this first time. She will need to get accustomed to the rougher play that pleases me: moans of pain, the flush of humiliation... my prick twitches inside her as I imagine her crying while tied open and left at the brink of release for hours. Her breath catches enticingly and I grin.

And while I do understand that being fucked and fed from with an entire demonic court in attendance is probably not the fantasy of the average mortal woman, I did not share her with them. I did not throw her into the gathered crowd after my release for them to use.

I growl at the thought of the rest of my court's spend leaking out of her available holes. Never before have I kept a bed partner for myself. In fact, I am tempted to make Sariel spend the night in the dungeons for merely being close enough to smell her arousal. What is it about this little Nephalem?

We reach my wing and I carry her to my bedroom. Even I must rest occasionally, at least as long as I maintain a corporeal form. I have never let anyone else touch my bed though; the thought always disgusted me. Not feeling any revulsion over my new belonging being the first, I turn toward it so I can lay her down.

I am far too old to dither over my feelings and question my motivations – taking her tonight showed me that I am far from done with her. I want to do every depraved thing I can think of to her – some of them in this bed.

As I lift her off my cock, a rush of wetness spills from between her legs to pour over mine and onto the floor. I growl and reluctantly place her on the mattress. She curls into herself and I cover her with a heavy blanket despite the warm air permeating my domain. The way she shivers now is not pleasing to me.

And no, I will not clean our mutual spend – I was not jesting when I told her that she is to be a vessel for my come at all times. I have an unusual thought then – of breeding her until she is swollen with my child, of having her birth me many children, a legacy for me. The fantasy makes me grab hold of my still-wet prick and stroke it. I shake my head trying to make sense of these notions.

I may have even had children over the eons, though if I did, it was never brought to my attention. I certainly did not raise any as my own. I never cared about descendants. The thought of having them with an Elioud is laughable. They would still be merely Cambion, though perhaps far stronger than most.

I release my member and turn to the bathing quarters, resisting the urge to make her clean it with her mouth.

By the time I return her breathing is deep and even. She is asleep. Being unaccustomed to sleeping next to anyone, I instead grab my robes and head out towards my throne room – there is always work to do when you are a ruler of Hell.

Knowing my lamb is confined to my bedchamber, her warm body available for my use at my whim, my spirits are better than I can recall them being in untold years.

I am nearly at my throne as I sense a presence behind me.

"I didn't know your face could do that."

Why can't I have a few hours without my son hounding my steps?

"What?" I growl.

"Smile when you're not torturing offenders," he replies with a smirk.

146

I have decided now – he will spend the night in the dungeons again.

"Wait!" he interjects, sensing my intentions out of centuries of habit.

"What?" I repeat, looking at him.

"The Fallen. I imagine her team member that Naamah, uh… occupied, will be returning to Abaddon at any moment. If you're keeping the girl here, you should prepare."

He is correct and I do have a plan, but perhaps I should set it in motion earlier than I intended.

"I will have a message sent to Maalik, assuring him that she will be mostly undamaged."

"Good," he breathes. "Would be a shame if that delicious-looking sna–"

His screams interrupt him as he plummets down to the cells under my throne room.

LIANA VALERIAN

CHAPTER 24 – KEVIN

I wake up slowly. Lifting my arms up to stretch, I feel the sore muscles, my well-used dick giving a twinge in protest to the friction against the sheets.

Huh. The last thing I remember was that hot as fuck succubus riding my face as she deep-throated me like a pro. I must have taken a nap after, and Lana's going to smother me with my pillow.

Wait, sheets? Why is there a pillow, how am I in a bed? Opening my eyes in alarm, I see that I'm also in my room. How the fuck did I get home? I don't remember getting here. Lana must have taken me home... somehow. *Fuck.*

I shoot out of bed, see that I slept in my leathers, and waste no time bursting out of my room and sprinting in the direction of the wing she sleeps in.

Hearing voices in the atrium, I poke my head through an archway to see Maalik, Daniel, Ramel, and Corson in conversation over a sheet of paper.

"Well, Romeo's awake," Corson snickers.

I speak through the lump in my throat to ask, "Where's Lana?"

"Now he cares," Ramel grits out.

"The archdemon Ashtaroth has her," Daniel supplies.

"What?" I gape at them, my gaze stopping on Maalik who's still holding the letter. I silently beg him to tell me this is all a joke, a little harmless retribution for Lana having to drag my ass home.

"You stumbled home walking like a cowboy, completely addled and pale," Maalik says.

"We presumed you were attacked and Lana taken," Daniel adds. "This letter confirms it."

A heavy weight sinks into my stomach and I flush, unable to look at them. I can't hide this. I fucked up and my friend and team leader is paying the price. "I, uh… I went to the succubus willingly," I confess.

Corson scoffs. "Well, I guess you learned not to put your dick over your team members, didn't you kid?"

I want to die.

Daniel walks up to me and grabs my shoulders. "It does not matter, Kevin. Being elsewhere likely saved your life," he says kindly, as always. I don't deserve the kindness.

"Maybe I could have done something…" My voice is pathetic and lost.

Ramel snorts. "You would have done something against what is likely to be the oldest archdemon in Hell?"

I squeeze my fists. There has to be something we can do. "What does the letter say?" I ask Maalik, nodding at the paper.

"Only that he has her, unharmed, and that we should consider your safe return a gesture of goodwill," he explains, and Corson laughs.

"She's going to return bowlegged and dehydrated."

"I didn't know he still cared to fuck anything, with how old he is." Ramel's voice is full of mockery. "Can he still get it up, you think?" he adds.

"This isn't a joke!" I yell. "She's in an archdemon's stronghold! We need to do something!"

Maalik shakes his head, "While we could likely manage to kill a good deal of his army, even all of us together are no match for him. It would end with us decimated and Lana still in the same circumstances."

"I do not believe he will kill her," Daniel adds. "He seems to be fixated on her, for whatever reason. He came to her aid twice."

"What if she's alive but doesn't want to be?" I snarl, and Daniel bows his head. "Whatever." I turn towards the armory. "If you're cowards, I'll go get her alone."

"Don't be foolish!" Ramel grabs my arm. "You will only get yourself killed!"

"Let him go," Maalik says, quieter than normal.

"Excuse me?" Daniel gasps at him.

"We can't imprison him."

But I'm already leaving, not caring to hear them finish the argument.

I arm myself and take some provisions from the kitchen. I'm not completely crazy, I know it's going to take me all day to reach the gates of his fortress.

No one tries to stop me as I leave Purgatory to find my friend.

LIANA VALERIAN

CHAPTER 25 – LANA

The sound of a heavy door clicking shut makes me emerge from the warm cocoon of sleep I'm wrapped in.

"You're awake," the most erotic voice in existence says.

I remember what I let him do to me, what I begged him to do to me, actually, and I flush. Not looking at him I ask, "How long have I been asleep?"

"A day."

"A day!" I sit up and the blanket pools on my lap, exposing my naked breasts. I scramble to cover myself but it's too late.

"Mmm," Ashtaroth purrs, the sound hitting me straight in the gut. Well, a bit lower. He grabs the tops of my arms and pulls me up. Now I'm completely naked. "Lovely," he says with a deep growl, then pushes me back against the wall. "I think it's time your mouth acquaints itself with the cock you will worship as your god."

I can't help it. I look down at his crotch. I didn't get a chance to see much of it while he was fucking me, but I would really, really like to.

A knock saves me from dropping to my knees and tearing his growing erection free from his pants.

"What?" Ashtaroth growls at the (un)timely interruption.

"My Lord," a timid voice sounds through the door. "There is a Cambion boy at the gates. From Abaddon. He, ah, requests to see you and we are uncertain how to proceed."

Kevin! It must be.

"Kill him," Ashtaroth clips and I shriek in outrage. He observes me for a second, then puffs out a breath. "Very well. Bring him to the throne room."

"I'm coming with you," I say, wriggling out of his grasp and ducking under his arm to get to the bathroom. That I'm successful means he let me escape.

His eyes are immediately on me when I return and the muscles in his jaw are ticking. He's clearly stewing over something. "What is he to you?" he asks with deadly intent.

"What? He's like... I feel responsible for him. And he probably thinks it's his fault that you took me."

He scoffs arrogantly. "Your entire army could not keep me from you." He's wearing that smug grin again and I want to slap it off.

"I know that," I grit through my teeth. "But he's just a twenty-three-year-old boy."

"And how old are you?" he asks, black eyebrow raised.

"Thirty-one, ancient cradle robber," I answer, turning to the dresser and picking out clothes at random. I wouldn't even know how old I am if Maalik hadn't been going to the human realm for provisions. No one bothers to really measure time here.

He laughs softly. "When I still freely roamed Above, women your age were grandmothers."

"That is... disturbing." Finished dressing, I pull on another pair of flats. I face him and see he's wearing an indulgent smile. My clit pulses and those sinful lips twitch.

"He could wait?" Ashtaroth suggests mildly.

"Let's go," I grumble, wishing he wore a paper bag on his stupid, stunning head.

Once we get to the throne room, I step ahead of him and immediately see Kevin in a silent showdown with Sariel and Armaros.

"Kevin!" I start running to him, but I'm stopped by a strong grip on the back of my neck. Ugh. Flipping caveman.

"Stop hurting her!" Kevin yells at the epochs old archdemon. He has zero sense of self-preservation.

"I'm fine, Kev." I rub the back of my neck once Ashtaroth releases it.

"What will you do when the council hears of this?" It's like a hamster facing off with a starving bear.

Thankfully, the bear just chuckles. "The Fallen will not bother the Council over one soldier. A soldier who is being fed and clothed. A soldier who sleeps in my bed and not in a dungeon." I blush over his words. Way to make it sound like I'm his willing concubine.

Kevin has no retort. That's unexpected. I look at him to see he's gazing at the archdemon, a dazed expression on his face. I snort. Yup, welcome to my world.

He shakes himself out of it and blushes. "Then I will go to them myself," he threatens. Idiot.

Ashtaroth sighs.

"Wait, Father." Sariel joins the conversation. "Don't throw him in the dungeon. I'll keep our prisoner secured. He's kinda cute." He winks at us.

"What?" Kevin expresses his confusion.

"Fine," Ashtaroth says on a long-suffering exhale.

"What?" I ask this time, but Sariel just grins like a kid in a candy shop and hoists Kevin over one shoulder, Armaros shaking with laughter behind them. He slaps Kev on the ass, then turns towards the doors, Armaros following. "Hold on," I say, but they're already gone.

"He's straight!" I say to Ashtaroth, thinking of Sariel and Armaros at dinner. "Very, very straight!"

"Do not fret, lamb," he replies in a salacious tone. "He will be begging to be fucked long before they do so."

"But..." I don't know what to say. I can't imagine Kevin at the mercy of two men. Two beautiful, toned, sexy fallen angels with centuries of experience in giving pleasure... hmm.

"Can I watch?" I joke. At least, I think I'm joking.

He gives a low laugh that I feel between my legs and steps closer, lowering his face to mine before murmuring, "Is that what you want to do, hmm? To beg on your knees, prostrating yourself before me, your tears falling onto the tops of my feet as you kiss them, writhing with the need to be filled to the brim? You would make yourself come by rubbing your cunt on my feet if I allowed it, would you not? You enjoyed my thigh so much after all. But I wouldn't let you find release, pet. Not for a very long time."

Who talks like that? And why am I panting? I don't have a freaking foot fetish! "You know what, I think it sounds more fun to watch than to participate," I say airily.

"You know what?" he mocks. "I know when you're lying."

"T-this is beside the point!" I stammer, making him smile all the wider. "Wait, have you been with males before?" I have to know.

"Of course." He's unbothered. "The constraints over sexuality mortals impose have no meaning here." Oh. That's... something. His impressive frame being caressed by calloused fingers. *Yum.*

I snap myself out of my salacious daydreams. "Kevin didn't consent to this. All of you need a lesson in consent, actually."

"Does it matter when he would enjoy it immensely in the end?" It's not a question, really. It's a haughty statement and my hackles rise. I'm no longer up for joking arguments away.

"It does when he'll hate himself after. I know that more than anyone." I did hate myself after that first time, but I find it's only half true right now, as most of my common sense has left my body sometime between dinner and dessert.

He doesn't like my semi-true proclamation though – his face twists into a rictus of contempt. "Your feelings do not matter to me. As long as you are ready to spread your legs at a mere glance from your owner, you may feel whatever the hell you want," he snarls.

I feel all the blood drain from my face until pinpricks are burning over every inch of it. It's one thing to know you're being used for the amusement of unfeeling creatures while you're being treated well. But the truth will always rear its ugly head, making sure there's no comfort in delusion.

He was always arrogant, presumptuous, pompous, and high-handed. But I realize now that he never truly hurt me until this moment. And this really hurts, like a slap to the face; a sharp stinging pain followed by a burn I feel in my throat.

Trying to hide the tears overfilling my eyes, I turn without a retort and pick a direction at random. He doesn't follow.

LIANA VALERIAN

CHAPTER 26 – LANA

This is the first time that I get to explore an archdemon's fortress alone and without sneaking through tunnels. Ashtaroth's sanctum is very unlike Asmodeus'. Instead of being an ancient ziggurat with little decoration, this domain makes me think of what a Gothic cathedral and medieval castle's baby would look like.

The hallway I escaped into is gloomy despite regular intervals of mounted candelabras. It's just too big to be properly lit, both wide and tall, horizontal support ribs meeting above me on the vaulted ceiling like archways. The ceiling itself is adorned with intricate carvings and, for all its austerity, I still find it incredibly beautiful.

I don't sit in any of the alcoves with their sturdy benches, decorated on each side by gargoyles. I'm full of a painful nervous energy and I want to push myself into expending it, try to relieve it somehow. If I wasn't worried that running would cause guards to stop me, I would have broken into a sprint. As it were, the guards and servants I encounter just bow out of the way. Why? Because their master had me for dinner and staked a claim over me publicly? I would tell them that I'm sure their behavior towards me matters nothing to him, but that would mean stopping to talk, and I can't stop. I need to keep going.

A small gray imp wearing scaled black armor bursts out of a room to my right. It must have pilfered someone's lunch because it's holding two squished cherry tomatoes, one in each claw-tipped paw. It's lightly furred and it can't be much taller than two feet – definitely below knee height. Its small wings have hooks on the upper tips and claws on the bottom of the phalanges extending from them. The membranes stretched in-between the delicate bones are a dusky claret red, similar to the tomatoes it still holds, juices leaking over its little fingers. It teeters back on its tiny clawed feet and its bat-like ears flick. The round black eyes look even bigger in the imp's surprise at seeing me, glittering above a button nose and a Cheshire-Cat-like mouth full of shark-like fangs.

The imp chirps, impales the tomatoes on its tiny gray horns, and darts away, a spade-tipped tail spinning behind it in the air current of its rapid departure. Blinking in bewilderment, I continue down the hallway, avoiding the occasional slimy drop full of tomato seeds.

Going aimlessly from one hallway to another, occasionally peering into the large halls revealed by open doors or entrance archways, I feel like I've been exploring for at least an hour, but I don't seem to be walking in circles. Just how big is this place? I didn't get to see it from the outside, having entered it by being squished into the size of a ping-pong ball and pulled through the ether.

How will I find Kevin and get out of here? Now I no longer have to worry just about myself and how long it will take for that unfeeling baboon's ass to be done playing with me – I have Kevin's wellbeing to take into consideration as well. I'm mad at him and I can't help it. While I understand his motivations, he acted without forethought, like a child, and just made everything worse.

Angry tears return to my eyes and as they slide down my cheeks, I find myself feeling tired... empty.

There's a balcony just ahead and, while it may give me an insight as to the appearance of the fortress from the outside, I mainly head there because I want to sit in a corner out of the way, and not have to worry about looking like I'm keeping it together.

The balcony is even wider than I thought. Vaulted archways support the roof, sharp tracery descends between the decorated pillars, throwing a thorny shade over the terrace, while the waist-high railing sports root-like decorations. It feels like I'm in a gazebo that nature overtook in its abandonment.

The balcony overlooks the Garbhodaka Ocean and, stepping close to the railing, I can see some of the fortress I'm in. It's as massive as it felt while walking through it, a black gothic monstrosity perched on the edge of a stark cliff, with numerous battlements and pointed spires – all black with an orange glow in some windows – in sharp relief with the stormy skies behind it.

Despite the emotionally numb state I'm in, my jaw drops, and, perhaps because of the state I'm in, I can't find it in me to process what my eyes are seeing right now. The sheer size and dark beauty of it. I back away from the railing and turn to the long sofa set against the wall. It's like the gothic negative of a renaissance sofa – instead of bright teal cushions decorated with *fleur de lys* and gold painted wood, this one is all heavy dark wood and dark, dark brown leather cushions.

I sit for another hour in a meditative (or dissociative) state, listening to the thunder and the crashing waves. Of course, I feel him before I see him in my peripheral as he sits next to me. He's quiet for a while, just sitting, his arms crossed.

"You must be hungry," Ashtaroth finally says, and I turn to look at him. His features are unreadable and no longer angry, the occasional wisps of fire in his amber eyes calm.

"Are you? Is that why you're here?" I return. And, okay, I sound a bit salty, but who can blame me?

His jaw grinds, a muscle under his eye twitching, but he hesitates. "I came to apologize."

My eyebrows crawl up to my hairline in surprise. "For what?" I ask slowly.

"You are upset," he remarks coolly in answer.

I scoff. "So you want to apologize because I'm upset, and not because of what you said? Typical man." I lift my palms up mockingly. "I'm sorry you saw me banging your sister, honey."

He huffs impatiently, uncrosses his arms, and leans his elbows on his thighs. "I do not believe I have ever apologized for anything to anyone other than the Dark Prince," he says with a bitter twist to his lips. "And there an 'I apologize' encompasses any transgressions made and all those one has yet to make."

I look at him until he turns his head in my direction, an imperious eyebrow raised in question.

I give him an evil grin. "I'm waiting."

"For what?" His expression is wary. It's a novel feeling to have someone who can go all 'Sodom and Gomorrah' on a city appraise you with caution.

"For the apology, of course," I say silkily. "I haven't heard the words yet."

He takes a deep breath, his lips twitching, and is that a hint of respect in those glowing amber eyes? "I do apologize, lamb." He keeps his eyes locked on mine. Unused to apologizing he may be, but he is certainly not a coward. Though it would have been better if he dropped the demeaning pet name.

"Alright," I concede. I straighten and he mimics my movement. I'd love to ask him if what he said wasn't the truth then, but I don't want to pour salt in the wounds. While an apology may start the healing process, an injury takes consistency to close. And still, it scars over.

"I saw a furry imp earlier." I change the topic. There's only so much emotional vulnerability I'm willing to show, and I'm not yet ready to argue over Kevin's wellbeing again. "I didn't know they come in a baby format."

He clicks his tongue in dismissal. "His kind breed like any mammal-adjacent creature. And the younglings require centuries to mature," he clarifies. "The one you saw is older than you."

Huh. I didn't expect to see anything that's not a warrior, servant, or courtier here. But I guess a palace this massive would house quite a few demons. Still, I ask, "Where are its parents?"

"Dead." He offers nothing further and stretches his long legs in front of him, crossing them at the ankles. I'm so easily distracted by him. Judging by the self-satisfied smirk on that angelic visage, he caught me ogling him again.

"It's an orphan?" I try to bring the focus back on the topic of the imp and not my inability to keep my eyes off him, no matter his behavior. It's a miracle he came to offer an apology knowing how weak I am when it comes to fighting my attraction towards him.

"He," he emphasizes, "is an aggravating pest. And his name is Puck."

"Puck," I repeat and smile. That's adorable. But hang on a moment. "I don't see you tolerating a creature of no use who is a cause for annoyance."

He harrumphs. "He will be both utterly useless and a bothersome vexation for centuries yet."

That's not what I meant. I narrow my eyes at him. Why hasn't he simply crushed the baby imp under the heel of his steel-booted foot? "I'm surprised that the demons living here haven't eaten him then, if he's so annoying." I hide my smile and caress the smooth surface of the leather cushion between us.

Looking up when there's no retort, I can see him staring at the movement of my hand. I stop and he clears his throat. "My domain is the nucleus for pride and promiscuity and my subjects glut on that. So long as I am here, they will not devolve."

"I see," I say thoughtfully. That's what happened in Asmodeus' court.

"Your friend," he begins, tone cautious. He's diverting my attention, but clearly unwillingly, judging by the way he forced the words out. Obviously, I'm not the only one not wanting to argue about it again. But why bring it up then? Fear washes over me faster than icy water from a bucket challenge. I jump up.

"Did something happen to Kevin?"

Ashtaroth shakes his head. "I offered to free him, but he refuses to leave without you." I guess that's to be expected. Though I'm surprised he offered to let him go after wanting to stick him into a dungeon.

"Is he okay?" I'm still standing in front of his lounging form and though I'm looking slightly down at him, he's the one exuding authority and dominance.

He hesitates and then says, "He was getting a... sponge bath from Sariel and Armaros when I entered the room." I can't help it – I snort in a very unattractive way. The sound seems to encourage him to continue though, as he says, "He was tied naked to the posts of Sariel's bed and seemed utterly terrified that I may have come to join the, ah, festivities." I burst into laughter, picturing Kev's shell-shocked face as the much larger archdemon stood near his exposed body. "As I spoke with him he... stood to attention," Ashtaroth adds, eyeing me with a mischievous smile, and tears of mirth start leaking out of my eyes. "You're not upset?" He stands up and observes me with some caution as if I'll start another fight over the matter.

"No," I say through my laughter. "He deserves it a bit for coming after me without a plan and putting himself in danger." I shake, picturing Kevin's embarrassment over getting an erection just from the presence of a *male* archdemon. "They won't rape him, right?" I sober up. He steps closer and lifts his hands to my face, brushing off my tears with his thumbs. My breath hitches in my chest and my mouth opens at the unexpected sensation of his calluses against the apples of my cheeks.

"No," he murmurs and takes a step back. "My niece Naamah charged into the room, proclaimed she had 'dibs' on the human, and absconded with him. While his sexuality is no longer in danger, I have seen her use her tail in ways that will probably alarm the boy. At first." I just nod, shell-shocked at how these demons play 'pass the ball' with living beings they deem beneath them.

I blink and my thoughts wander again, catching on the way he said the word dibs. I should have had my attention span checked out while I was still living in the human lands. "You speak in a very outdated way and rarely use contractions. I don't think I've heard you use any modern slang unless it's a quote."

He purses his lips and scratches at the stubble that's shadowing his chin. I wonder if he shaves or just wills it away. "All Celestials are created with an innate capability to understand and speak every language. I guess I don't see the point in colloquialism." He raises his eyebrows, waiting to see my reaction. While he did sound less stuffy with the last sentence, he ruined it by using 'colloquialism'. Still, I give him an encouraging smile. I won't delve too deep into my motivations for wanting him to feel like his effort is appreciated. I'm probably just dicknotized. Though I still haven't really seen it. I automatically look down at his leather-covered crotch and he growls quietly.

"You must eat; you only had a bit of soup over the course of two days and I prefer you conscious. Though taking your soft and utterly pliant unconscious body would also please me greatly."

I open my mouth in affront, ready to yell with the speed and volume of a marketplace hawker, when he suddenly lifts me and cradles me to his body, holding me against him like he did after the dining room live porno show. "I can walk!" I squawk indignantly.

"You wandered far from my wing and your mortal body needs sustenance," Ashtaroth decrees, and walks back inside like a conquering warrior making off with his plundered prize.

I don't bother nagging him over his heavy-handedness. What's the point? Instead, I relax against his firm chest, resting my head under his chin, and breathe in his sweet and woodsy smell. I'll flagellate myself over my desires some more tomorrow.

CHAPTER 27 – ASHTAROTH

I toss my little lamb onto the thick mattress and she bounces a couple of times, her breasts shaking in a most alluring way. Pushing the thought aside, I snap my fingers and bring forth a platter of cold cuts from the kitchen.

"Eat," I command. Over millennia, I have seen what and how much humans eat – as far back as the first attempts to find edible berries and roots. I do not believe a few spoonfuls of soup is enough to sustain a soldier like her. Perhaps I should do some research on modern human nutrition.

She gives me a suspicious look. "Are you fattening me up like a pig before slaughter?" My lips curl into a smile at her impertinence. Anyone else would suffer the consequences of questioning me in such a manner.

"You will die many times tonight." I wink at her. "*La petite mort.*" She snorts like the pig she alluded to and rolls her eyes. It should be off-putting, and yet... I find myself charmed by her mannerisms, the novelty of her.

As she eats sitting cross-legged on the bed, I remove first my cloak, followed by my bracers and boots, and finally my chest armor, grinning at the way her eyes track my movement. I step in front of her wearing only leather trousers and a black silk shirt. She looks down at my feet and flushes. It confuses me until I remember our earlier conversation, my painting a picture of her bringing herself to orgasm by rubbing against them and I exhale a quiet laugh.

"Are you done eating?" I ask, knowing I should let her eat more, but I'm far too impatient to be inside her again. She has been so close, yet the sweet flavor of her arousal hasn't graced my tongue. I take away the tray of mostly eaten food and stand before her, arms crossed as her eyes lock on the growing bulge trapped by my trousers.

"Would you like to taste it on your tongue?" I croon and her breath catches. "Have me slide down the velvet tightness of your throat until I find my pleasure there? Tell me, would you swallow down all of me?"

She nods slowly, dazed by my words and by her own desires. I climb onto the bed in front of her and she scrambles back against the pillows. I stalk her slowly until my face is level with hers.

"You see, you may have your consent," I murmur quietly against her lips. I have never shared my mouth with another unless it was a tool for duplicity in seduction. I never saw the appeal before I saw her trembling mouth.

"What would you do if I said no?" Sweetly predictable.

"Then I would have feasted on your cunt until you begged me to suffocate you with my cock to the point that you're desperate for a single breath of air."

She gulps and I see the wheels turning behind her wide eyes. "I changed my mind."

I grin in triumph and sit back on my legs. "As you wish."

"Wait," she gasps as I tear down her trousers. "Was this what you wanted all along?"

I do not deign to confirm her theory as I find myself distracted by the sight of her luscious center. I lick my lips and she releases a breathy moan, enthralled by the action. I know she's captivated by my mouth.

While I merely wanted to claim her at the dinner, only preparing her with my fingers so that she could take my girth, I now want to experience fully the sight, smell, and taste of her sweet cunt.

I roughly push back her thighs and spread her legs as she yelps. Positioning my face at her already glistening flesh, I drape her calves over my shoulders, then growl as they slide off, my shirt offering no bracing friction. Impatiently, I rip it off and she gasps at the sight of my revealed torso. She will have to admire my physique later. I reposition her legs again and bury my face into her warmth. Groaning, I inhale deeply, the neat triangle of auburn curls at the apex of her center tickling my nose. Unable to wait any longer, I chase her taste with my tongue, pushing it inside her tight channel.

"Fuck..." she moans softly.

I've only just begun. I feast on her slick folds like a starving animal, fucking her with my tongue, then sucking on her flushed nub. I've not been in Heaven in an eternity, but between her legs, my memories of it feel sharper.

Wanting to drive her to release, not only so I can feed, but also wanting more of her sweet screams of ecstasy, I enter her with two fingers and twist them so I can press against the sensitive spot behind the upper wall of her clenching tunnel. Her back arches and I press down on her stomach with my other hand, keeping her in place for my mouth and fingers.

"Shit, shit, shit," she whines, and I can't find it in me to feel smug over my prowess when she has so utterly bewitched me. I rub my groin against the mattress, growling when it's not enough. I should have removed my trousers. My cock feels like it's confined in a chastity cage.

I stop flicking my tongue over her nub in favor of sucking it, my fingers now moving in a rapid beckoning motion against its flat counterpart on the inside.

Her breath is sawing in and out between her lips and she keens, "I'm gonna... fuck, Ash!" I suck harder as she calls out for me, thrashing her head on my pillow, chanting, "Ash... Ash... Ash!" Her breath stops after an inhale, then releases on a moan so raw, she truly does sound like she may be dying.

Taking the nourishment her release gives me, I slow my fingers and ease the pull of my lips, gentling her through the pleasure as she trembles uncontrollably. I pull out my fingers once the maddening contractions of her channel abate and cover her hole with my mouth, sucking out her arousal. I could release in my trousers at my little lamb's taste.

Licking her once from her ass to the curls adorning her delicious cunt, I lay Lana's trembling legs down on the bed and jump up to tear my breeches off. My sex expands in its new-found freedom and I hiss through my teeth at the nearly painful sensation.

I pull her to the edge of the bed until most of her head hangs off but her neck is still supported, then place my fists at the side of it. "I will allow you to call me Ash while you are climaxing," I declare, then straighten so I can feed her my leaking cock. She gasps and I paint her lower lip with the fluids gathered at the tip. A growl vibrates in my chest at the sight; her lips are still trembling and the depraved visual of innocence corrupted is a shot of lust I feel in my balls. She swipes out her tongue to taste the wetness and moans.

"Good girl," I praise. "Open." I tap her mouth with my cockhead.

She obeys like a good pet and I slide in until her lips envelop the turgid head. Her tongue rubs against the sensitive flesh and I grit my teeth. "Fuuuck. I knew you would be a whore for my cock." She moans at my hissed words and I grab hold of her head. "Take a breath," I warn. She trembles in apprehension. *Fear not, sweetness. This won't take long.*

I push my prick as far as it can go and feel the tip of her nose near my sack. Her throat tightens convulsively and she chokes, her teeth digging into sensitive flesh with the movement. She could chew on it like a corn cob and I would still fuck her mouth until completion. Saliva is leaking out from between her lips, lubricating the way. I slide back and advance farther until I see myself stretching her throat from the inside. I growl, losing sense of everything other than the drive to achieve release. Pumping faster, I grunt like a wild animal. I place a palm on her neck, feeling my cock nudging against it, and my head tips back on a feeling of possession so strong, I want to beat against my chest like a primate.

The noises she makes are desperate, making my blood sing. Her knees draw up as she runs out of air and the thought of her losing consciousness as I continue to use her throat selfishly pushes me into release. With a shout, I buck my hips forward and release my come down her throat. My muscles tense and release in pleasure and, once some clarity returns, I pull halfway back, still pulsing in her mouth. As she swallows me down, I caress her abused throat.

Finally, I pull out and crouch in front of her. Her cheeks are red and wet with tears, and her breathing is hoarse. I caress her wrecked face. "You please me tremendously, my little lamb."

Her pupils are dilated and she reeks of the lust I stoked within her with my rough use. It is my nature to know exactly which acts of depravity arouse her and I will use that knowledge until she is enslaved to the sensations only I can provide.

"I am not done with you yet, sweetness." I position her back in the center of the bed and flip her onto her stomach. Spreading her legs enough to enter her, I fist my still-hard cock and drag it between her cheeks. She tenses and I chuckle before continuing to her soaked entrance. Without preamble, I mount her in one thrust. She moans weakly at the intrusion, the sound amusing me.

"Poor thing," I mock as I lay myself on top of her, her round ass cushioning my pelvis. I swivel my hips and grind against her, the head of my cock rubbing against her sensitive front wall until she purrs in pleasure. "That's it," I praise her. "Take it for me."

I build her up slowly, enjoying the wet sounds of our joining, the desperate edge of my lust now blunted enough that my behavior is no longer bestial. Feeling her build towards completion, I slide a hand under her body and rub at her center.

Her breathing picks up as she tries to push back against me, chasing sensation. "There you go," I whisper. "Come on my cock." I roughen my strokes. "Come on my fingers." I speed up my ministrations. "Come for your master."

I would laugh at how easily I push her over the edge, unintelligible keening coming from her mouth and her body shuddering under me, if the powerful clenching of her cunt didn't squeeze a release out of me as well.

"Fuck!" I growl and embed myself deeply, flooding her womb with my spend.

We both pant as we recover, and I would stay inside her for hours, were I not crushing her with my weight. I push up on my hands so I can sit back, then spread her cheeks to watch myself leaking out of her pink hole. Mmm.

Since she is depleted, I move away from the enticing sight to hand her the glass of water that came with her dinner. Her swallows look painful and she hands me the glass only half empty. "Can you not heal your throat?" I ask, bewildered.

"Just a little bit." Her voice is completely ruined and my spent balls jump. "You should have thought about that before you skullfucked me," she rasps, mistaking my wince for remorse – I feel none. I laugh at her crude dry humor. Perhaps Sariel was right – my mood *is* better these days.

"Sleep," I command, and lean forward to lick the water drops clinging to her lips. She tenses but says nothing as I move back, her eyes heavy and already closing. Soon her breathing is deep and even, and I pull the blanket up to cover her cooling skin.

I suppose both of my hungers are sated enough that I could attempt to sleep in the bed with her. After dimming the lanterns, I climb in next to her. The fact that she sleeps through my weight shifting the mattress tells me how much I drained her. I may have to be more careful. I scoff at myself – the notion is foreign to me.

As I look at her in the darkness, I contemplate. A leopard cannot change its spots, but I am willing to paint over some of mine to keep her content and amenable.

CHAPTER 28 – LANA

Something thumps onto the bed near my head and my eyes pop open. I'm faced with my reflection in two huge, wholly black orbs. I scream, my throat protesting, and the creature in front of me shoots back, the extended wings at its back making the motion comically slow. Once it lands, it runs towards the door.

"Wait!" I rush out, sitting up – and clutching the blanket to my naked chest, thank you very much. The rascal stops and turns his head slightly so one wary eye is visible.

"Puck, right?" I ask gently. "I'm sorry I scared you. I didn't expect to see anyone, especially not that close." Puck faces me fully, holding his arms behind his back under his wings, and peers up at me from a lowered head. How can a demon be so gosh darn cute?

"What are you doing here?" I try to keep my voice soothing, not wanting him to run again. He just chirps at me. Right. "I don't speak... whatever that language is, sorry." He doesn't seem to mind and starts exploring the bedroom instead, poking his head into my dresser.

"Do you know where Ashtaroth is?" The imp pops back out of the dresser, wearing one of my flats like a hat on his thorns. I bite my fist. Judging by the excited chirping and hopping, he does know where Ash is, so I carefully wrap the blanket around me and, after telling Puck to wait in the bedroom while I get dressed, close myself into the bathroom to make use of the facilities.

Refreshed and dressed, I come out to see that Puck has strewn clothes from my dresser around the room. I can see how servants may call this demon the bane of their existence.

"Let's go, little hurricane." I open the door and he darts out, heading out of the wing and, judging by the familiar décor in the hallways we take, towards the throne room.

On the way, Puck bumps into a candelabra, and a candle topples off, right onto some gigantic creature's hide. The fire must be enhanced somehow, because neither the fall nor my frantic stomps extinguish it. I try smothering the flame with ether as a last-ditch resort. Thankfully, it works and I blow hair out of my eyes before giving the imp a stern look. He's affected a pose of such pitiful regret that I can't bring myself to yell at the little pest. "Come on," I say instead. "Walk in the center of the hallway."

I hear murmurs of conversation coming from the throne room as we near it and see demons – courtiers – exiting, whatever gathering that occupied Ashtaroth probably concluded.

Puck and I walk in and I stop dead in my tracks. The archdemon is sitting on his throne and there's a half-naked sex demon perched in his lap. Her skin is a milky green color, her hair a deeper emerald.

"Maybe you can jog my memory?" she purrs in his face.

He sighs and rubs at his forehead, eyes closed. "You know nothing, Itra. Leave."

"Aww," she whines in a voice that rakes over my nerves like a rusty pitchfork. She scoots forward and starts grinding on his crotch like she's giving him a lap dance. My ears start ringing and I start walking towards the throne. If he thinks I'm going to join his little harem, he is sorely mistaken. I feel disgusted. Right? Definitely not jealous.

The demonic stripper looks down between their bodies. "Do you really not wish to feed, My Lord?" *Gag*.

His eyes meet mine as he answers her. "All my needs are being taken care of." She follows his gaze and jumps off so she can look at me. Instead of returning the look, I drop my gaze to his now-visible crotch. It's still clothed and remarkably unstirred.

The demoness steps closer and sniffs loudly. "Her?" she shrieks. "You're turning me down for a mortal child?"

"Stop shouting in my face or I'll show you some of the ways this child can shut you up." I may not have my swords – something we'll be rectifying immediately – but I can take down this succubus, no problem. Their expertise is home-wrecking, mine is fighting infernal creatures.

She squawks like a vulture and turns her bare tits towards the archdemon on the throne. "She can't speak to me that way! Punish her!" Her tone then changes from the shrill one back to the seductive purr she used earlier. "We can teach this trash some manners together, My Lord." She looks at me slyly. "Fuck over her bleeding corpse, like we used to," she adds on a croon.

My back straightens at the implication of past trysts and the grotesque manner of them. I take a step back before Ashtaroth shouts, "Enough, Itra!"

"But –"

His roar interrupts whatever objection she was about to voice. "Leave!" His eyes are wholly black now, no whiteness visible, the tendrils of violent flame in them so vivid, they appear to be leaping out of their confines. They're nothing compared to the flames engulfing his throne now, though. Despite them, the room is suddenly icy, my rapid breaths misting in front of my face – I'm viscerally reminded of the power discrepancy between us.

Itra, ignoring the danger, unwisely charges at me instead of departing. I lift my hands in time to deflect her extended claws before they could bury themselves in my eyes. Tilting us sideways, I disrupt her balance and use my leg to throw her on the ground.

She's clearly even crazier than I thought, because instead of staying down, she shrieks like a harpy and launches herself up. I redistribute my weight in preparation to hold my ground, but the only thing that reaches me is a gust of hot air and a wave of ashes. The archdemon obliterated her without even moving and I'm not nearly as bothered by it as I should be. Good riddance. A not-so-small part of me wishes he had let me do it myself.

He turns his gaze to me, hands clenching the ends of the throne's armrests so hard, I can hear the metal protest. As I stand my ground, either from stubbornness or fear, I'm not sure, the flames die out and his expression slowly returns to its coolly neutral mien.

"You fucked on a bleeding body with her?" I ask, my voice cold and steady. My priorities may be a *tiny* bit out of whack.

Sighing, he pinches his nose between his eyes. Can archdemons get headaches? "While I have availed myself of her before," he starts, and I throw up a bit into my mouth, "I have no specific memory of the circumstances she speaks of." I exhale and he lowers his hand to look back at me. "But I am a primeval being, Lana." I startle at hearing him say my name for the first time, but he continues before I can reflect on it. "There is not much depravity left for me to explore. If you can imagine it, I mastered it."

"Right." I nod dumbly, unable to look at him up on his throne. How do I always forget? How do I get so wrapped up in what his body does to mine and forget about everything I was brought up to think of as good and moral? As if he wasn't pressing me against his hardness with Nick's body mere feet away not too long ago.

Like the last time I was faced with a mirror showing me my own sins, I don't fight the urge to leave his presence and find some clarity. Before I'm sucked in again.

"Wait," he says softly. I stop but don't turn around. "I was holding court to try and gather more information on Asmodai. Asking about events further back than I have, when before we only focused on his last known appearances."

I do turn around now as this is important and, unlike the demoness implied, I'm not a child. "And?" I ask, attempting to stay impassive myself.

He crosses his arms and sits back. "There was mention of a woman he held prisoner."

"A human woman?" This wasn't on my bingo card today. Well, none of it really was.

"Elioud."

What? "When?" I ask, both needing to hear the answer and dreading it.

"She was spoken of a year ago. Apparently he kept any information about the nature of it close to the vest." Could it be? Simone disappeared over two years ago.

I clear my throat. "One of my teammates went missing less than a year after we arrived in Purgatory. We looked for her, first in the area close to home that she was designated to patrol. It should have been an easy task for a novice. When we didn't find her we searched wider, the Fallen even wider than that. It was like she just disappeared into thin air."

Ashtaroth hums thoughtfully. "I know."

"You know?" I repeat inanely.

"It was brought up at Council meetings."

Of course. The Fallen had asked for the Council to help in the search for any information regarding Simone's whereabouts or fate.

A loud bang in the now quiet throne room startles me and I spin towards the noise. I forgot Puck was here. He somehow managed to detach an ancient-looking shield from the wall and it clattered to the ground. It looks dented. Ash clearly doesn't care about the shield as he continues our conversation like nothing happened. Probably used to it. "I believe it is time to visit my brother's home myself. Perhaps confirm some old suspicions."

"Can you do that?" I'm surprised – after all, I went there with Akira because the archdemons claimed to not be able to do so themselves without risking war.

"I have no interest in conquering his domain or interfering in any way. I will ask for forgiveness for my intrusion once we locate him." He stands up like he's going to leave right now.

"I'm going with you," I say quickly. I'll need my leathers and weapons.

Before I can ask him about their whereabouts he's shaking his head. "No. Remain here. You would only serve as a distraction."

I grit my teeth. "That could be my team member he held and I'm responsible for her wellbeing. I'd feel like a failure if I didn't do everything I could to find her."

"What you feel has no impact on my decision. You will remain here. Puck," he calls out to the imp, "guard her."

I bristle. Not only had he high-handedly decided I was a liability on his task, but to also think a walking calamity of a baby imp could keep me safer than I could myself? I stomp towards him, fists clenched, ready to tear into him. If there's any chance that this is Simone, it's my right to be there. But he only takes one last look at me, from my feet to the top of my head, as if making sure Itra really didn't touch me and disappears.

"Asshole!" I yell, my throat giving up the ghost and making my voice break halfway through.

I'm breathing like an enraged bull. "Come, Puck." I storm out of the throne room. "There must be a room full of priceless art we can destroy before he's back."

CHAPTER 29 – LANA

We didn't actually go destroy art. I'm not a monster. Just banging one. Instead, I take advantage of Ashtaroth's absence to check up on Kevin.

I ask a guard for directions to Naamah's quarters and, surprisingly, one goes as far as to even escort us. The demon looks like a satyr, with the lower body of a goat and horns poking out from his wild mane of hair. I wonder if Ashtaroth's home is usually populated with the somewhat human-appearing demons I've been seeing, or if the lack of hellhounds and other, more grotesque-looking creatures is for my benefit.

By some miracle, no furniture was damaged on our trek through the fortress. The guard stops at the door I presume leads to Kevin, bows, and leaves us.

Wondering what fresh horror I'll uncover on the other side of it, I knock on the door. A gorgeous succubus with curly black hair opens it. "Uh, hi, Naamah?" Yeah, I sure do sound confident. I clear my throat. "Your uncle told me my friend Kevin is here."

Her glistening red lips open into a wide, mischievous smile. "Hi," she purrs and I shiver. Her voice goes down like caramel-covered chocolate. "You must be Uncle's pet."

I wonder if I'll leave here with a stitch of dignity intact. "My name's Lana," I supply, in hopes that she'll use that instead.

"Lana." It's like she's tasting the name and I try to control my body's reaction. Freaking sex demons. "Your friend is tired, Lana."

"Uh-huh." I bet he is. She leads me through her quarters and I wonder if they're her permanent rooms or ones available to guests. I expected more BDSM equipment from a succubus.

As we enter the bedchamber I hear Kev murmuring, "You said I could rest for a couple of hours." He sounds so pathetic that I burst into laughter. Kevin is tumbling out of the bed when I lay my eyes on him, his legs tangled up in a sheet he trips over. "Lana!" He stands and cups his probably abused – not that I want to think about that – groin. "I didn't expect to see you."

"Clearly. Can you put some pants on?" I turn to the demoness with a wry smile, "If he's allowed, of course?"

She just smiles, devastatingly seductive, her lilac eyes heavy-lidded and speaking of long, sweaty nights of passion. "I'll leave you two to catch up. Come along, Puck," she adds to the imp who was halfway up a carved bedpost, the top with its red canopy clearly his destination.

Once we're alone, and Kev has his bits covered, we sit at the lush sofa adjacent to the bed. "You look... better than me," he grouches, eyeing me up and down.

"You look like you've been locked away in the bunny mansion as the only guy there," I cackle, looking at the hickeys all over his chest.

"Ah, well..." Kevin runs a hand over his close-cropped brown hair. "Better the devil you know than two fallen angels, I say."

I try to cover my smile with a fist, but it shows in my voice. "I heard they're incredibly skilled, actually."

"They gave me a sponge bath!" Kevin throws his arms up, frustrated with my lack of understanding about the ordeal he went through. "And they cleaned every inch of me, Lana. *Every* inch," he finishes, horrified. I can't help it anymore, I start laughing again, arms wrapped around my middle as my stomach muscles clench from the force of it.

"Yeah, yeah," Kevin grumbles. "And you? Are you really just okay with sleeping with that absofreakinglutely terrifying archdemon? I nearly pissed myself when he talked to me," he blushes.

That's not what I heard, I think, but spare him. Isn't it impossible to pee while having an erection, anyway? I'll need to find someone to confirm or deny. I don't think Ash needs to pee. The toilet in his bathroom looks awfully new.

I clear my throat again instead. At this point, it's becoming a tic. "He hasn't hurt me," I say. "Other than my pride." And it's true, I know that, but does that justify me enjoying him when he *has* hurt others?

"Doesn't make him good." But I think he realizes it's a bit of a 'stones and glass houses' situation as he nervously grips the back of his neck.

"Oh, by that definition, I should fuck Daniel." I grin at him and he scrunches his face adorably.

"That's just wrong," he says with feeling, and I have to agree – looks like having a daddy demon kink is more acceptable to my psyche than a daddy angel kink. "Don't scar me like that, there's enough going on already."

"Anyway." I change the subject to a more important one. "What the fuck were you thinking coming here alone? Lucifer's burning ballsack, do you realize how idiotic that was?"

Kevin stands up and starts pacing restlessly. "Well, yeah now I do. Wasn't thinking much at the time."

"Yeah, *duh*? Now we're both stuck here and Liam, Ethan, and Jessica are alone. Oh." The information I got from Ashtaroth should have been the first thing I said to Kevin. As always, I got distracted. "There may be a chance Simone is alive."

He stops pacing and whirls towards me. "What? How? It's been years and we've heard nothing."

I nod. He's not saying anything I didn't consider myself when Ash told me about an Elioud woman. It feels dangerous to hope. "According to Ashtaroth's informants, Asmodeus was holding one of ours captive about a year ago."

"A year ago?" He seems to deflate and his shoulders drop.

"I know," I commiserate. "Ash went to get some information now."

Kev gapes at me. "*Ash?*" he repeats incredulously. "And why does 'Ash' care, anyway?" The invisible quotation marks are obvious.

I decide to just gloss over the embarrassing nickname thing. "He considers him a brother of sorts," I explain. "Actually, I'm pretty sure your girl is Asmodeus' daughter," I add, with no small amount of glee.

Predictably, Kevin blushes. "Not my girl," he mutters, and sits back down, the burst of energy having clearly left him.

"Right," I scoff. "I'll let you know what I find out." He nods, his eyes growing heavy. I punch him in the shoulder. There's too much nervous energy inside me and since he was dumb enough to follow me here, he's going to be the one I talk it out with.

"Ow!" he hisses, eyes now wide open.

"You deserve it. Now tell me what happened at Abaddon after I got kidnapped by one of the oldest creatures in existence to be his sex toy."

***

I'm roused by a now familiar feeling of being carried bridal style and held against leather armor. The smell of warm sugar and crisp outdoors confirms that Ashtaroth is the one carrying me.

"You will no longer sleep outside of my bed," he decrees, once I wrap my arms around his neck. I don't say anything, just roll my eyes sleepily. Clearly I fell asleep with Kevin. I hope he's alive.

"What did you find out? Did you see a rift into the human realm?" I ask about his trip to Asmodeus' ziggurat instead of asking about Kev's wellbeing, a part of me knowing he wouldn't hurt my friend. If nothing else, it wouldn't put me in the mood to make the two-humped camel. He's being awfully considerate for a notorious ancient monster.

He looks down at me, eyes narrowed like he suspects where my thoughts went. "No. And he did not hold her there."

"But you know where, right?" I intuit. He must have carried me for a while before I woke up because I see we're in his wing already.

He nods, opening the door to his chambers with the ether. "There is a cave system on the other side of Asmodai's domain. The confined lieutenant I spoke with suggested that may be where he would have taken her to hide her from the court."

"Why would he do that?" I ask as he sets me down on the bed. "And could you free the caged demons?"

Ash crouches in front of me and shakes his head. "No. And I do not know why. He has had lovers aplenty, as is shown by his numerous progeny. Perhaps he did not trust his subjects around this one. Regardless, we will scout the caves tomorrow for any evidence of her stay."

This wakes me up a bit and I brace myself on an elbow. "You're taking me with you? I thought I was a 'distraction'," I ask, still surly.

His eyebrows raise. "You would have been a distraction in his stronghold, seeing as I would have been protecting you from hundreds of starving demons, rather than asking them questions," he says, like it should have been obvious.

Oh. Well, if he had just said that earlier, maybe I wouldn't have pictured his balls on a chopping block for half the day. "I think you need communication lessons to go with the consent ones, Your Majesty." I blink at him innocently. He scoffs and his face scrunches slightly in affront. My hand reaches out unthinkingly and I smooth the frown lines between his eyebrows with my thumb. Blushing, I cover the action by asking, "Uh, do you need to feed?" Wait, how did I possibly think that question would make things less awkward?

The effect of it is instantaneous as flames leap to life in his eyes and his mouth hardens. "While I do not need to feed daily," he begins, and brings the hand I moved away to his mouth so he can nibble on my fingers, making my breath catch, "I would." He grins salaciously at my lust-drunk expression. "But you are unaccustomed to the expenditure. It's making you tired," he finishes.

That explains why I've been sleeping so much. I was worried I had narcolepsy for a minute there. "That's very selfless of you," I accuse teasingly and he scoffs in denial. "Am I... less potent than a demon would be?" I ask hesitantly, half dreading the answer, wholly dreading the reason behind the question. I'm actually feeling insecure.

"You being mortal has no effect on that." He shakes his head and surprises me by kissing my palm before he sets it down to stand up. "You must, however, recuperate more frequently."

He throws the blanket over me and I dare to ask, "Does your niece know that? Kev seemed a bit... wrung out."

I'm glad he seems to have calmed down about Kevin's presence, because he just shakes his head and says, "He'll be fine," sounding less Ancient Sunday School Teacher than normal. "I must take care of a few matters before we depart." He ruined it again.

Throwing a slightly confused, but still incredibly regal look over his shoulder at my giggle, he leaves and I plop down onto the pillow.

While I'm looking forward to being more useful again tomorrow, in the grand scheme of things, I can't help but worry about what working with Ash will be like. He's probably going to be overbearing and frustrate me.

I sigh into the pillow and try to fall back asleep. And ignore the part of me that wishes he had taken me up on my offer to feed him.

CHAPTER 30 – LANA

"This armor is the shit!"

I'm looking at myself in a large mirror in Ashtaroth's quarters, having just put on the armor he brought me. He's lounging in the seating area, looking like a bored monarch, the familiar mildly indulgent smirk in place.

I can't help the child-like joy I feel. The armor which, of course, fits like a glove, is the most badass thing I've ever seen. Well, apart from his own. Mine is clearly its feminine counterpart though – tight at the waist with reinforced cups to protect the breasts. While the décolletage isn't armored, it is protected by intricate metal ribbing, interlocked with joints that ease shoulder movement. The ribs meet at the center of my sternum in a spine made of interlocked circles. A diamond hangs from the last ring, just above and between my breasts, shaped like a jagged fang. A silken black shirt protects from any chafing the slim, layered shoulder guards may cause. Reinforced bracers are snug at the wrists but flare out at the elbow, and my hands are protected by supple black leather gloves. A large red ruby decorates the steel-ribbed corset at the spot just above my navel. Fire seems to churn inside it. The wide belt draped over my hips has attached hilts on each side. Everything, from the shoulder guards to the boots on my feet, is decorated with gorgeous gothic designs.

I notice Ash walking up behind me in the mirror, not disguising his admiration for my backside in the tight leather pants that showcase it. "You'll need these," he says and extends two black short swords. The metal seems to absorb light, just like the crown that's occasionally on his head. The guards are decorated as ornately as my armor and the hilts end with more of those blazing red rubies. They're beautiful, but...

"I had swords of angelic steel with me?" I question, my palms hovering over the hilts he offers.

He grunts and shakes his head, unbound hair gently caressing his face. "I had these made for you. Try them."

I eagerly take the swords from his hands. The hilts feel like they were molded to my palms. I flip the blades from a standard grip to a reverse one and then back again, moaning. "Perfection," I say reverently, and he smirks, pleased with himself. I would roll my eyes if I wasn't pleased with him as well. While everything in Purgatory was in my size and well balanced, these items clearly took into account the way I move and even just my posture. I beat down the urge to hug him.

"This can't have all been made while I slept?" It's just too detailed.

"Some of it," he hedges.

Huh. No point in poking, I guess. "How are we getting there?" I ask instead and his mouth moves slightly in a hint of a wince.

"It's too far to walk and even flying would take a couple of hours. You will have to endure traveling by ether again."

I focus on the important part of his answer. "Wait, you have wings?" He just raises his brows in that kingly way that says 'obviously'. I'm afraid asking to see them would show too much of the insatiable curiosity I feel when it comes to him. Instead, I inquire about something that's been bugging me for a while, but I couldn't bring myself to ask the Fallen at Purgatory. "Why do some of you have wings and others don't? I mean, you all had them at the start, right?"

"We did not have physical wings upon creation," he corrects. "They, as is all of us in our true forms, are made of ether. When assuming a humanoid form was required, great feathered wings were the physical manifestations that human minds of that era chose to accept." I nod to show that I'm following along so far. "During the Fall, either the first one when we archangels rebelled against our Creator, or any subsequent ones, the power to summon wings was taken away as but one of the punishments bestowed upon the outcasts. Humans witnessing the ostracism said they saw the wings of the exiled burn. It is an apt metaphor. Those siding with Hell see that power returned."

So since Daniel is not on the side of Hell in the Heavenly Conflict and because he hasn't been taken back into the angel's fold, he can't use his wings. That's just wrong. "How come some of the Fallen have snake eyes and some don't?"

"Some characteristics of demonkind can manifest quickly once the Fallen venture into Hell."

"So, Maalik was on the path to becoming demonic?"

"He served Belial briefly if I'm not mistaken," Ash supplies.

"Belial? The chatty one? I can't imagine Maalik serving anyone, he's too... Maalik." Too dominant, too strong-willed. I scrunch my nose.

Ashtaroth just smiles at me. It's that 'you're a cute little lamb' smile. *Ugh.* "Are you done asking questions so that we may leave?" he asks.

"Actually, one more question. Are Fallen all male? Or mostly male?" Since he's being open, I may as well take advantage and ask this stuff. In fact, I don't think I've heard him string together so many words at one time before.

"As ether we're genderless and, furthermore, we did not have the many names you know us by today. We communicated in the Celestial language – or Malachim as it is sometimes referred to in human tongues. It has no translation. When taking a physical form, various factors were considered, such as the superiority of male physical strength and the various prevalent beliefs at the time. Once we became known to mankind in our humanoid forms, we adopted the names bestowed upon us."

"You're being awfully forthcoming," I remark with suspicion.

He gives me a neutral look. "You asked nothing that would need to be concealed from you for your own wellbeing."

That doesn't sound ominous at all. "There are things that would harm me if I knew them?" I ask, mouth ajar.

"Certainly. Now, may we proceed?" He holds a hand out and I offer him my own, cutting off the graphic image of my brain leaking out of my ears via knowledge. But I'm not mentally prepared to be squished like a bug again either.

"This will be brief," he clips, grumpy again.

Naturally, there's only one possible response: "That's what she said."

***

My nose doesn't bleed this time, which is good. What isn't good is me retching out my breakfast into the red dust under me. Lovely start. I straighten up and Ash offers me a canteen and a linen cloth. Wonder if his all-powerful magic can conjure up a breath mint.

"Thanks," I murmur after rinsing my mouth, and take a look around. We're standing in the desert under a twilight sky. There's no sign of life anywhere. "This is cozy," I remark, and he smirks at my dry words.

"This way." He turns towards the red cliffs behind us. There's a large cave opening in the direction he's heading. I ask him about the areas in Hell that were clearly shaped by erosion, a process that should have taken far longer than the realm's existence, but he's not as forthcoming as before – he's focused on the cave opening. There's a red glow coming out, I imagine from underground lava flows or vents.

We enter the cave and the sand under our feet turns to stone. The arid desert heat turns to cold dampness instantaneously, but pockets of lava still illuminate the cave. "How is this possible?"

"You're in Hell, lamb." He unsheathes the greatsword strapped to his back in one elegant move. Like everything else with him, it's a thing of dark beauty, and I can't help the primal tingle I feel at the way he looks with it. He can probably destroy any threat found here with a thought, yet he plans to use that sword. There's something so masculine about that. Judging by the look he throws me, he knows the sword in his hands is not the only one I'm thinking about.

"Do you think you can manage to keep your eyes ahead?" he asks in that self-assured mocking way he has, and I unstrap my swords, looking anywhere but at his grinning face. He moves closer and murmurs in my ear, "I'll take care of your aching little pussy when we get home." I moan and, predictably, he chuckles, but I couldn't hold it in. It's the first time I've heard him use the word pussy and it just does something to me. I'm on a serious mission and my panties are soaked.

At that moment a screech comes from my other side and a leathery form, a blur of claws and fangs, launches itself towards me. Before I can lift my weapons, the creature stops with a wet sound of steel slicing through flesh, and the only thing in front of me is Ash's now bloody sword. The creature lies in two spreading puddles of blood at my feet, cleaved in half.

He flicks the blood off. "Let's go," he orders calmly, while my heart is still trying to beat its way out of my chest cavity.

We walk in silence, with me now carefully observing the dark corners of the cave. Stalactites and stalagmites cut the orange glow from the lava vents making the shadows flicker around us. Our steps and the *drip, drip, drip* of moisture are the only sounds I hear. There's a giant cobweb in the corner, dew glistening on the strings. I shudder to think of what a spider in Hell might look like.

"Are you afraid?" Ash asks tauntingly, his voice lilting.

"How could I be afraid? The most dangerous thing here is walking right beside me," I tease lightly. But it's the truth.

"Hmm. Perhaps I need to instill fear in you again. You've been taking far too many liberties in the way you speak to me. Maybe it's time you start addressing me as Master at all times, and not just when you beg to be fucked."

I flush in embarrassment at being reminded of the instances I did so. "I will kill you in your sleep," I mutter.

He scoffs. "Not only do I rest infrequently, but I am also virtually indestructible."

"Indestructible?" I mean, I knew he couldn't be easy to kill, but I figured there must be a way; even Superman has his kryptonite.

"There is one being that could end me. But Father is not a murderous god. He merely sent us here for all our transgressions, after all."

That doesn't jibe with all I've been taught. "How about the Old Testament then, divine judgment? Noah's Ark and The Great Flood, Sodom and Gomorrah?"

"The Bible was written by humans, sweetness," he answers, slicing through a cobweb in our way, none of the strands sticking to his sword. "Not a lot of it is accurate. I was there, after all. Humans like to exaggerate, and history changes to fit the current narrative."

Right. "How about Evolution versus Creation then? The Earth can't be both six thousand and five billion years old at the same time. So which one is it?" I could be the first historian to answer the age-old question! Not that I could share it with anyone back home.

"Can both not be true?" he smirks over his shoulder.

"What do you mean?" I jog up to catch up with him. "What do you mean?" I ask again, but he just smiles beatifically. "Wait, is the answer one of those things that would melt my brain?"

"You may take care of those." He points ahead with his chin instead of answering. Two soul amalgamations are floating ahead of us. Guess the subject is closed.

"Such a gentleman," I sigh, rotating my wrists to loosen them. I dart forward and lower myself to my knees as I land between them, a sword out to the side in each hand. They disintegrate, and I hear a snort behind me. He even makes snorts sound majestic. "What? I can show off, too."

"The difference is," he says, passing me and walking on, "that I do not need to try to show off. I am simply innately superior to all others."

This time I snort. "That's the kind of arrogance that got you kicked down to Hell, you know." I'm walking beside him again and see no change in expression from my statement. "Do you regret it?" I ask carefully.

"Regret is not an emotion I practice," he answers coolly.

Hmm. "How old are you?" I ask, innocently. Maybe I'll glean the answer to my previous question that way.

Seems I'll have to live with disappointment though, as all he says is: "Time does not have the same meaning to me as it does to you."

Guess chatty time is over.

LIANA VALERIAN

CHAPTER 31 – ASHTAROTH

As we explore the cave system for hours, Lana does not complain. In fact, after asking so many questions, she became silent and I find the absence of her soft voice and dry humor... uncomfortable. Grudgingly, I must admit to myself I no longer prefer solitude and silence where she is concerned. I will simply have to make her desire to give me everything I want, including her willing company.

Deciding not to question the reasons behind these desires, I instead pour that energy into strategizing how to achieve my goals of not only making her amenable to me physically, but also cleaving her to me emotionally. I never entered battle unprepared, after all.

Her mortal stomach growls – interrupting my scheming – and I remove a large piece of cheese I stored in the pouch on my belt. I noticed she does not often voice her desires. A matter of pride, but also not wanting to inconvenience others. I vow to teach her how to demand what she needs.

I extend the food toward her and her round innocent eyes meet mine. With gratitude painted over her transparent expression, she takes the cheese and proceeds to nibble on it.

I withdraw my earlier sentiment – she should always let me think of her needs and allow only me to slake them. The thought of Lana on her knees, while I feed her only the best morsels with my fingers, hardens my cock. She would look up at me in worship and say, 'Thank you, Master'. And I would reward her for being my good little pet with my hungry mouth between her luscious thighs.

I groan and she snaps her gaze to me. I pretend not to see it and walk faster, trying to outpace the reactions of my body to a mere fantasy. I feel as if I am thousands of years younger and introduced to the pleasures of flesh for the first time.

"Uh, Ashtaroth?"

I cannot recall an instance of her hailing me by my name. The punch of lust I feel at her doing so now is ridiculous. "Yes?" I encourage, when she stays silent.

"I need to… pee." She avoids my gaze, obviously feeling embarrassed by the needs of her body.

"Then go?" I keep my voice monotone, knowing that if I were to take advantage of her awkwardness and tease her now, we would be standing here until tomorrow.

She gapes at me, reminding me of a fish with the way her mouth is opening and closing. "Right here?" She motions to the ground with her hand.

"You may as well. I am not leaving you alone here." I sigh when she just stares at me, eyes wide, and pull her to me by her belt, which I start unbuckling. "You truly believe relieving yourself in front of me will make me lose interest in fucking you?" I click my tongue dismissively. "You won't be free of me so easily." Once her belt is unbuckled, I spin her around and squeeze her behind before nudging her toward an alcove made of stalactite curtains.

She yelps and hisses at me over her shoulder, "You overbearing prick!"

"Prick sounds too small to describe me, don't you think?" I grin at her. "Rod, perhaps? Or baton?" She stares at me in bewilderment, embarrassment pushed aside, so I continue: "A bludgeon? A mace? Oh, I know, a battering ram." Having arrived at the category of siege weapons, I was about to escalate to 'trebuchet', but she spins around and covers my mouth with her hand. So impudent. If it were anyone else, they would already be a scorch mark on the ground by now. But as it is her, I will just have to punish her with my cock later. The fantasy makes me smile against the palm of her hand and her breath hitches, widening my smile further.

"Don't quit your evil demonic overlord day job to become a stand-up comedian," she quips. "And turn around, will you? This is awkward enough without you watching me."

I grant her this small measure of privacy and turn around. I even take a few steps – enough to appease her but not so far that I could not be by her side in an instant if she screamed. These silly human notions will have to be conditioned out of her, however. I will not allow her to hide anything from me. Once she rejoins me, I hand her the canteen of water which she waves off. "Humans need to drink over two liters of water daily," I chastise.

She takes the offered water with a lifted brow. "Have you been researching human needs?"

"Nonsense. It's common knowledge," I deflect, as my answer would be far too revealing, but she is observing me with a small grin.

"Did you read a book or search the internet?" She is teasing me again and my body feels lighter somehow, like removing plate armor after a long battle.

"What is this internet you speak of?" I frown at her and delight at the aghast expression on her face. "I'm jesting," I add before she has a coronary. The invention of internet pornography has made satiating demons that feed on lust a far easier job than it was before these modern inventions propagated sex so prolifically.

"Asshole," she mutters. Since it makes her eyes gleam, I don't punish her for it.

Mood lighter, we continue our venture into the cave's depths. When we arrive at forks, we choose a direction at random. After eating a few apples and some dried meat, she scowls into the darkness. There are no lava vents in this narrower tunnel and I summon fire to hover over her shoulder – I can see as well in the dark as I do on a bright summer day. Not that I witnessed one personally in a few millennia. Being banished from the sun by the Almighty has that consequence.

"There has to be a simpler way to get to wherever we're going," she grumbles.

"Well, we could manifest through the ether, but it would be slow going in a closed space. We would have to make hundreds of stops." I know what her reply will be before she utters it, but I laugh at the sheer flair of her insults. I catch 'insensitive oaf' and 'diabolical sadist' in the barrage of barbs.

We run into another pair of souls given physical form, as incorporeal as that form may be. I allow her to dispatch them once more – I am nothing if not a magnanimous creature.

"That's the second pair in these caves, as far as we know of at least. Why are they gathering like this?" she asks.

"I do not know. While I hold a vote on the Council, I admit to not giving this issue much thought. Most of my brethren did not. It was at Belial's insistence that we came to a consensus over the matter of bringing your kind here."

"You're on the Council? Did *you* want us to come here?" She sounds impressed, though I always found it a tedious position.

"Yes," I sigh. "Heaven believes that an exodus from Hell due to overcrowding would lead to Armageddon on Earth. While our side may find the chaos of the process enjoyable, those of us in command know that the extermination of the human species would staunch the flow of sinful energy coming from Above. Demonkind would be forced to feed off each other. Most would eventually starve."

"Yikes. Speaking of overcrowding…" She ducks into a narrow passage and I wait until she is nearly at the other side before I materialize there. "Show-off," she grouses. "But, overcrowding, can you explain that to me? Because the majority of human souls don't become demons, right, just incorporeal? And while we dispatch manifestations daily, and I see a minor demon or two almost as often, it doesn't feel that cramped here, you know?"

I turn and she stops before she would have crashed into me. "You know how the manifestations come to be, correct?"

She frowns up at me, either because of my sudden stop, or because she believes I'm questioning her intelligence. "Yes, of course. Several human souls that have been sent to Hell have to be occupying the same space to become dense enough to evolve into the ghostly blobs we see." She comes to the realization and her mouth forms a tempting little oval. "Oh."

"Yes, *oh*. If you saw what I see, you would be hesitant to stroll around so casually." Point made, I turn and start walking again, but not before I see her shudder.

"You see every soul? How bad is it?" She catches up to me, her beautiful spring-green eyes wider than usual.

This time I frown. "Not so bad that there should be two or more manifestations so closely together. But while Heaven is perpetually expanding, accommodating the ever-increasing influx of souls, Hell is static. Frozen just as Father made it eons ago."

"That part I know." She nods. "Why isn't Hell expanding, though? It's like building a prison and just adding more and more inmates, not changing the size or number of guards."

"Mm. That is a fitting metaphor. But I do not presume to know Father's plans…" My voice trails off as I sense something – someone – ahead. The infernal opening to the Pits under my brother's house indicated that he is in the heart of Hell, but could we have been wrong?

"You still call him Father," Lana muses. "After all this time, after everything?"

"I do not hate Him," I reply absentmindedly. "Not like some of my brethren."

My curious pet would probably have dug deeper with her endless questions (and I would have indulged them because she clearly has me by the balls), but she stops and straightens in alarm instead. "There's a demon ahead. Judging by the similarity of your power outputs, I would wager a week of Abaddon's kitchen duty that it's an archdemon."

Her senses are as sharp as the Fallen claimed. "How loud of a temper tantrum would you throw if I asked you to stay here?"

"Like releasing Puck in a china shop," she replies, her voice singsong. Fine. I would hesitate to leave her unguarded regardless. She is safest with me.

Another twenty minutes and we reach a cavern with a high ceiling, an underground stream steaming from subterranean lava flows gurgling on the far side. There is furniture, though nothing would make the cavern appealing to a woman used to human comforts – which is what Asmodai attempted, judging by the less Spartan additions of pillows heaped on the bed, bookshelves full of colorful volumes, and a plush seating area.

I determined the identity of the archdemon standing before that bed, back turned to us, before we entered. And it is not my brother.

CHAPTER 32 – LANA

"Belial," Ash greets the crowned archdemon occupying the cavern we walked into. While he's tall, it's not his physical presence that chokes the air, making the chamber feel smaller, but that oppressive aura. I suddenly realize that, while I always felt Ashtaroth's aura of static and heat, it never felt as intolerable to me as the one I feel now. It's making me feel worthless, thinking of all my failures, losing Simone at the forefront of my mind. We're here looking for her – she's likely alive. Did we stop searching too soon, and let her suffer for years?

As he turns, I realize it's not the most horrible thing about his presence after all. Because Belial is not wearing a form that's remotely human, and is far, far from the angelic perfection of Ashtaroth's face. His skin is leathery and a pale, sickly gray. His eyes are slanted, red on the outside, and orange where an iris and pupil should be. His nose is nearly flat, the diagonal nostrils reminding me of a goat's. In fact, I can see why demons were often depicted with goat-like features, if Belial's face is any measure – the ears protruding to the sides, the curved-back horns. There's a horned ridge bisecting his forehead and disappearing to the back of his head. It looks like it burst out of his skin. More horns extrude from the jawline and his jagged mouth is lipless and full of thin razor-sharp teeth.

I can't help feeling the primal dread that's twisting my stomach. I'm also very grateful that he's hiding the rest of his body with the heavy robes he wore when they visited Purgatory – I just wish he had also left his hood on.

Probably seeing the horrified disgust on my face, Ashtaroth seethes through clenched teeth, his voice low and full of anger. "Change forms." When Belial just tilts his head at the command, he snarls, "Now!" I haven't seen him like this before. He's not just angry, he's practically vibrating with something I can't quite name.

"Why?" Belial drawls in that honeyed voice, so at odds with his grotesque appearance. "Are you afraid your mortal pet will see what truly lies beneath the beautiful flesh she takes inside her body?" He's virtually cackling like a villain in a cheap horror movie at Ash's reaction, the clenched fists now aglow with hellfire.

Seeing him so unsettled, this normally insouciant and overconfident male, a sense of protectiveness wells inside me. Maybe it's the way he thinks of my needs: the food and water, the extra sleep, and the toilet he doesn't need. And perhaps I've set the bar real low if I take into consideration how he didn't kill Kevin and how he'd ripped Nick's spine out before he could kill me. Look, I know it's absurd. Not only has he done more horrifying things himself – spine in point – but I'm just a speck of dust compared to his mountain range in age. He doesn't need me to defend him in any way. Still, I stare up at him until his attention shifts to me. "Just so you know," I say when his fiery eyes lock with mine, "I'm not that into monster porn. We could maybe introduce a tail here or some horns there, though," I say, tapping my index finger against my chin in thought. "Oh!" I exclaim. "Can you do the forked tongue thing?" I ask sweetly.

Ash's eyes warm – don't ask me how I notice that, given that fire burned there to begin with – and a corner of his mouth twitches, betraying his signature almost-smile. But then he turns to Belial, the fire wreathing his hands extinguishing as he crosses his arms, and he looks back like his normal conceited self. "Why are you here, Belial?" he asks in a long-suffering voice that seems to piss the other archdemon off.

"Looking for Asmodai, just as you are. *Ashtaroth*." Clearly unhappy that he didn't manage to wedge a divide between us, Belial's voice loses its sugared sweetness for a moment. He regains his usual demeanor though and sighs. "Clearly, he's not here." He spins with a hand extended, palm upturned, like a game show hostess presenting a prize.

Ashtaroth doesn't point out that the opening to The Pits indicates Asmodeus is with Lucifer anyway. Belial was the first one to find out what it was Akira and I saw on our scouting mission, after all. Ashtaroth just waits for Belial's dramatics to end, his face set in an air of boredom.

"Though," Belial prolongs the word, enunciating slowly, "I have heard a rumor that the woman's family got involved. According to my sources," he simpers, "they're all well aware of their ancestry and trained their whole little mortal lives to prepare for conflicts with Celestials."

The archdemon beside me, arms still crossed in a way that feels distinctly disrespectful, grumbles dismissively. "Even if they somehow entered Hell in search of her, they would hardly pose any threat to one of our kind."

"True," Belial crawls slowly again. I wish I had brought my earplugs – his voice is giving me the heebie-jeebies. "It is, however, a lead worth following, no?" He grins and I see those sharp teeth are even longer than I thought. *Fucking hell.* "After all, we can't go inquire with the Prince unless he decides to honor us with his presence."

Ash sighs and pinches the bridge of his nose. "I will have it looked into." I wonder who he'll send, seeing as he can't enter the human realm himself.

Belial bows at the waist, the movement quick and as smarmy as the rest of him. "But of course!" His eyes, the color of lava, narrow on me calculatedly. "I will leave you and your... *delightful* companion now, so you can proceed. Our angelic counterparts," he snickers, "aren't pleased with the lack of progress on our parts."

With that, he disappears into the ether and I shudder with my whole body. "He probably has a reality TV show called Hell's Cliché."

The corners of Ash's lips curl into a small, indulgent smile, and he walks deeper into the cavern, obviously not taking Belial's word that there's nothing to see here.

There are obvious signs that a woman had stayed here, but I don't see anything that would indicate that it was Simone. Judging by the little touches of comfort in this chamber, whoever it was, she wasn't being neglected while staying here.

"It doesn't look like she was kept as a prisoner, Ash," I call out to him from the other side of the large living area, browsing the books on the shelf. It seems that, whoever she was, she liked circuses and clowns. *Blech*. I bet all clowns are demons in disguise.

"Ash, is it?" he whispers in my ear and I launch three feet into the air.

"What the fuck!" I shriek over the sound of his laughter. The bastard is lucky I didn't break his nose when I jumped. I have been told that my head is exceedingly hard. "And I thought you said I *may* call you that," I grumble, emphasizing the allowance.

He smirks at me and grabs my waist. "You were climaxing at the time and gasping for air. But very well. I will permit it outside of those circumstances as well. Are you taking that with you?" He's nodding towards the novel I'm still holding. I look at the cover; a clown with yellow hair dressed in a red and white striped onesie grins from it. I shudder. Pure evil.

"Fuck no," I blurt and push the book back among its creepy companions. When I turn back into Ash's loose embrace, I tuck my head under his chin to brace myself for being beamed up. I try not to think about why I find the position comforting.

CHAPTER 33 – LANA

Ashtaroth's hands on my arms are the only thing keeping me steady as we materialize in his rooms. I groan but mercifully don't vomit this time, sparing the plush red carpet in the sitting room.

"I must talk with Sariel," he says, sounding distracted already, like his mind is mostly on whatever plan he's thinking up and not on the task of slowly herding me towards a sofa. The teasing smirk is gone and he helps me sit before vanishing without another word.

I rest my elbows on my thighs and lower my head into my palms. The nausea is horrible, but I feel something else as well and tally the days in my head. While Maalik somehow manages to keep me supplied with my birth control shot, I still get my periods and they're still an ordeal. Though the bathroom had soap as well as bottles of shampoo and conditioner in visible places, I somehow doubt my demon stocked up on tampons and maxi pads.

I whine into my palms, thinking of the conversation I'll need to have with him once he comes back. Maybe I should talk to Sariel instead, the Fallen who actually has contact with the modern topside world. The thought gives me a spike of anxiety, though. Some primal part of me knows Ashtaroth wouldn't appreciate me making such an intimate request of his son.

I stand up and drag my sorry carcass to the bathroom. I get there just in time to strip my pants and sit on the toilet – I'm glad that particular consequence of my monthly visitor didn't occur in the caves. I do not want to discuss period poops with the sex god, no sir. I knew without a doubt that he wouldn't let me leave, but I also didn't want to see his handsome face twist into a look of disgust.

I know feeling self-conscious over whatever your captor may think is far from a feminist mindset, but I always was this way; my moods were so dependent on those of the person I was sleeping with. That's why, once I left university, I rarely slept with the same person twice. My attachments are often toxic, so I only let myself form them with people I'm not attracted to: Mike, who considers a vagina only slightly more attractive than dog feces on the sidewalk, Kevin, whom I instantly started mothering, the lack of parental love in his life tugging on my heartstrings.

But Ash... he's everything I shouldn't want but am always weak for. His face and body are an icy perfection, such a contrast to the fire underneath that skin, all that passion. The imperious, confident way he carries himself, like he's the master of all that he surveys and nothing will throw him off balance, he'll always be strong and reliable. The real danger is how he is during sex though, giving me everything I need to feel the most pleasure I can. Even when he used my mouth with seemingly no consideration, it was what I needed. How can I feel guilty for pleasuring an archdemon, when I'm just a vessel, when I'm not lowering myself to my knees in front of him and taking him as deep as I can to make it good for him, using every trick I ever learned to wring out as many sounds of pleasure as I can?

I cut out the train of thought, because it's making me wetter than I already am under the circumstances, and because it's barreling towards a certain end station – that man, male, demon, Celestial, whatever he is, he's the perfect package for me to fall obsessively in love with.

I finish up on the toilet and strip my clothes, then look around. I know the big cabinet holds towels, but I haven't opened the smaller one under the sink yet. Once I do, I snort – of course there are things for me there. Boxes of tampons in all sizes, pads, more toilet paper, razors, tubs of lotion, and little bottles of perfumed oil. It's like he used the search words, 'how to take care of your mortal female captive'.

I take out what I need, including one of the razors; I've been here for a couple of days now and grooming hasn't really been a priority. I run a hot bath, add plenty of bubbles, and tie my hair up so it doesn't get tangled.

Groaning, I lie down, feeling tense muscles loosen, the warmth soothing my aching lower back and belly. I close my eyes and try not to think – I'm feeling too cowardly to pick at my feelings and ponder my actions.

Once the water loses some of its heat, I shave, but before I can start on washing my hair, I hear footsteps approaching. I shoot up and reach for the towel I set out when the door opens and Ashtaroth walks in with no hesitation. He stops when he sees me standing there, naked and wet from the bath, and I see him take a deep breath as his eyes rove over me. Not removing his gaze from me, he unbuttons his shirt, deft fingers flying over the buttons with practiced ease. I stand frozen under his burning gaze, my nipples peaking under his watchful eyes, goosebumps tickling as they emerge. He unbuttons his leather pants, not taking them off, instead leaning to remove his boots.

When his intentions finally become clear to my numb brain, I jolt and sputter, "I'm on my period," then squeal when he steps into the bath, paying no attention to my protest. He crowds me against the tiled wall and I lose my balance. His arms are instantly on my waist and lifting me up. I wrap my legs around him and grab his shoulders on instinct.

"Mmm," he rumbles, lowering his head to his preferred spot at the crook of my shoulder. "I need you now," he breathes into it, hands now holding me up by my ass, squeezing the cheeks and spreading them. The carnal and possessive action makes me moan and when I lower my gaze, I see I left a smear of blood on his sculpted stomach. I flush as he transfers my weight onto one arm and uses the other to push down his pants. He groans as the head of his released cock, now pressed between our bodies, rests against that smear of deep red.

Kinky bastard, I think, but I'm a hypocrite because the sight makes my pussy clench. I'm as bad as he is, marking him with blood. He lifts me higher and I wrap my arms around his neck. His gaze is still on our sexes as he uses my body to wet his cock in a mixture of my blood and arousal. His face twists, but it's not with disgust, it's pure lust, and it's so beautiful that my head drops back and I moan loudly.

He positions me over his dick, lowering me slowly, hands clenched hard enough on my body that I know there will be bruises in the shapes of fingertips on me, despite my Nephalem healing. Once he's fully sheathed, I breathe out a sob and rest my forehead against his, lost in a haze. After giving me a second, he moves his hips slowly, looking up at me with brows drawn, gauging my reaction. His amber eyes are crackling with embers of fire and he's so close our noses are pressed together, our breaths mingling.

Whatever he sees on my face gives him leave to move and he presses me down against his pelvis, rocking his body into mine. Every swivel of his hips drags my clit against his skin, the glide slickened by water, blood, and arousal. I bite my lip and whine, his eyes zeroing in on the action with a predator's gaze. The urge to close the last inches between our lips is overpowering my sanity, so I tilt my head back against the tiles instead.

Ashtaroth starts using my body like an instrument for his pleasure, now roughly lifting and pulling me down onto his cock, his hips pounding up in concert. But he's unusually quiet, his normally filthy mouth only releasing grunts of pleasure and exertion. I worry at the change, stupidly, and look at him again. My mouth opens at what I see, his eyes not looking down at where we're joined, but fixed on my face, taking in every minor change in my expression, every twitch of my lips, every time I shut my eyes when it feels just right. He's so inhumanly beautiful, and he's looking at me like he's worshipping me with his body and making sure he does so with the consummate skill he does everything else.

I can't, I can't, I never felt anything like this before, like my soul is being fucked along with my body; what I feel inside is as powerful as the feelings of my clit dragging over slick skin – *his* skin – of his thick cock pushing so deep inside me that lightning streaks of pleasure spear through my body from my core. I start sobbing with every breath punched out of me, my nails clawing at every part of him they can reach.

His mouth opens in a snarl and my willpower snaps, along with the tether that was winding up my pleasure. I press my mouth against his and cry out at the pleasure exploding from my core. He growls, takes my mouth in the same possessive manner that he took everything else from me, and kisses me through my orgasm, now fucking me with something close to violence.

"Fuck," he breathes as his mouth releases mine. His eyes are closed, brows furrowed with what seems like anguish. He then snaps his head back, tendons straining on his neck, and shouts, "Lana!" before lowering his mouth back to my shoulder, biting down, and shuddering against me. My pussy clenches hard against his pulsing cock and it feels so good that I don't know if I'm still in the throes of my first orgasm or if this is a new one.

His mouth returns to mine again, like that first kiss shattered some barrier where both of us held back from the intimacy, and now he can't get enough. He's still moving his cock inside me, gently, slowly, making me moan into his mouth. *This feels different*, every cell in my body is whispering to me. Gone is his sardonic humor, the lazy indulgent way he handles my body. This feels like something I don't want to name.

Whatever it is stops as he moves back and sighs, gently lifting me off his body. He takes a step back and looks me over in a perfunctory way before disappearing again. I slide down into the water, now hot again – his parting gift. I expect to feel insecure over his abrupt departure, but I don't. I don't, because the caring he shouldn't be able to feel is always obvious, going beyond the bare necessities required to keep me useful, for him to feed.

I'm also preoccupied with the fact that I care too, more than I should. Over the last few days he went from a gorgeous face and devastating body, to a person with interesting thoughts, incredible experiences, a unique sense of humor... and perhaps even wants and feelings that go beyond the selfish.

Seeing an archdemon as a person, being attracted to his personality – that's going to be more dangerous for me than whatever he could do to my body.

CHAPTER 34 – ASHTAROTH

I drag a hand through my steam-damp hair, then take a seat at the head of the table, Sariel and Armaros' eyes tracking me.

"So hard up you had to leave mid-meeting?" Sariel smirks, hands clasped in front of him on the tabletop. He then freezes, nose wrinkling as he takes in my scent. "Is she alive?" he asks, eyes wide.

"That's not blood from a wound, dumbass." Armaros rolls his eyes at my son. They're hardly ever apart, yet they take pleasure in disagreeing with each other at every turn.

Sariel whistles and wags his eyebrows. "Sailing the Red Sea, eh?" Once he takes my mood in, however, he frowns. I must be showing some of the agitation I feel. Like remorse, fear is something I have not experienced... until her. I never had any reason to. I never put a value on something so delicate. "Why don't you look like a dude who just nutted?" Sariel asks, confusion clear in his voice, on his expressive face.

I click my tongue and glare at him. "Your mastery over vocabulary never ceases to astound me, son." He just snickers, but there is wariness in his expression. He enjoys pushing me with his jokes, taking the punishments in stride, but he is loyal to a fault.

After a second of pondering, he leans forward, now serious. "You know we'll protect anything that's yours, right? Keep it safe?" He doesn't like to show it, but my son is incredibly astute. After centuries together, he anticipates my needs without requiring much input from me.

When exactly did Lana become mine to care for and protect? When has she started to influence me? t should have been impossible. But her presence makes me see the world, my world, in a new light. Pride feels keener, lust feels sharper. My ennui has lessened, the present becoming clearer. I feel millennia younger, but equipped with the knowledge that this is not common. I want her to bask in all that my power can give her. I want her to not only crave my flesh in return, but also to find my entire being as vital to her existence as air.

Armaros must catch on and rests his palms on the tabletop, nodding with a grave expression. I hold both of their gazes for a moment. "Yes," I acknowledge, ending the discussion to move on to the matter at hand. Or at least I thought I did.

"So, it's perfectly okay that you're catching feels." That Cheshire grin is back on Sariel's face. "For a girl young enough to be your great, great, great, great, great, great, grea–" I cut him off with a thrown goblet, which he sadly dodges with ease, his shoulders shaking with laughter.

"Do not make me throw you in the dungeon; I need you to go to Purgatory." My order sobers him up marginally.

"What do you need from us?" Armaros asks, elbowing my son in the ribs.

"Inquire with the Fallen about this Simone, and perhaps any other female offspring they misplaced over the years."

"Like the one recovering in your bed?" Sariel quips.

"She's not missing, numbnuts, they know perfectly well where she is." Armaros sneers at him.

"Find out what you can about her family," I continue as if the interlude never happened. "We will see if what Belial claimed is true."

Sariel shakes his head. "I still don't like that he had information we didn't. Probably sucked every cock on the Council for it."

"Neither do I," I agree. I should pay more attention to Council matters. Something does not feel right; a puzzle piece jammed in the wrong spot. And why did we never find the rift claimed to be open in my brother's domain? "Leave now," I command, dismissing them with a wave of my hand.

As they rise wordlessly, I catch the eye of a servant lurking in the corner. "Prepare a tray of food." The servant bows so deeply that their horned head nearly kisses the ground. I decide to walk back to my quarters to clear my head of the last vestiges of my unease.

I pluck Puck off a candelabra right before his weight can unbalance it and send him off as my niece rounds the corner, a leash attached to the Cambion boy loosely held in her hand. While the boy looked simply resigned to his fate at first, once he sees they are no longer alone and that it is, in fact, me who is seeing him like this, he flushes a red as deep as Puck's preferred treat.

Stepping over the threshold to Elysium would be easier than not showing my enjoyment over the blow to the male's pride, so I do not bother to hide my grin. "What are you doing with that child, Naamah?" I ask with a drawl that visibly infuriates the boy.

She stops, places her free hand to rest on her curved hip, and cocks her head with a sultry smile. "Walking my human, obviously."

"I see that." I smirk but ponder the situation. I walked my human a lot today in those caves. Does she need more? She is used to regular physical activity. I decide to spar with her – I will undoubtedly teach her more than those young Fallen. I shake my head. Naamah is waiting patiently, but my thousand-yard stare clearly confused the youth, his brows now drawn. "Is the leash necessary?" I ask, returning to the present.

My niece clucks her tongue and bats her hand dismissively. "Necessary? No." Her smile spreads to the point where it unveils her true nature. "But it's so much fun. For me, at least," she croons.

I chuckle at her theatrics – Naamah is certainly my favorite among my brother's brood. Before I make my retort, the flushing boy interrupts us. "Did you learn anything about Simone? And where's Lana, is she alright?"

All mirth gone, I pin the brash young male with my stare. "Teach your pet to respect his betters, child," I snarl through gritted teeth, addressing Naamah, but not moving my eyes from the now-pale mortal. "My Nephalem is attached to him. My mercy, however, only extends so far. It would be a shame if he were to be returned to dust the next time he interrupts an archdemon's conversation."

Naamah glares at the boy and hisses. He stumbles half a step back but corrects his posture and does not cower.

"Apologies, Uncle." The succubus dips her chin at me solemnly. My rage is always close to the surface. She knows many creatures have met their untimely end for talking to me at the wrong moment.

For being brave enough to hold his ground and not piss himself like the majority faced with my ire do, I reward him with an answer to his brazen questions. "Not yet, and yes, naturally."

That he even considered Lana may be unwell implies he thinks there is a chance she could be hurt while under my protection. I clench my jaw until I feel a muscle in my cheek ticking. The boy's eyes widen in fear again. I leave his punishment to my niece and nod a curt farewell to her before materializing to my wing, reminding myself to keep my lamb content and sweet – I should not kill the boy.

Lana is reading in the sitting room when I enter – a tome on the Heavenly War. At least anything in my home is mostly accurate. At the snap of my fingers a tray of food appears before her on the low table. She's peeking at me behind the large book's covers, no doubt sensing my mood. My lamb is perceptive and already highly attuned to me. Now smirking, I sit next to her on the settee, ordering her to eat. Rolling her eyes at the command she no doubt found too imperious – I will enjoy punishing her for that later – she lowers the book and gives the cold cuts her attention. I should make sure she eats more cooked food.

"I will show you to the kitchens tomorrow. Or you may relay your wishes through any servant. You must eat even when I am not around to feed you." She snorts, chewing slowly. The pleasure I derive from watching her eat the food I provided makes me worry that I will next start thumping a bat against the ground before dragging her to my lair by her hair.

"Don't worry, when I need food, everyone will know." She smiles, her eyes twinkling. "I get hangry," she clarifies. "What did you decide to do about Asmodeus and Simone, if that's who he has?"

"Sariel and Armaros should be at Abaddon now, gathering more information from your Fallen mentors." I have no need to hide my intentions from her.

She purses her lips, considering her next words carefully. "I'm guessing I can't go talk to them about it, too?"

Does she think that I could not reach her in Purgatory? That I would not let her visit for fear of her leaving my grasp? I suppress my laughter. "You are staying here because I want you in my bed tonight."

I can see her pulse speeding up at my words, her lovely neck flushing, the redness traveling up to her cheeks. She ignores my statement and I cross my legs, then lean back, indulging myself by watching her eat. I should have insisted she eats the food from my fingers. Her luscious lips close around a piece of cheese and she reaches for another olive.

"Would you choose to stay here, if given the choice?" My question surprises her, the olive slipping through her fingers. Not taking my attention from her, I use the ether to stop its fall and float it back to the tray. She is too busy gaping at me to notice. I would have floated the olive into her mouth were I not worried she would choke on it in her current state of astonishment.

She blinks a couple of times, her beautiful eyes still locked on mine. "What would I do here?" Her question is soft, tentative.

"You may continue with the purpose you have been brought Below for if you wish. I will allow you to keep your Cambion boy to do so with if that is what you desire."

She bristles, her spine straightening. Such a joy to see her provoked. "First of all, Kevin is not a pet to be kept. Second of all, neither am I!"

I feel that sharing my opinion on this would be detrimental, so I merely maintain a neutral smile. After a while she turns back to her food, her eyes not quite focused as she contemplates her answer. Finally, she gives me her reply, while still not looking at me. "I don't know," she whispers, then busies herself with her meal again.

When she throws a glance my way to gauge my reaction, she does a double take. Clearly, she expected me to be mad. But how could I be? She did not say no, as her mortal heart must be telling her she should have. I may be 'catching feels', as my son described so eloquently, but I have not taken leave of my sanity. I will coax, I will convince, and I will be the devil on her shoulder, as ironic as that may be. I can be patient – as long as she remains here, by my side and secure.

After she is done eating, she excuses herself to the bathroom. It was a strenuous day for her and I am rather well fed from our bout earlier. Still, she finds me waiting for her by the bed, unclothed. I strip her of the sleeping clothes she had just put on in the bathing room, then throw her onto the bed to have my own dinner, despite her reservations and objections.

CHAPTER 35 – KEVIN

The succubus closes the door to her chambers with a loud click. I tug at the collar around my neck with a finger and groan in frustration. While I'm always up (literally) to try all sorts of kinky shit, being paraded like this in an archdemon's fortress, in front of the evil bastard himself... it's really fucking demeaning.

I turn towards Naamah and her lavender eyes flare at the sight of me collared, as if she briefly forgot she was literally holding my leash. She visibly catches herself and glares at me instead.

"That is the last time you will speak in Uncle's presence without being invited to do so."

I bristle at the chastising tone of her voice. It's not that I can't stand women in charge. Heck, my best friend is female and my team leader. But I never expected to be in a submissive position in a sexual relationship. This demoness would have me performing tricks on command if it was up to her.

"It's not like he was gonna tell me anything if I didn't ask!" Am I whining? Seriously, who have I become? I take a deep calming breath. "If there's a chance our missing team member is still alive, I wanna know. And of course I'm worried about Lana!" I can feel myself winding up again like a toy soldier. "He could have hurt her and I'd never even know!"

Naamah blows air out of her nose, only it actually comes out in puffs of smoke. "You would know, my pet, as you would be out on your sweet little ass. If you carry on like this, said ass will be encased in a funeral shroud. And that would be such a waste." Her voice started out as angry, but in the end it turned into a seductive purr.

I'm practically vibrating with a mix of frustration and humiliation as I bring my face to hers. "Don't call me that," I growl.

Instead of getting mad right back, her lips stretch into a devilish smile. Her tail wraps around my thigh, the tip pressing against my crotch and making my dick twitch. A puff of air, too close to a grunt, escapes from my lips and she squeezes tighter until I'm lightheaded from all the blood rushing down south.

"A punishment is in order, I think," she whispers against my lips. "A spanking will do nicely."

CHAPTER 36 – LANA

"Ugh," I groan, feeling stiff as a board from the long trek in the caves. I stretch my arms above my head, giving a baleful look at the dim gray light peeking through the heavy, dark red velvet curtains.

It's hard to tell the time of day in most areas of Hell, seeing as the sky remains unchanged. Purgatory is always blanketed by darkness and the ever-present red celestial lights. And when you leave the fortress, you walk under a sky of glowing, burning red and orange. Ashtaroth's domain is bleak and gray, but it does seem to grow darker and lighter in regular intervals.

My bladder is urging me to the toilet, and as I clumsily descend from the tall bed, I nearly land on the tiny curled-up beast sleeping by it. I swallow back my yelp and skirt around a lightly snoring Puck. I wonder why he isn't sleeping on the bed – he had no problems climbing into it yesterday.

I wash and dress, ignoring the slight ache in my lower belly. Truthfully, my period cramps are usually a lot worse, but a good workout on the first day does wonders. I flush at the thought of the workouts I had yesterday. That demon is ravenous and nothing deters him from having what he wants.

I decide to visit with Kevin first – if he's not otherwise occupied – and walk down the corridors I was shown by the guard yesterday, a now-awake Puck traipsing by my side. We find Kevin dressed, mercifully, but walking somewhat stiffly. He refuses to tell me what that's about, though the spectrum of reds and pinks marking his face makes me think up a few likely scenarios.

"Out with it," I grumble after watching Kevin fidget with pursed lips for several minutes once I caught him up with the search for Simone. We're sitting on a cushioned bench on Naamah's balcony, sipping the coffee I asked for from a passing servant in the hallways. The coffee was delivered so fast that I had to wonder if there are hidden passageways throughout the castle — most Celestial creatures aren't strong enough to use the ether for transportation.

Puck took one look at a plush velvet sofa and plopped onto his belly to nap.

"Are you sure he doesn't hurt you?" Kevin finally asks.

I lift my brows. "That question sounds like I may be confused as to whether he is or isn't," I reply, smiling at him teasingly. Predictably, Kev flushes again, stammering. It's so familiar to me and comforting, this camaraderie we share, and I ruffle his soft brown hair.

"I just... we ran into him in the hallways yesterday. Uh, Naamah and me," he clarifies, shifting awkwardly and I have to bite my lip to hide my smile. "I kind of butted into their bullshit conversation to ask about you and Simone. He said he would've killed me if it wasn't for you."

He's watching me with a weary look, so I refrain from calling him an idiot. "Would you have interrupted an archdemon's conversation, if it wasn't someone I was, eh... entangled with? If it wasn't the uncle of someone you're entangled with?"

Still flushing, his eyes now widen in realization, that he may have, again, acted recklessly. "I guess not," he mumbles.

"Well, then. Don't do it again." I stick my tongue out at him to pull him out of the maudlin mood. "I'm not scared of him," I add. "Well, that's a lie, I am scared of some things, but not that he'll hurt me. Not anymore."

Kev sputters. "How? Why?"

I shrug. "I know how that sounds, believe me. It's just..." Now it's my turn to flush and fidget under Kevin's wide-eyed stare. "He makes sure I eat. And drink." I see him rolling his eyes at me. "Oh, I know how that sounds, Kev. But it's not just that. He tries to do it... perfectly, you know?"

"Like when you buy an expensive cat with a pedigree and want to make sure you treat it accordingly?" he asks dryly.

"Fuck off," I grumble.

"Sorry, sorry, go on." He places a hand on my arm and squeezes gently.

"What I meant to say is, he seems to willingly go against his nature and thousands of years of habits to make sure I'm well."

"That's the problem, isn't it, Lan?" He's speaking softly now, holding my gaze. "You can't change thousands of years of habit, let alone your nature in a month, or however long he's been obsessing over you."

"Mm," I reply, agreeing though I don't want to.

"It's just sex, right?" Kevin asks, brows up. "It *is* just sex, Lana?" he repeats when I don't reply. "Please tell me you know that however he acts, it's just an affectation that won't last."

"Since when are you the mature one in this partnership?" I quip.

"Don't deflect with a joke now."

He's still giving me that stern look so I reply, "Yup. We'll be home soon."

I don't tell him about Ashtaroth's question last night, whether I would stay if given the choice, but the way he's looking at me now shows me he's not quite convinced anyway.

***

I find Ash in his throne room. Armaros and Sariel pass me with a wink, clearly already following new orders.

I walk up to the archdemon, admiring the way he looks on that massive black seat. The armrests are decorated with wrought metal demonic arms, hands ending in grasping claws. I remember now the metal groaned under his hands the last time he was angry and sitting there. I don't see it now, as he covers most of it, but I know the backrest holds a depiction of those same clawed hands ripping open a ribcage.

He's looking down at me from the raised dais the throne is set upon, a lazy and indulgent smile decorating his devastating face.

"Come here." He pats one of his strong thighs in invitation. He's wearing his leather armor, still menacing, but more comfortable than plate.

I look around in a mocking search. "Are you sure no demonesses will fly out of the walls to try and rip off my face?"

His smile grows, dimples gracing his sculpted cheeks, and his eyes glow with heat and satisfaction. "I will hold my temper next time. I find that watching you annihilate any competitors for my attention would serve as a titillating memory every time I'm inside you."

"Oh, get over yourself," I snort, but climb up the steps until I'm on even ground. "Why would I have to fight for your attention when I have it all to myself without lifting a finger as it is?" My voice is sugary sweet and I sit on the proffered thigh, back resting on the arm he wraps around me. When I look up at him, I see he's still smiling, gazing at me with a look that scares me with its warmth.

I gulp and try to slice through the tension. "What did Sariel and Armaros find out?"

"It could be no other female offspring other than your teammate, Simone."

I roll my eyes at him. "I could have told you that. A disappearance would be impossible to hide at Purgatory. We're like a high school, only less hormonal."

He's smiling at me like I'm his favorite kitten in the litter. Since I can't pinch him through the thick leather armor, I just scrunch up my nose, likely compounding the whole high school thing.

"So, what now?" I ask.

"They're on their way to the mortal realm to begin investigating her family."

His expression betrays some consternation. Naturally, I tease him about it. "It's not nice when you're left out of the action, eh?"

That sly smirk makes its reappearance. That's much better. "Do you wish to participate in the briefings then?"

"Mhm," I hum, tracing the curlicues of his armor over his breastbone, just as I traced the lines of his seal in a grimoire not long ago.

"Very well, lamb." His grin bares his teeth and there's a smidgeon of evil there. "But don't complain when you fall asleep at the table once I drag you out of bed for a briefing in the middle of the night."

I tug at the lock of raven black hair falling over his cheek and he laughs in surprise and delight.

"What do you do in the middle of the night? When you're not having briefings or holding court, I mean." I tuck the lock of hair behind his ear, caressing its shell once I'm done.

A purr rumbles in his chest. "Perhaps I count your freckles. Then again the next night to make sure I did not err the night before."

I side-eye him. "That's just creepy." And romantic.

He chuckles at the mocking expression on my face. "Of all the things I did for you, that is what you find creepy?"

I freeze for a beat, then throw my head back and laugh, the sound echoing in the empty throne room. The fact that I really shouldn't be laughing just makes me unable to stop doing so.

When I look at him I find his eyes fixed on my mouth. He gently pulls me closer, a suggestion instead of a command, and I loop my arms around his neck so I can bring my mouth closer to his. I love that mouth, truly. When it's between my legs, just the thought of it being there pushes me to the edge with the speed of a fighter jet. Instead of kissing him, I slowly lick his upper lip, following its contours, lingering over the cupid's bow.

He must have been holding his breath because he expels it in a burst with a sound close to a moan. I swear my eyes roll to the back of my head. I have a feeling this demon could make me come just by moaning in my ear.

Wanting more of the sound, I stand up, his hands letting me go with reluctance. Holding his gaze, I lower myself to my knees between his feet and casually spread legs. He watches me with a clenched jaw, his fiery eyes so intense it almost looks like he's furious. But I know those eyes now and I'm not afraid. I slowly drag my palms up the tops of his leather-clad thighs. "Let me," I whisper.

He's immovable, observing me intently, either looking for something in my expression or memorizing the sight of me on my knees before his throne. Slowly he moves his hands to the buckle of his belt to unfasten it. The clinking of metal on metal is loud in the quiet room, as is the whisper of leather against skin once he lifts himself just enough to slide his pants low enough to free his cock.

He's completely hard already, skin stretched over the veiny shaft, the tip glistening. I scoot closer, then lower my lips to the root of his dick, pressing a gentle kiss to the top of his testicles before angling my head. I drag the tip of my nose up the heated flesh of his rod, inhaling the clean musky scent. His breathing turns ragged and I look up at him to give him a smug smile of my own, enjoying the power I hold. His mouth is slightly parted, his eyes restless, bouncing from my mouth to my eyes, then to the tops of my hands at the junction of his thighs, and then starting over. His hands are already clenched on the armrests.

Keeping ahold of his gaze, I extend my tongue and lick over the frenulum. The loud hiss he releases and the clenching of his muscles under my palms spur me on, and I angle my head again and close my lips over the area, gently sucking and swiping at it with my tongue.

"Fuck!" he growls, releasing the armrest to grip my hair. "You have a... wicked mouth," he says between panted breaths.

With a wink at his flabbergasted expression, I extend my tongue fully and lick a path from root to tip, then suck out the bead of precum waiting for me at the top. His thigh muscles spasm and I smile, my lips gently caressing the head of his cock. I draw back a couple of inches and spit on it.

He yells lightly in surprise, then uses his hands in my hair to tilt my head back. "You are a filthy, filthy girl," he rumbles. "I believe I will need to clean you with my tongue."

I moan and wrap my right hand over the bottom of his shaft, squeezing tightly until his head kicks back, tendons straining. Once the grip on my hair loosens, I bring my head down over his cock again and, mouth open wide, I take him as far as I can. My lips meet the thumb and forefinger I have wrapped around him. I suck hard and rub my tongue over as much of the shaft as I can. I pull back a bit so I can start stroking his dick and sucking on his cockhead to the soundtrack of his groans.

It's not long before he pulls me off him and stands up. "No," I whine in protest, but he's urging me up.

He's shaking his head. "Not now, my hungry little slut. I need to fuck you." My pussy clenches at his degrading words, but he's already behind me, tearing my loose pants and pressing on my back. "Bend over. Arms on the seat, ass in the air."

Moaning, I position myself as he ordered, his hands pulling my hips back into his groin and kicking my feet further apart. "You're so fucking wet already," he growls, fingers now dragging roughly through my folds. With a quick tug on the string, he pulls out the tampon I forgot about, then I hear the whoosh of fire as he burns it. I feel embarrassed for all of a second before he has two fingers inside me. He bends over me so he can whisper. "You love sucking your master's cock, don't you, my filthy little whore?"

I whimper, the sound pleading, and he pulls back. But instead of pushing inside me, like I expected, a sharp sting over my pussy makes me yell out. He just slapped me between the legs! A tiny part of me is telling me to protest the degrading behavior he's subjecting me to today, but my body overrides anything else and I find myself begging. "More..."

He chuckles but doesn't give me what I asked for, this time lining himself up with my opening and pressing inside. The glide is embarrassingly easy. "That's it," he growls once he's fully seated, then grinds in so deep I squeal.

He pauses to run a soothing hand down my back, tracing my spine. "I'm not quite sure which sight I prefer: you on your knees before my throne, or bent over it." His hand reaches my ass and he squeezes a cheek with propriety. "Luckily, I can have both."

With that, he starts pounding inside me and I have to brace my palms against the backrest despite his firm hold on my hips. I love the pain from his tight grip and merciless thrusts as much as I love the grunts that accompany them. I push back against him, wanting more of everything, anything.

"Good fucking girl," he snarls behind me. "Show me how much you love having me inside you." I cry out every time our flesh meets with loud sounds of skin against skin. He releases my hips to hold me by the front of my neck with one hand, the other snaking around to my pubis so he can nestle my clit between his fore- and middle fingers.

Every time his groin meets my ass the impact rocks me forward into his palm, depriving me of air while rubbing my clit between the fingers of the hand between my legs. "You have ten seconds to come or I will leave you suffering all day." His voice is as ruthless as the hand around my neck.

"Ten," he starts counting, fucking me faster as all the air is pounded out of my lungs and my mouth opens with empty heaves.

"Five." I need air, but I need to come even more and then I need to feel him coming inside me.

"Three." The black spots dancing in my vision are making me dizzy so I close my eyes. My clit feels like it's going to catch fire from the heat of his fingers.

"One. Come. Now." The words are a growled command my body has no choice but to follow and I tense just as he releases his hold on my throat. I gasp for air at the same time as agonizing pleasure explodes through my body, the rush of oxygenated blood and dopamine transporting me to another reality.

I can vaguely hear Ashtaroth shouting behind me as my muscles tense and release, his hold of me the only thing keeping me from slumping over in a heap.

I'm still floating minutes or hours later, blissed out, as he withdraws, then pulls me up to spin me around. "Sit," he commands, voice raspy from shouting. "I want to know I'm sitting on our come the next time I have to entertain the rabble."

I moan weakly at his words and look down between my legs at the small puddle of our combined fluids. Ash growls like a starving wolf who just found itself in a sheep pen, drops to his knees and roughly pulls me forward towards his mouth.

Despite the excruciating skill he uses to build me up to a peak again, it takes a long time to reach it after that mind-shattering orgasm. Not to mention that I'm still mostly zoned out. But Ashtaroth savors every second and every drop of moisture as I alternately caress and tug on his silken hair, dazedly enjoying the sight of the king kneeling before his own throne.

CHAPTER 37 – LANA

"No," Ash says mildly after I move my knight closer to his queen.

We're playing chess in what must be his main study, judging by the lived-in feel of it. The chess set is a thing of beauty, made out of the same black metal as the swords he gifted me, the pieces themselves carved out of black and white pearl.

"You're not thinking ahead." His voice and body are relaxed after the throne room rendezvous, but the way he chastises me stings my pride. "You know all the rules and you react with the most efficient move each time. But you don't see the whole picture."

The words are somewhat disheartening. "Some team leader I am," I huff, trying to hide my fears of inadequacy with sarcasm.

Ash shrugs and moves his bishop. "Making the right call in the heat of battle is what a good commander is for. Knowing where to move your soldiers to maximize their usefulness. Taking advantage of openings. Short-term strategy." He's grinning at what must be a lovestruck expression on my face. I'm a whore for praise. "Just trust the generals to plan the battle," he adds, then points to the board. "Checkmate."

"Ugh," I groan. "Why am I even bothering, you've been playing this game since it was invented."

"We're not playing for you to ever win, sweetness." He's resetting the board with a smile that he probably can't keep from being patronizing. "We're playing for you to learn something. We could however spar if you prefer?" His brow lifts in question.

I snort. "That will be over even faster than this is."

"That wouldn't be for me to win. I was observing your fight with that boy until he got the upper hand. Your moves are good, but there is more to add to your repertoire."

I blush, hating that he saw that particular incident – I wasn't at my best.

"You could have won." He correctly interprets my embarrassment. "But you held back." The last is said with a harder voice than he's used these last couple of hours.

"I know." I make the first move as my pieces are white this time. "I was just hoping until the end that it was all a joke. Or that we'd fight it out and he'd calm down." I shrug, then bite my lip, not looking away from the board, even though he hasn't made a move and there's not much to think about yet.

"Next time you find yourself in a situation like that, you do not hesitate – you go for the killing blow." I look up at him and his serious gaze. "Even if it's the Watcher," he adds.

I'm taken aback. "Daniel? He wouldn't hurt anyone. He's a healer."

"Regardless," he counters, voice steady.

"*If*," I emphasize, "Daniel is suddenly possessed by a demon strong enough to do so and attacks me, I will go for an incapacitating blow."

"You will learn both," Ash decrees, and we all know his decrees are law as far as he's concerned.

As if to emphasize his words, books crash from the top row of the shelf behind him, where Puck is now curling up in their previously held lofty place.

***

"Keep your distance," Ashtaroth chides in a slow drawl. Weapons training with him has been just as fun as I imagined it would be. That is to say, not at all. Well, I do get to see him swing his greatsword around – the other greatsword – but it would have been better if it wasn't in my direction.

It's been a while since I felt like a novice in a fight. "How can I out-speed your greater reach, if you can move faster than my eyes can track even with that ginormous sword?" I grumble with ample amounts of frustration.

Ash is circling me, the giant sword held casually in one hand, like it's not taller than some people I know. He's always watching me, observing my stance and correcting my posture. My back hurts and I resist the urge to sheath my swords and pop my vertebrae back into place. We've been at this for days now. Sometimes Kevin joins me instead, but it's not often Naamah lets him leave her clutches.

Sariel and Armaros have been spending most of their time in the human realm observing Simone's family. Apparently, there are strict rules in place to prevent exposure and they can't just pop in and question them for whatever information Belial thinks they have. Still, they found time to train with me as well.

True to his word, Ashtaroth had been letting me sit in on the short briefings when the two Fallen visited home. As he predicted, those visits were often during the miserable hours of the night and not nearly interesting enough to keep me awake. I held my tongue about it stubbornly, refusing to let the smug bastard know he was right, but one such night – after a grueling afternoon of sparring and an energetic round of sex right there in the courtyard – I managed to fall asleep while walking and entangled my clothes in a candelabra, taking us both down. The candelabra, not Ash. He just carried me back to bed and promised he'd let me know what was discussed when I was awake.

"The idea is that you learn to hold your own for long enough against more powerful beings, not just soul manifestations and demonic minions." He stops in front of me and pulls up his sword to rest it over his broad shoulders.

I bite my lip to stifle a moan. *Hot*. Judging by the arrogant smirk on his face, he knows the effect he so effortlessly has on me.

His words fully penetrate my lust-addled brain and I frown. "Let me guess," my words are staccato and singsong. "Long enough for you to come rescue me?"

His smirk turns into a wide smile, showcasing perfect white teeth. "Precisely."

I take a step closer and rest one of my shortswords on his upper thigh, pointing towards his dick in a threat that needs no words. "I'll be pretty pissed at you if you swoop down like an evil version of a guardian angel every time I'm in a fight."

He leans forward, heedless of the sword tip pointed menacingly at his family jewels, and presses a kiss on my forehead. He's been doing that a lot these days, ever since that first kiss in the shower. Little intimacies that aren't sexual in nature. I noticed that he does it when I'm being especially 'cute' – by his definition, at least. "You can be mad at me and still ride my cock. In fact, I may find it to be quite invigorating." I can feel his lips stretch into a smile and I growl, the sound not very threatening when compared to the deep rumbly ones he tends to produce. I can't push him away because I have a sword in each hand and he's too close for me to sheathe them.

"Misogynistic prick," I hiss at the general vicinity of his neck. Shoulders shaking with laughter, he steps back and winks at me.

"Footwork." He continues with the lesson. "Evasion. When battling someone who so greatly supersedes your physical strength, do not attempt to parry. Use that quick strategic mind of yours to find openings and destabilize your opponent. Use the terrain – as you did with the golem."

I still flush every time he compliments something, despite hearing some daily. He calls out mistakes and praises correct moves with equal generosity.

"What's the point of this, your evil lordshipness? You could turn me into a raisin with a thought, couldn't you?"

"I prefer you as a moist grape." His voice is irreverent and as beautiful as ever. Still.

"Please, do not ever use the word *moist* again." I shudder theatrically. "Not even you can make it sound hot."

Ash throws his head back and laughs, then sheaths his weapon. He shakes his head – either at me or at himself for finding me amusing. "When wielding ether as a weapon, you prefer air as a medium?"

I fidget, feeling like it's a trick question. "Uh, yeah. Things on fire tend to be loud. And I'm not strong enough to incinerate them like you."

He crosses his arms and looks down at me. "No penchant for torture, little lamb?"

I sheath my swords and poke him in the chest with my forefinger. "I may decide to torture you one day if you don't stop calling me that."

Wrapping a couple of his own fingers around mine, he tugs on it with a fake beatific smile. "Water," he says, bringing the conversation back on track. "There is plenty of it in my domain. Easier and more effective than wind on a strong opponent."

I pull my finger out of his grasp and stick my tongue at him. I'm mature like that. "And do what?" I ask. "Drown them?"

His eyes twinkle with a sadistic glee that would send a smart person running to the hills. I'm an idiot, though, and the sight, one I often see while he's pleasuring me, sends a pleasant pinch to my clit. He looks at the apex of my thighs as if he can see it through my clothes. Thankfully – as he's downright insatiable – he ignores it and continues with the training.

"It's hard to chase someone when there is water being forced down your nose and throat." He drags his eyes up to my face with slow reluctance, as if convincing himself not to act on the carnal urges right this moment.

His glowing amber eyes finally meet mine. "Start by summoning a ball of water in, let's say, the size of an orange."

CHAPTER 38 – ASHTAROTH

I find myself regretting this plan before I even implement it fully. This is what happens when I listen to my son's unsolicited advice.

Sariel claimed that I should take Lana on a 'date'. As if I need to woo my woman with more than my sexual prowess and every luxury she could ever desire. But... what if he is correct? He does have experience with modern humans which I have been sorely lacking these last several millennia. Since Father banished the first Fallen from the radiance of the sun, I have hardly ever allowed myself to be summoned Above. Not that I would have been observing the nuances of human desires even if I could walk their realm freely. No, it was not until I saw a Nephalem with red in her hair and freckles on her face that I wished to learn more about Father's favored children. Admittedly, I was drawn to her posterior first – I am who I am and even my lamb's incredible prowess of getting under my corporeal skin has not changed that.

At this very moment, there is a picnic basket set atop of a picnic blanket under one of the mightiest trees in my realm – a rather soggy realm, with a soggy ground, hence the tree.

My kitchen master assured me he would not disappoint this time and has prepared the scene with meticulous care. There are red roses, which I was told now symbolize love. Last I knew, red roses denoted sacrifice and bloodshed, but apparently I am 'living in the Stone Age'. Then there is chocolate and I have to wonder when that primitive currency became known as an aphrodisiac. Lastly, there is champagne. How fermented wine which notoriously exploded bottles has come to represent the pinnacle of beverages among lovers is a mystery greater than the creation of the universe (no, we do not know either, but it is certainly not as far back in history as humans believe).

"Why exactly are we trudging through the fog this early in the morning?"

Lana's question makes me doubt any benefits this excursion might have when it comes to her feelings for me. Surely this is not the way to make her fall in love. Feasting on her cunt for a day straight until she pleads for mercy has to be more effective and also more enjoyable for the both of us.

"We are 'trudging' because using the ether to travel is detrimental to your wellbeing. It is only a moment longer, sweetness, under the tree up ahead."

"What is? And what tree?"

I grind my teeth together. This is ridiculous. I call up a breeze to sweep the fog away, revealing the designated picnic spot.

"That tree," I say with a measure of smugness. The servants did well. A soft blanket is surrounded by thick burning candles, which cast a warm glow on the closed woven basket.

"Wow," Lana sighs softly. Perhaps this will be good for us after all. I barely start towards the tree again, when I hear an out-of-place thud behind me. Turning, I am met with the scene of Lana on all fours, her gaze both bewildered and embarrassed, having clearly tripped over some critter's den.

"You are grace incarnate." Smirking at her clumsiness, I pick her up and cradle her soft, warm body in my arms. Much better.

"I do seem to have the best balance when I'm in a fight for my life, don't I?" Her mischievous grin allays the spike of fear in my chest by only a fraction. I must ensure she is never in a fight for her life again. Somehow. I walk past the border of the candles and set her down next to the basket.

"Did you do all of this?" I can all but see the hearts in her eyes, remembering a 'meme' Sariel once showed me on a stolen mortal's portable telephone device.

Being completely honest with your partner is something loudly touted by human relationship experts. I have read about the disruptive power of lies in a marriage. Not that we are married.

"Yes." I dip my chin to relay my (fake) humbleness.

"It's wonderful, Ash." Lana takes my hand into both of hers and caresses it affectionately. This is clearly working! By the day's end, she will be hanging on to every word I say. "It's just not very..." I look at her from under my lashes, not moving my face an inch. What could be missing? "I mean, it's not very archdemoney, you know?"

I chuckle, attempting to disguise the sigh of relief I expel. "I merely wanted to take you on a date."

She narrows her eyes. "Uh-huh." I widen mine. *Uh-oh.* "Thank Sariel for me." I shut my eyes altogether. She is too perceptive to be easily fooled.

"Very well, it was Sariel's idea, and the kitchen servants set everything up," I admit.

Her smile is as brilliant as I remember the sun to be. Or Heaven. "What matters is that you're the one here with me." I cannot help returning her smile and her expression turns dreamy. She leans forward and brings her face close to mine. "You are so beautiful," she murmurs. I can feel the whisper of her soft lips against mine and the warmth from her breath.

Suddenly she flinches with a sharp inhale, nearly crashing our noses against each other. We both look at the picnic basket which just moved on its own. It shudders again and I place it before me, prepared to protect Lana from whatever threat is held inside. Materializing my sword in one hand, I use the other to open the basket's lid.

Lana yelps as Puck scrambles out, blinking into the only slightly brighter light of day. His belly is hugely distended and I grab him by the scruff of his neck before he can run off. Lana peeks inside the basket and scrunches her nose. "Looks like he ate most of the strawberries. There are a few trampled ones left behind. Oh, and the chocolate looks like Swiss cheese."

I very slowly turn my glare onto the small demon. He tries to extricate himself from my grasp in jerky movements and his round black eyes are full of fear. Dematerializing my weapon, I instead call up a ball of fire. No one has mentioned that barbeque is *not* an aphrodisiac.

"Wait," Lana laughs at the soon-to-be murder scene in front of her. She is clearly not taking me seriously. "We'll just have some strawberries and chocolate brought down later."

I stare at Lana, attempting to gauge just how upset she would be if I annihilated this imp. Puck, sensing where his deliverance lies, now struggles to reach her, tiny arms straining in her direction. The way my little lamb's eyes soften as her mouth gently opens lets me know that, damn it all, I cannot immolate the pest. Today.

As I release the imp, he flies into Lana's arms, his bat-like wings nearly smacking me in the face.

"There, there," she soothes the two-legged calamity. "The big bad archdemon isn't going to hurt you."

I raise my brows and fix her with a droll look. "Lana, he has lived with me for decades. He knows very well that, were it not for you, his innards would be hanging off the branches above us." Then again, if it were not for her, neither I nor the imp would be here. She scowls at me while still gently patting the imp's back as if it were an infant. How am I supposed to woo her when my first course of action will always be chaos and slaughter?

"Well then." Her smile is a devious thing. "You'll just have to ask yourself WWLD before you give into the impulse and choose violence. What would Lana do?"

I scoff in affront. "That is ridiculous, you are..." The look on her face stops me in my tracks. Her eyes are completely narrowed. "And

I am..." Now she is pressing her lips together as if begging for patience. "Would you like some champagne?" I finish.

"Why, I'd love some."

Wonderful, that is... wonderful. It is all going wonderfully.

I take the bottle of chilled sparkling wine out of the basket. When I see the cork, I reach back into the basket in search of the corkscrew. It does not take me long to realize the kitchens did not pack one. Or champagne flutes for that matter. WWLD? Massacring all of them is likely out of the question, but some mutilation is surely called for. I exhale slowly through my nose.

"What's up?"

"No corkscrew. Or glasses. Or plates, not that the latter matters anymore."

Lana places Puck on the blanket before jumping up with much enthusiasm. "Bet I can open it with the ether! I *am* pretty good with air."

I look at her, then back to the cork before reluctantly handing it over. "Be careful not to —"

But I am too late. Lana attempts to open the bottle right where she stands. I manage to throw a quick shield of ether over her before the top of the bottle explodes from too much pressure. Lana jumps back in surprise, having clearly overestimated her fine motor skills with ether. She trips over one of the fat candles and kicks it atop the woolen blanket. Puck chirps in alarm before darting towards the fortress, just as the blanket catches fire with a whooshing sound. Lana, still protected by my shield, scurries back on her elbows.

Surrounded by the inferno, I observe the wicker basket bursting into flame. I could extinguish the blaze, but I find it a fitting end to this disaster of a picnic. I walk out of the fire, until I am standing above my baffled Nephalem.

I lean down and pull her up by the front of her shirt. As I'm crowding her towards the trunk of the tree, she gazes up at me with a delicious expression – part fear, part lust. My cock is instantly rock hard and she feels it too, judging by the gasp she unleashes as I press her back against the trunk with my front. In a moment she will feel it inside her as well.

I lean down until our faces are level. "Now we're doing this date my way."

CHAPTER 39 – LANA

I'm woken by a thunderous rumbling. I've lost count of how long I've been here, but it feels like it's been a long time since I last heard thunder this loud, on that day when Nick tried to kill me. As I sit up, the room starts shaking, paintings are rattling against the walls, and the glass of water Ashtaroth left for me by the bedside tips over. Quickly righting the mostly empty glass, I jump out of bed and drag on the sleep clothes I often don't even bother to wear anymore. They never last longer than a couple of minutes before being unceremoniously removed.

I burst out of Ash's quarters, still threading one arm through the sleeve of my top, and sprint towards the throne room. If he's not there, he'll be in the meeting room behind it. I'm not sure how I know that it's his power shaking the palace and not an attack. It just feels like him. And it feels furious.

Something thuds into the window I'm running past and I yelp, freezing in place. Hail. A massive hailstorm started raging outside. Running once again, I sling around corners, dodging the occasional running servant on my way towards the shouting I now hear. I feel a sliver of apprehension at the tone of that roaring voice. Maybe I should go back and wait for him to tell me what's going on? No, I would never be able to go back to sleep and wait to find out what's wrong.

As I enter the throne room, the sight before me makes my bare feet skid to a stop. Sariel is on the ground in a heap, his majestic black-feathered wings slouching half on the ground. His head hangs down and I can't see his face, but the rest of him is covered in soot and blood.

Standing before him, whole body heaving with furious breaths, is Ashtaroth. His eyes are a pure red, reminding me of Belial's that day in the cave, and yet somehow even more unnatural. They're an alien, glowing crimson color. Every tendon in his body is strained and his clenched fists are wreathed in hellfire. He doesn't look at me, eyes fixed on his son's form on the ground. Wanting to see that he's alright, I slowly cross the distance between us. "Sar?" I whisper, sliding down to my knees and placing a hand on his shoulder. "Are you hurt?"

He doesn't move for so long that I contemplate sending whatever meager healing power I have over his body to check for injuries, when he lifts his head just enough that his eyes meet mine. I gasp, the sharp sound loud between two of Ash's growling breaths.

Sariel looks completely devastated. While I can't see any wounds on him, his eyes are dead, his face a rictus of pain. "What happened?" My voice cracks at the anguish emanating from him. Ashtaroth doesn't seem inclined to reign in his fury enough to explain. I look around. "Where's Armaros?" I ask, a heavy stone of dread sinking into my stomach. I don't think I want to know the answer to my question.

I don't have a choice, however, as Sariel replies, his voice as dead as his expression. "Gone."

"H-how?" I sputter in disbelief. What could have killed a fallen angel up in the mortal lands?

"The humans." His voice is ragged, like he broke it screaming. "They knew we were watching them and set a trap. They tortured a child so his screams would draw us out to a barn." He drags a hand down his face, smearing the soot on both, then tugs at the collar of his armor, like it's suffocating him. "They had... some kind of an accelerant. Liquid," he continues, every word sounding like it took immeasurable amounts of effort. "He charged forward to the kid. I was keeping watch. They were both doused and instantly engulfed in flames." His teeth are clenched now and in the lull of his speech, I can hear that Ash went wholly quiet. A glance up confirms that he doesn't seem to be breathing at all, that demonic red gaze fixed on Sariel's face.

"I tried to help," Sariel sobs out, and shows us the undersides of his palms. There are burns from the tips of his fingers to his exposed wrists. For them to not have healed instantly must mean he was burned to the bone. My gorge rises. "The kid... I couldn't do anything. But Arma, he would've healed." When I look back at his face, I see there's now a clean track through the smeared soot. A single tear. "I pulled him out." He looks at his hands again. The agony he must have felt. "His insides were completely burned. Like it was hellfire. But no demon." He looks up at Ashtaroth, who is as still as a statue carved by Michelangelo. "By the time I managed to get the fire out, his melted internal organs were oozing out of charred fissures." The scent clinging to Sariel adds to the mental image his description provided, and I turn away just in time to empty my dinner onto the mosaic floor.

"Belias!" Ashtaroth roars over the sound of my retching, the ground echoing it with a tremor. Darkness swirls on Sariel's other side, like black smoke being whipped into shape by razor-sharp winds. Out of the darkness steps a warrior. He's dressed in black plated armor that somehow manages to look frightening on a soul-deep level, without having any macabre adornments. Something about the sharp lines and decorative grates makes me think of a furnace in a medieval crematorium.

"My Liege." The demon bows deeply to Ashtaroth, not even looking at me or Sariel on the ground. Judging by the power output I can feel from him, he's a demon lord, likely a general. Ashtaroth's next words confirm my speculation.

"Take a detachment Above to the dwellings of the humans Sariel and Armaros observed. Slaughter them all. Kill any human that sees you. Do not leave a trace of your presence behind for Heaven to find." His voice grows colder with every word.

The warrior bows again. "It will be done." He confirms that he understands the order and doesn't ask for the reason behind it.

"They have something like hellfire," Sariel croaks. The demon nods after a beat, then disappears into an implosion of that black smoke.

I clear my throat of the viscous remains of my stomach's contents and speak up softly. "If we kill them all, we can't question them about Asmodeus and Simone, or this fire."

Ash still hasn't looked at me once. "Go to the bedroom," he finally says, voice low and contained.

"I'm not saying don't kill them, but maybe wait to see who could be useful?" I'm trying to keep my voice as steady as I can.

Ashtaroth finally turns towards me. His eyes, still laser-red, pin me to the spot and my lungs seize. He's never looked at me like that; with such hatred. "Leave!" he roars at me. I flinch and can't help the burning I feel behind my eyes, in my flushing cheeks. I place a hand on Sariel's shoulder and give him one last comforting squeeze. After standing up on shaking legs, I hold my head high as I turn to leave. No doubt he can feel the hurt he caused, but I'll be damned if I react.

I walk back to the quarters I've been living in these last weeks, unable to stop thinking of that image Sariel painted. Of the friendly fallen angel burned beyond recognition. I grew close with both Fallen since coming here, and I'm mourning him, so I can't imagine how it must be for Sariel and Ashtaroth, who spent hundreds of years with him.

This time I don't encounter anyone: not a servant, or Kevin and Naamah, or little Puck. I wonder if the demons felt the fortress tremble enough times to not go prying when it does.

After cleaning myself in the bathroom, I pace the sitting area for a couple of hours, then lie down on a sofa when I can't keep myself upright anymore. I can't go to his bed – I may be able to empathize with the pain he's feeling, but it doesn't take the hurt of his shouted dismissal away.

The sky lightens infinitesimally as my eyes close and I fall into a fitful sleep.

LIANA VALERIAN

CHAPTER 40 – ASHTAROTH

"Father?"

Sariel's wary voice barely registers on the periphery of my awareness as scene after scene flits in my mind, as if I were watching one of the silent late nineteenth-century films Sariel and Armaros used to bring Below.

Armaros…

Cutscene: a millennium ago, the first time I saw the fallen angel. My son had instantly taken a liking to the handsome male who exuded a boyish charm. The two immediately became inseparable, one rarely found without the other.

Cutscene: Sariel and Armaros made a wager as to who can seduce a greater number of sex demons in a fortnight. Leaving lovesick demons unable to perform for Lupercalia in their wake, Lamia, the mother of all succubi and incubi, decreed their punishment should entail imprisonment in her bedchambers for a moon. Neither sought out a partner for decades after being released from captivity.

Cutscene: the boys decided Samhain should be celebrated as my birthday and threw a masked ball, where they attached Batman masks onto the most grotesque demons serving under me.

Cutscene: Armaros vowed to protect Lana with his life once it became obvious she was important to me.

"Father, Aim is here."

I lift my head and seek out my master of intelligence. My army commanders loiter near the edges of the room, and my son stands beside my throne, bracing an arm on the backrest to balance on weak legs. I stand and clear the seat.

"Sit."

Sariel flinches at the gravelly sound of my voice. "Father, no –"

"SIT!"

My voice fills the throne room, shaking the chandeliers until candles pelt the gathered, none daring to move.

As Sariel limps towards the seat I vacated, I approach Aim.

"Report."

Aim begins speaking without preamble. "The humans acted on Lord Belial's orders."

My soldiers begin voicing their outrage and demands for revenge until it sounds like we are encased in a hornet's nest.

"Leave." I dismiss them. Those not wearing a helmet show their shocked reluctance to do so, but no more than two seconds pass until the three of us are alone.

"How?" Sariel asks from the dais.

"His agents acted for years, possibly decades. We found barrels of what appeared to be the archdemon's own modified hellfire. Belias and I took it upon ourselves to dispose of them personally."

"What does this mean?"

I grind my jaw and face my son. "It means the rift was never in Asmodai's domain. Belial took advantage of his disappearance, likely even precipitated it." I see the dawning realization in Sariel's eyes. "This was an attack against me. The schemer knew I would send someone of high rank in my court."

Did he know it would affect me so? I cannot recall the last time I felt this much rage. It took Armaros' demise to show me I had been forming attachments even before Lana entered my world.

At the thought of her, I clench my fists by my sides. "Lana must leave this place. Our domains are about to become staging grounds for a war the likes Hell has not seen in an eternity."

Sariel hesitates for a moment before voicing his thoughts. "Are you sure, Ash?"

Clenching my teeth to the point where it surprises me they do not shatter, I nod sharply.

Aim's calm voice interrupts my fantasies of the many ways I would rip that overgrown rat apart for the damage he has caused. "It must ostensibly appear as if she left you of her own free will. If you overtly send her away for her own safety, you will be painting a large target on your weakness."

Sariel leans forward and bites his fist in thought, paying no heed to the various substances covering his skin. "How are we going to do that?"

I meet Aim's gaze. "Return to the mortal realm. Find and eliminate as many of the humans Belial influenced as you can over the course of a single night. It will not take long for the Council to take notice and send for the girl."

Sariel appears unconvinced. "She may resist, Father, she loves you."

My voice has never sounded as bitter as it does now. "You cannot love a soulless monster who massacred dozens of what you consider to be your kind."

LIANA VALERIAN

CHAPTER 41 – LANA

I don't know how long I've slept when I wake up with a headache and stiff neck. My bladder is full and my stomach's empty, so it may have been several hours.

Once I freshen up in the bathroom, I realize what the familiar sensations nibbling at the edges of my consciousness are. The Fallen – my Fallen, my mentors. They're here.

In a sense of déjà vu, I find myself running towards the throne room again. Raised voices greet me, just like they did yesterday, only now there are several voices trying to talk over each other, and they're all familiar to me.

I don't slow down as I run straight towards the blonde and blue-eyed fallen angel in drab gray robes and hug him, my arms wrapping around his waist.

"Child," Daniel says and he sounds so much like a worried parent. "Are you alright?" he asks when I look up into the familiar kind eyes.

I nod and step back, realizing we're at the center of everyone's attention. "I'm fine," I reply, and turn towards Maalik. "I'm not gonna hug you, have to mind your blood pressure, old man."

But Maalik doesn't smile at my joke. Looking around, I can see Kevin, with Naamah's hand on his shoulder, as if she's holding him back. Ramel is positioned behind Maalik, arms crossed, a scowl on his face. Sariel is standing near the throne, beautiful face still ravaged by grief, but he at least cleaned himself since I saw him last.

And of course, on that throne sits Ashtaroth. He's looking at me with an expression so indifferent, I would have rather seen the anger from yesterday. "Why are you all here?" I ask, not looking away from the archdemon, but addressing my mentors.

I'm willing his expression to change when Daniel clears his throat. "We are here on behalf of the Council. Regarding the murder of humans at the Great Duke's command."

I sigh at Ash, even though he's looking right through me. It was all too hasty, and now there's trouble with Heaven.

Maalik doesn't miss my reaction or lack thereof. "You knew?" he asks cautiously and I nod at him solemnly.

"They tortured and killed a child. And a friend." My voice is harsh but not defensive. "I'm not going to mourn them. I just wish I could have questioned them first." I'm tempted to throw the archdemon still sitting quietly a glare, but it's painful to keep looking at him. His acting like I don't exist is painful enough, but he's also doing it in front of my friends. Like any tenderness between us was just a dirty secret.

"Hmm." Maalik steps closer to me, his dark skin gilded by the many candles in the throne room. "And do you also know that once Belias was done, Aim was sent to kill every single person related to that family? One hundred and eighteen humans."

I feel the blood drain from my face. I slowly turn towards the throne, my head spinning. Ashtaroth seems to almost be waiting for my outrage, anticipating it. "Why?" I ask softly.

He's still for a moment, then smiles in a way I haven't seen since our first encounter. "If someone in your family were to be ripped apart by a demon, would you not kill any of its kind you came across?" He speaks in a mocking tone that somehow manages to still be icy cold.

I shake my head in disbelief. "It's not the same! These were innocent people, they did nothing to you!"

That dreadful smile is still on his face as he crosses an ankle over a knee. He's sprawled on the throne like nothing of consequence is happening. "Could the same not be said for most demons? Would you be equally affronted if I killed a hundred of my own kind?"

My mouth falls open and it takes me a second to form my reply in the face of his ridiculous question. The Fallen are silently observing our volley. Even Kevin and Naamah are standing completely still, their eyes wide open. "You're comparing demons, some that spawn with an ingrained instinct to rip into any living creature they come across, to people? Humans aren't born good or evil, they have souls."

His eyes flash, but then he smirks and I have a feeling he manipulated this conversation to go exactly as he wants it to. "Can one not love without having a soul? Angels do not have souls. Father does not have one. Even the Watcher whose apron strings you cling to is soulless."

I flush at the insult and take a step back. Sariel is frowning at his father with what looks like disappointment. "That's not what I meant," I snap. "What is this conversation really about, Ashtaroth?"

Any hint of animation wipes from his face. "Nothing. There is nothing for it to be about."

I can feel myself trembling at the implication of his words. *Nothing.* Daniel steps closer and nods at Maalik who smoothly breaks the silence in the room. "As I was saying before you joined us, Lana." There's a steadying quality in those golden snake eyes that I really appreciate right now. "The Council has decreed that any Purgatory warrior held here by the Great Duke is to be released."

My eyes instinctively snap towards the archdemon who shrugs leisurely, his smile not reaching his calm amber eyes. "They were always free to leave at any time."

I clench my jaw. Bastard. Either he's putting on one hell of a performance or I'm the most gullible person in both Hell and on Earth. I look away from him before my mask slips. Catching Sariel's eyes, I nod at him in farewell, then turn on my heel, not waiting for the others.

My breaths increase in volume, the air sawing in and out through my clenched throat. I want to scream and rip at the flesh of my chest until I can pull my lungs out and stop feeling like I'm drowning. I pick up the pace, but Maalik reaches me, his long legs eating up the distance. "Do you need anything from here?" he asks.

"No," I reply, my voice as dead as Sariel's was last night. "There is nothing."

CHAPTER 42 – LANA

Rolling over to my other side, I pull the covers over my head. Two days ago, we walked until late into the night, across all of Ashtaroth's territory, before crossing the fire river into the lands I've patrolled hundreds of times. Everything hurts now and I'm somehow more exhausted than when I returned from Asmodeus' ziggurat fortress, which now feels like years ago.

I settled into living with demons with alarming ease and now feel displaced in my own room. There's no breakfast waiting for me to share with Puck. No water left by an archdemon to ensure I'm hydrated after our nightly activities. Growling, I throw my damp pillow onto the floor. I'm not usually a crier. I tend to run or fight away any anguish I feel, and I haven't cried since those first weeks here, but my exhaustion has left me unable to get out of bed for anything other than a stumble into the bathroom.

A familiar weight lands on my ass, and it takes me a second to realize that it's not meant to be there. "Puck?" My voice sounds like I deepthroated a cheese grater. "What are you doing here?"

Chirping and squeaking, Puck answers my question in great detail. I just don't understand any of it. He clambers over me until he's so close to my face that I go cross-eyed trying to focus on his baby bat features.

The door bursts open, bouncing off the stone wall and two muscular figures try to enter at the same time.

"Why is there a demon in your room, Lana?" Corson asks incredulously, while Maalik looks like he's trying to hold back laughter.

"He's mine!" I hiss and tug Puck closer, hugging him like a teddy bear, as his wings bat against my arms and muffled chirps vibrate through my body. Oops. I slacken my hold a bit so he can breathe.

"Of course he is," Maalik drawls. I have a feeling he would have rolled his eyes if he didn't find it beneath him. He grabs the handle and, shooing Corson out, starts closing the door. When it's just his bald head poking in, he gives me an evil smile. "You have until morning to finish moping. I'll be dragging you onto the training grounds in your pajamas if you don't show up dressed and ready after breakfast."

With that, he shuts the door and I groan pathetically. "I should never have gotten that beer with Mike," I tell Puck. "I should have changed my last name and moved to Zanzibar." Puck chirps solemnly.

I look into the huge black eyes which are focused on me unwaveringly. "Did you leave, sweetie? Or did he kick you out?"

Of course, Puck can't answer me. Instead, he burrows under the covers and settles down for a nap.

**

The next morning, after breakfast with Daniel, Puck and I head out to the training fields outside of the fortress. Daniel accepted Puck easily enough, but it wasn't him I was worried about.

We're followed by curious glances and, yes, some hostile ones too. The way they glare at Puck like he's the fox in the henhouse makes their feelings clear. I disappear for over a month into an archdemon's stronghold and come home with a baby imp. Nick's old friends look especially miffed. I just smile stiffly at everyone and try to steer Puck away from objects that aren't nailed to the ground or wall.

Outside, I see Jess, Ethan, and Liam waiting for me, standing by Maalik's side as Kev is stretching on the ground. He hasn't noticed me yet, but Jess is practically vibrating with excitement. I reach them and pull her into my arms. A couple of seconds later, I feel more sets of arms around both of us. "Group hug," I mumble into Jess' citrus-smelling hair.

"Alright," Maalik interrupts our reunion. "Let the girl stretch before I wipe the floor with her." When I extract myself from the many limbs around me, I can see the relieved look in his eyes. Guess he didn't expect me to show up so easily.

"Oh, it's on," I tell him, then turn to Jess. "Hold my baby," I tell her, pointing towards an oddly subdued Puck. He's peering up at us clutching the tomato Daniel gave him at breakfast, before promising to request some of the cherry variety for him.

Ethan's choking pulls my gaze away from the imp. "R-really?" he sputters. I eye him with confusion until it hits me.

"No, you dumbass! He's mine and a baby, but not my baby. Do I look like an imp to you?" I growl at him.

"Well, I don't know, Lan." Ethan raises his hands defensively. "You've been gone a while, doing who knows what with who knows whom."

"I know who she was doing what with," Liam's sly voice interjects and I gasp.

"Liam! *Et tu, Brute?*" I place my palm on my chest in a show of betrayal.

"It was too easy," he says semi-apologetically.

I shake my head and begin stretching out my stiff muscles. It's only been a few days since I last trained, but Armaros' death and Ashtaroth's dismissal took a toll on my stamina.

Everyone including Puck takes a seat while I unsheathe my spare shortswords. They don't feel as nice as the ones that were made especially for me, but I shoo that thought away. I don't want to think about all the things that will never feel as good anymore.

Warming up my wrists, I ask Maalik what his weapon of choice will be today. He ponders for a moment, then summons a greatsword using the ether. I press my lips together to hold my thoughts in. Cracking my neck, I fall into the familiar stance.

Not giving Maalik a chance to consider my moves, I dart forward and test his reactions with a few quick jabs. Trying to push me into the defensive, he executes an overhead swing, which I easily sidestep. He's not half as fast as the opponent I trained with most these last weeks.

I arch a brow at him in a challenge. He grins and sweeps his weapon, cutting the air between us with a whoosh and I barely jump back fast enough. Guess the challenge was accepted. When he advances again, I duck and slash at his exposed torso, sword hitting leather. The only thing that kept it from penetrating the cured hide was the thin shield of ether Maalik called up in the last second. Emerging behind him, I aim a kick to his back, but he spins around and grabs my foot.

"You've been training," he says, releasing my foot with a slight push that has me stumbling to catch myself before I hit the ground. Asshole.

"Yup," I confirm. When I see the fight is over, I sheathe my swords, then tuck stray strands of hair behind my ears. Free to turn around, I can see that more than just my team has been watching the clash, conversations and exercises stopped. Great. I'm the main attraction again.

"Against a greatsword," Maalik continues. "Wielded by an archdemon?"

"Mhm." I hum and tighten my ponytail, not knowing what to do with my hands.

His brow furrows and he steps close enough that only I can hear his next words. "Why did he let you go without a fight?"

I try to swallow the lump that seems to have taken up permanent residence in my throat. "I know as much as you do, Maalik."

"Mmm," he muses quietly, then raises his voice back to its usual booming quality. "Looks like Lana will be teaching you today, everyone!"

"Oh, no you didn't!" I hiss through my teeth.

The evil grin on Maalik's face fades as fast as chalk being wiped off a board. "Belial is here."

"What?" I look around, not seeing anything at first. But then a cloaked figure emerges as if from a fog, the oppressive aura reaching us at the same time.

Belial strides straight towards Maalik. Thankfully, he's wearing his cloak, hood pulled up, so no screams of terror ring out across the field. Just some whimpers. I grit my teeth through the feeling of wrongness that surrounds him like a cloud of cheap perfume.

"Why are you in Purgatory, Lord Belial?" Maalik sounds on edge, much more so than he was in Ashtaroth's stronghold. And he's in his own territory now.

Belial tuts. "Granted, I do not remember much of your time at my court, Fallen, but I daresay you were more respectful then, seeing as you're still alive now."

Maalik doesn't back down from the thinly veiled threat. "I was given responsibility over these soldiers by the Council. An archdemon showing up in the middle of Abaddon is alarming."

Belial lazily gestures at me. It's impossible to know where he's looking with the way his head is tilted down under the hood. "What if another archdemon came? But, oh, I have heard he's done with you now, girl. I had forgotten."

I refuse to show any kind of reaction to his drawled words, even though it feels like someone shoved a dagger down my throat. Forgot, my ass. Did he just come here to gloat?

"Why are you here?" Maalik repeats his question in a clear voice.

"Since the girl enjoys demonic company so much," he says, nodding towards the side where Puck is half hiding behind Liam's thick legs, his boots nearly as tall as the imp. I have to fight the urge to pick the bat baby up like a football and run inside with him. "I thought I would extend the option to live at my court," Belial finishes.

While his offer stupefies me, the sensible part of my brain must still be online and I blurt *nothankyou* without even thinking to form the words.

Belial doesn't even twitch, surely expecting my denial. "Are you sure?" His voice is singsong and so sweet it turns my stomach. "Your grandfather was the commander of my legions for centuries."

I shiver and wonder what kind of person he must have been to lead this slimebag's armies. My mother was adopted as a baby, barely a few weeks old, and never knew who her biological parents were or what they were like. I guess if they were a demon and angel, they didn't exactly have social security numbers to find them by anyway.

"It's such a shame he's not around to do so anymore," Belial continues, interrupting my thoughts. Something about the way he said it brings my hackles up.

"Well, apparently I'd be a shit general anyway. Something about reaction versus long-term planning. So, best of luck elsewhere." My voice is breezy despite the anger I'm starting to feel.

Belial pulls his hood down, exposing that monstrous face. I hear yelps and gasps from the soldiers but show no reaction myself. He grins widely, exposing those shark's teeth. "It is not for underlings to plan wars, girl." A patronizing voice if I ever heard one. Movement at the corners of my vision makes me turn my head in time to see the rest of our mentors and any other Fallen in residence joining us on the field.

But Belial merely looks at Maalik before issuing a command: "Give her to me, boy."

I cough in shock at both the outrageous demand and equally absurd moniker; Maalik is as far from a boy as anyone could get, with that towering build, his dark, menacing looks, and a deep, rumbly voice. He schools his reaction better and speaks calmly. "She is not mine to give. And she already politely declined your invitation."

Daniel steps up to my side, back ramrod straight, and an anger in his eyes that I'm not used to seeing.

Displeasure is now obvious on the archdemon's face and he takes in the two Fallen who taught me the most, baring his horrifying teeth. "It would be better for you and every pathetic creature living in this ruin if you bowed now." A shiver of fear skitters down my spine. Is he going to attack Purgatory? The rest of the Fallen step up into a line of defiance between the archdemon and our home.

I have a second to feel guilty and contemplate just going with him to spare my friends a battle with an archdemon – he could wipe us Elioud off the map in a minute. Maybe the Fallen could get some strikes in, but they're no match for that power either.

Belial, however, doesn't attempt to grab me and he doesn't start decimating our numbers. No, he instead disappears and then materializes at the edge of our realm's border to Hell. Soon he's no longer a lone figure as dozens upon dozens of demons file into rank. He's not going to risk himself, as minuscule as that risk may be, the coward.

My body feels numb as I slowly unsheathe my twin swords again. Somewhere behind me, Ramel is yelling at the soldiers who expected to train today, not fight an archdemon and his army. "Arm yourselves!"

LIANA VALERIAN

CHAPTER 43 – LANA

Ichor sprays over my face as Ethan dislodges an axe out of a hellhound's thick neck. In any other circumstances, one of us would be making a joke about it. But we're overrun by demons and no one is taking a break to speak beyond short commands and warnings.

I plunge both of my swords under a beefy demon's chin. The flesh-eating monster gurgles, black blood spilling out from between its sharp teeth. It scrabbles for my swords with its talons, slicing them off on the angelic steel. I grimace and pull the swords apart, eviscerating it.

Before I can catch a breath, unearthly screeching sounds behind me. I whip around to see a female-looking demon floating towards me. I've encountered a lot of different types of demons before. Or at least seen drawings of them. But this is a sight that will give me nightmares for weeks – if I survive this. The head of a beautiful woman floating seven feet above the ground, her entrails trailing under it, dragging over the dirt. While she rushes toward me, I can only discern lungs and lots of intestines. I don't need to see more, though. Before it reaches me, she's cleaved in half by Maalik's greatsword, the severed organs landing on the sandy soil with a plop. My stomach roils and I turn around before I throw up my breakfast, trusting my mentor to finish the demon off.

Liam is fighting several imps, so I run to him to help. While imps are easily dispatched and a type of demon we encounter often, they could overwhelm you with numbers to bring you to the ground. I gather moisture from the air – a rainbow of spilled blood and ichor – and force it into the lungs of four of them. As they start digging into their chests with their clawed hands, I relieve them of their heads, one by one.

"Thanks," Liam pants, bent over and bracing his hands on his thighs.

"Where's Puck?" I ask, taking the moment of reprieve to observe my surroundings. Elioud and Fallen battle minor demons all around me. I don't see many of ours on the ground, but the gore is starting to pile up. This is how I pictured Hell before I even knew it was a real place. Belial is still standing on the edge of the realm, as if he's waiting for something. Why not just kill us and be done with it?

"That your imp? He disappeared as soon as the demons showed up." Having caught his breath, my teammate jogs over to Jessica and the fanged demon she's fighting. A few feet behind them, Daniel is healing Darla, who has a nasty gash running down her thigh, too close to the femoral artery for my liking.

I contemplate helping Daniel heal her, when I'm brought to the ground, a heavy weight settling on my back. Saliva drips onto my neck and I instinctively send a punch of ether-called air to knock back my assailant. I turn to my back just as the hellhound recovers and thrust my swords out so that it impales itself on them on the next charge. Claws dig into my torso and I push my swords in deeper, twisting until the creature stops moving.

"Fuck," I grunt, using another blast of air to roll the demon off me. Dragging myself off the ground, I hiss as scratches that burn like hellfire make themselves known on every side of my body. I send only enough platelets to the wounds that I'm not actively bleeding – I can feel myself draining, my grasp over the ether becoming loose.

I don't know how much time passes as I fight back-to-back with my teammates, dispatching some stronger demons I've only ever read about, and a lot of lesser ones I encountered frequently. All I know is that we never had to fight for so long and we're all exhausted. Our swings are becoming slower, our strikes sloppier, and I don't think I could even heal an inflamed hangnail right now.

The Fallen are all fighting a massive behemoth with a body the size of an elephant. The monstrosity sports a horned head like a bull's and giant bat-like wings. Shaking my head, I head towards a cluster of fire imps harassing an exhausted soldier from Corson's team. I tag Peter out to take a breather and start dodging the hurled lava rocks the imps are creating using whatever demonic powers they possess, while slicing off smoldering limbs. I can hardly feel my body anymore and my lagging speed allows the last one to get a hit in just before I use my crossed swords to shear off its head.

"Motherfuck!" I yell at no one in particular and summon just enough moisture to douse the fire kindling on the sleeve of my leathers. The dirty liquid reveals a hole the size of a tennis ball, blistered red skin underneath.

"It would be a shame if you died on this battlefield."

The smarmy voice raises every hair on my body – and even that is painful in my state. I turn around to face the archdemon that, perhaps, waited until I was at the edge of the battle, separated from my allies.

"Still better than enduring whatever you want me for, I'm sure," I reply coolly. I didn't expect to make it through this alive, not with an archdemon gunning for me.

"And what if I looked like this?" Belial waves a hand towards his face, which changes between one blink and the next. He now looks like every romantic interpretation of an angel; clear cornflower blue eyes and short, wildly curly golden hair. His sensual pink lips are curled into a beatific smile and his cheeks glow with a healthy blush.

I laugh weakly – seems like even Hell has incels – and the smile instantly transforms into a snarl of rage. *Touchy, touchy.*

Belial swings out his arm and a blast of ether lifts me off my legs, hurling me through the air. I land on the ground, spinning, the impact knocking my breath away, my bones grinding against each other. Sand scrapes over my face and neck, burning viciously, invading my open mouth.

Once I stop tumbling, I groan and try to lift myself up from my sprawl, spitting sand. Before I manage more than a couple of inches, a kick lands in my side, flipping me to my back. I both felt and heard a rib snap.

I can't help the whimper that comes out of my mouth. Sensing a looming presence, I open the eyes I had shut tightly with pain. Belial stands above me, upper body moving with his furious heaving breaths.

"You are owed to me, you pathetic bag of blood." He's all but seething, hands clenched by his sides, like he wants to pummel me further into the ground.

"What are you talking about?" I wheeze, blinking to clear the spots from my vision.

"I did not give your grandfather leave to breed an angel and leave Hell!" He's growling with fury, as if it hasn't been decades since my mother was conceived. "Then when my soldiers tracked them down to bring him back, that meddling do-gooder got in their way and they slaughtered her for it."

My eyes are tearing up, both from the implications of his story – the tragic end my grandparents met because of this monster's pride – and the pain in my side.

"So he killed twenty-five of my best soldiers before they brought him down. He would not let himself be captured."

"And you killed him, too," I finish the story.

"They killed themselves!" he snarls, eyes starting to glow orange. His voice is now far from that artificial sweetness. "They managed to hide their spawn, suppress its powers so it would go through life unnoticed."

My mother. That explains her complete ordinariness in spite of being a full-blooded Nephalem. I clench my teeth and wrap an arm around my aching torso.

"But you," he continues, that evil grin bearing his sharp teeth, horns emerging from the top of his brow. "I felt you. It took me decades to convince the council to enlist Elioud children. Years of herding the souls together until enough gained a form. But the council moves slowly..."

He could do that? It explains the clusters of manifestations in those caves... right before Ash and I ran into the archdemon now giving his villain speech.

"Why?" I ask, genuinely curious. "I'm just a quarter Neohalem. Rare, yes, but not that much stronger than my teammates. At least not in a tangible way." My senses are sharper than any of the other soldiers and that's about all I can claim as an upper hand.

"You will take the punishments of your grandfather. But you love spreading your legs for archdemons, don't you?" His lip curls in disgust. "He must have mounted you a thousand times for his smell to reek out of your every pore."

Belial holds his arm out to the side and a spear taller than the average man appears in his hand. The shaft is made out of the same demonic black metal as the swords Ash had made for me. The tip is fashioned out of a ruby, fire burning at its core.

"I think I'll start penetrating your body right now." He throws his head back and laughs at his own lousy pun.

I can feel my lower lip trembling in fear. I know it's better that I die today than to let this asshole torture me for years. But I don't want to die. I want to eat more quiet breakfasts with Daniel, laugh with Kevin on our patrols. Get drunk with Jessica and watch Ethan try to make Liam lose his temper. I want to find Simone. Make Maalik smile at my stupid jokes. Cuddle with Puck in the mornings.

But most of all I want Ash. I want to see that smug smile when he manages to get me flustered. The focused way he looks at me when I eat, like he's writing a research paper on all my favorite foods. I want to touch every inch of the taut smooth skin that covers his warrior's body. Want to lie in his possessive hold every night as I fall asleep.

A big part of me hoped that he'd find me on my next patrol, once his anger settled and whatever punishment he got for having all those humans killed was over. That he didn't mean for me to leave. Lying here, I don't even care about those deaths anymore. He'll never be the hero. But I clearly have the capacity to fall in love with a villain.

Belial presses the tip of his spear under my clavicle. His face is now that of the aberration he truly is. "Make sure to scream loudly," he chirps, the high-pitched voice so at odds with his horrific form.

He pushes the spear down, the sharp tip cutting through my leathers like a knife through butter. The next second it's embedded into my skin. I clench my teeth, pressing my tongue to the roof of my mouth. As the ruby scratches against bone, I can't hold my pain in any longer.

My mouth opens in a shattering scream, every ounce of agony reflected in it. He twists and blackness starts overtaking my vision. The spear is pulled out just as a deafening boom of thunder vibrates through my body. I force my half-closed eyes to open and sob at the sky behind Belial.

Enormous crimson wings catch the air like mighty sails as Ashtaroth unsheathes his weapon and roars, "Belial!" Thunder emphasizes the fury in each syllable.

The psychotic demon giggles. "Oh, finally," he says, and throws a wave of Hellfire at my archdemon. Ash doesn't even try to dodge it as it hits him, and he explodes in a supernova of red light.

That's when darkness engulfs me and I lose consciousness.

CHAPTER 44 – ASHTAROTH

I pull myself out of my true form and back into a physical body. I want to be able to hold a weapon, to crush Belial's skull with my hands, to rip him apart, limb by limb.

Reforming right in front of him, I grab his head and twist it before pulling it off. I want to feel his blood covering my body like an unholy baptism, but I am not the only one who cannot be destroyed.

Belial's ethereal form, orange tendrils trailing behind it, leaps back before reforming once again into the flesh and bone demonic visage. The Fallen and Elioud, having mostly dispatched the rest of Belial's troops with Sariel's help, move closer but maintain a healthy distance. The ones that are not injured or tending to the injured, at least. I look at Lana, bleeding and unconscious just a few feet behind the archdemon who hurt her.

"You wanted to fight, betrayer," I taunt in our original language, making his nostrils flare. I beckon him closer with one hand and unsheathe the blade that reformed with my body with the other. I need to exhaust his power enough that he flees.

Belial laughs fanatically. "What took you so long? She's all but dead now."

I growl under my breath. I miscalculated terribly and my little lamb paid the consequences. A trembling Puck reached us with his warning, and, pausing only long enough to send Aim to the Dark Prince, I grabbed hold of Sariel and materialized us in Abaddon. Perhaps too late. Perhaps the last time we spoke was when I was pushing her away, making her believe she meant nothing to me.

I grit my teeth. Lifting my sword, I give Belial no choice but to engage me or flee. He charges, spear extended, and our weapons meet with a thunderous clash. I disengage and swing horizontally, aiming to cleave him in half. But he moves too fast, deflecting my strike and making it go wide. Belial then thrusts the spear forward, my own torso the target, and I easily sidestep. Using the opening, I swing my sword overhead. As he dodges, I summon ether-born wind to send arrow-fast particles of sand at his face. Shrieking, Belial releases the bounds of his mortal form again, reforming only when my winds die down. When he summons hellfire to throw at me again, I don't expend energy on reforming. Instead, I use the ether to disappear from the fire's path and emerge behind him, kicking him in the back – a move similar to the one I practiced with Lana just days ago.

Stumbling, Belial jumps through the ether himself, moving to a safe distance. A few mocking words from my side are enough to have him charge me again recklessly. We dance for long minutes. But Belial always enjoyed politics more than fighting, leaving the leading of his armies to Lana's grandfather. I expect him to make a mistake soon.

After executing a feint, I surprise him enough to cleave off one of his arms at the elbow. I take in his roar of fury with a grin. Still smiling, I swing my sword in an undercut, his shriveled balls the next part I want removed. He jumps back fast enough that only the tip of my sword makes contact, cutting a long slash into his robes.

I click my tongue in annoyance and grip my weapon in both hands, ready to end this game. At that moment the ground begins shaking beneath us and I take several steps back on instinct. A hole opens underneath where we were standing, just as I'm clear of it, and Belial disappears with a wail of terror, straight into the Burning Pits.

Aim must have reached Sataniel and, briefly, I wonder if my assassin still lives. But I'm already turning away from the glowing depthless pit and the moaning wails rising from it. I run towards Lana and drop to my knees, dumping my sword to the side like it is worthless kitsch.

I gently tip up her head with my palms on her jaw. Her face is bloodless and the wound under her shoulder is to blame. "Watcher!" I yell for her mentor, the one whose healing abilities she lauded during the weeks we spent nearly every hour together. Turning around, I see that the blonde angel is tending to Lana's mortal companion, Kevin. The boy is bleeding from a long gash across his sternum.

Sariel kneels next to them and ushers the other Fallen towards us. My son may have given into lust centuries ago, but he still has some light in him, enough to have maintained the ability to heal flesh wounds. All I could do would be to cauterize the wound with fire, hurting her more in the process.

Daniel reaches us and leans over Lana, immediately placing an already glowing hand over the hole in her chest. It has been eons since I saw that kind of power at work – most of the once-angels residing in Abaddon or Hell cannot connect to Heaven's light this easily.

This angel did not fall lusting for the carnal pleasures of mortal flesh. No, he was merely made more feeling than most angels, the empathy creating a capacity to love, that capacity leaving a void where there should have been only light. But angels are not given that choice; the free will to act on needs they should not have. It is why most of us joined Sataniel in that first schism. None of us had the same needs... but we should not have had needs at all. We should have been obedient guardians and messengers, existing for no other purpose than to serve the Most High. Perhaps Father had come to regret some decisions if he had left so much of his love in this being despite the angel's imperfections.

Although he had used a lot of his energy fighting demons and doing battle mending, the Watcher makes quick work of the perilous injury and Lana stirs just as it closes, leaving behind a mark of a healing wound that would have taken a normal mortal several weeks to achieve on their own.

Beautiful eyes the color of a newborn leaf open slowly, unfocused at first, dazed and dreamy. The eyes of an angel, inherited from her grandmother, but most often burning with the indomitable will of her general grandfather. She leans her cheek into the palm I placed to support her head.

"I thought he killed you," she whispers, her voice faint and raw from screaming. I growl at the sound of it, wishing I could have had more time with Belial, to torture him for centuries for causing her pain. But what I can do to him is nothing compared to what he is hopefully enduring at the hands of the Dark Prince.

"I believe I told you, sweetness, that there is only one being who could rid you of me." I stroke the apple of her cheek with my thumb and her eyes close again.

"She requires rest," Daniel explains. "The healing wounds are leaching her strength. She has none of it left." The Watcher's tone is calm and unafraid, though haggard from depletion.

I sheathe my discarded sword, then gently gather Lana in my arms before rising. "You have my gratitude," I murmur to the solemn healer, then turn until I am facing the rest of the Fallen. "We are leaving." I sweep my gaze over her mentors and colleagues, daring anyone to defy my proclamation. They all look ragged and not many dare to even meet my eye. I find Maalik standing close, arms crossed, and address him next. "Sariel will stay here to assist."

My son is supporting the Cambion boy, who perhaps finally got past his aversion to the male's touch. "Yes, Father," he acknowledges my command, his black eyes still full of painful loss.

I unfurl my wings, making several soldiers gasp in awe. While pride would have normally given me a burst of energy, I am fully preoccupied with the precious being in my arms and ignore them. I propel myself into the air, Lana sleeping through the force of it.

Turning towards the Phlegethon, I do my best to hold a steady elevation so as to not jostle her, and use the ether to shield her from the wind.

LIANA VALERIAN

CHAPTER 45 – LANA

I feel like an elephant is sitting on my chest. Groaning, I try to lift my hand to it, but it's trapped. With a gasp born of adrenaline, I open my eyes and see a familiar red velvet canopy. To my right I see a familiar bedroom, and to the left a face that has, in the last couple of months, become as familiar as my own.

"Am I dead?" I croak, enjoying the way Ash's lips curl into a small smile. But, *ugh*, I think I have morning breath from Hell, my current location having nothing to do with it.

"You certainly slept like the dead for three days. If your face and hair feel sticky, it is because I attempted to feed you broth and honey water and not because I orgasmed over them while you were unconscious." He grins wickedly, but I see there's cautious relief in his eyes. "Or did I?"

I groan and pull my hand out from underneath the cocoon of covers, so I can slap my palm over my face. "Your jokes are the worst, Ash, please stop embarrassing yourself."

His low chuckle stirs that fire in my belly, one he kindled and ignited and poured fuel over until it rose like a phoenix from the flames – my own creature but also his. A dinner bell ringing for my own personal feast.

But, first… "I need to use the bathroom, STAT. Or should I say *statim*, Father Time?"

My teasing doesn't ruffle him and he just smirks. "If you want to make that point, you will have to go further back than Latin, sweetness."

Before I can deliver a riposte, he's no longer lying next to me and I feel his arms sliding underneath my body, scooping me up from the bed. "Hey!" I protest halfheartedly. I fucking know I can't walk right now. To be completely honest, I may pee all over myself if I tried. He's not paying any attention to my objection anyway, and soon we're standing in the middle of the bathroom.

"Shoo." I wave him off. "Privacy. It's a thing."

He looks heavenward (and isn't that ironic), and mutters as he turns towards the exit. "I should let you piss yourself." Just before the door closes behind him he adds, "There will be no privacy from me in the future."

As soon as the door is between us, I rush to the toilet, glad I'm in a nightgown and not my leathers. But while I thought this would be easy, I find myself in a bit of a panic instead. It's like my bladder forgot how to relieve itself. As I try to let go, I just grow more frustrated. Remembering an old trick from my more voracious drinking days, I bite my arm, and, finally, a too-slow trickle starts.

Once my bladder is blessedly empty, I sigh in relief and take care of the next pressing tasks: brushing my teeth and bathing. He must have cleaned me as well as tried to feed me because I'm not covered in dirt and dust. Still, I don't feel clean until I scrub every inch of my skin with his pine-scented soap.

When I come out, Ash is sitting on the edge of the bed, a placid expression on his face. I plop down next to him, though he only jostles slightly, since he basically weighs as much as a wall of bricks.

"So..." I give him the cue to start explaining. He turns towards me, his lips set in a very fake looking Mona Lisa smile.

"I suspected Belial was behind the ambush on Sariel and Armaros," he begins without preamble, as if he had the words on the tip of his tongue all these days and now he's finally saying them out loud to me. "The information about your Simone's family came from him, after all." He bares his teeth and I feel that the disgust isn't only aimed at the other archdemon, but himself as well. I want to tell him Armaros' death wasn't his fault, but there's still a wall between us, one born from his behavior the day following that loss.

"I sent Aim to investigate," he continues, leaning forward to rest his arms on his thighs, the rings on his fingers glimmering in the candlelight as he interlaces them. "What little he could find out, confirmed that Belial had been communicating with the cretins and arming them, and thus his culpability." He sighs and slowly angles his head to make eye contact with me. "Because he was the culprit there, I assumed he was also the culprit in whatever situation Asmodai found himself in. I deduced that I was his target, for whatever reason."

His jaw clenches and, when he doesn't immediately continue, I finish the thought he began forming. "But it was me, not you."

He stands up and begins prowling around the room, his clenched fists belying his slow and steady steps. "Yes," he says at length. "It was you, and I sent you away from here, thinking you are safer at Purgatory, far from my side and any possible fallout."

I shake my head. "He's a master manipulator. He had been planning this for decades. He's the reason we're here, the Elioud. While Hell *is* overcrowded, he somehow manipulated the damned souls to congregate and merge into manifestations, making it seem even more dire to the Council. He whispered in their ear for years, tugging strings left and right, making everything unfold just so."

I stand up as well and plant myself in his path, making him stop walking. "While he couldn't have predicted that I'd end up here with you, he probably had dozens of different contingency plans. You couldn't have known."

He growls in frustration and places his hands on my shoulders, squeezing lightly. "I have known him for millennia. I should have thought beyond the obvious. I let my grief and anger spur me into hasty decisions."

"He said he wanted me because he felt my grandfather owed him his service and abandoned him to be with my grandmother instead," I share, and Ash inclines his head. "Why the argument, though?" I ask the archdemon before me. "The one you had with me. If you wanted me gone, telling me to fuck off would have been just as effective."

Ash closes his eyes and, letting go of my shoulders, starts pacing again. I cross my arms and wait for him to speak, unwilling to help him explain, even though I have my own suspicions about his behavior that day.

"I am indestructible," he begins. "And for countless millennia, I did not feel nuanced emotion, not as the majority of humanity does, not even while living in Elysium." He stops pacing in front of a window and pauses as if to gather the right words to explain this to someone who has only lived a few decades and spent all of those decades feeling a certain way. "We were not created to love anything but our Creator, nor to feel pride in anything but our work for Him. But feelings can be shaped, influenced, and corrupted — they evolve." He turns back towards me and something in his expression keeps me rooted in my place across the room. "For the next several millennia, I only felt a perversion of the little emotion we were given. Lust in control, pride of self, greed for power."

He starts walking back to me slowly, and for some reason, I have to fight the urge to step back. "I desired to control you and your pleasure from the moment I saw you attempting to outsmart that golem." I flush and swallow audibly, my throat suddenly dry. "But I also knew quickly that your presence... centers me. Eons of memories reside in my head; it is not a quiet place. I haven't felt at peace for so long." His last words are said so quietly, they're nearly a whisper. He tilts his head and gives me a wry smile that never fails to cause pirouetting butterflies in my stomach. I mentally douse them with bug spray. Not the time to jump his bones. "I wonder if that is why Asmodai took his Elioud," he finishes his thought, and I bristle.

"It doesn't justify keeping her by force for years," I growl, feeling indignant on behalf of the girl I barely just got to know before she disappeared, presumed to be dead.

He winks unapologetically. "Perhaps not for you. But..." His expression sobers and he drags his hand through his messy hair. It almost looks like he's been taking better care of me than himself these days. "Caring about the safety of someone who is not as indestructible as us is maddening. When Armaros was killed, it was obvious that I had formed such attachments in the last centuries. You, pet, are more vulnerable than demons and fallen angels."

My eyebrows pop up and I take a step back, shaking my head. "So, what, you were being a dick because you wanted the attachment gone?"

"No," he refutes instantly, stepping closer and placing a hand behind my neck, preventing me from putting more distance between us. "I was a *dick*." His brows lift at the insult. "Because, while I was trying to push you away for your safety, I also wanted you to fight it, to say you do not believe our lives to be less important or us incapable of caring because we lack a soul. To say you wished to stay, despite the measures I took after Armaros' death."

I sneer in his face. "You know I don't think only humans are capable of love. Or that having a soul makes them – us – more worthy. And if you thought I was going to beg you to let me stay after you acted like a total bastard, you really don't know me."

Instead of getting mad, he lifts his other hand to cup my cheek, smiling at me triumphantly. "You acted exactly the way I expected you to; walked out of my throne room with your head held high." He rubs the apple of my cheek with his thumb and peers down at me. "I apologize for causing you pain by handling my own so poorly," he adds softly.

I blink up at him. What am I supposed to say to that? I'm more used to people lashing out than admitting their faults in a conversation. I settle for evasion and joking – it's enough that one of us is being mature. "Are you going to send me home every time you have this demon menstrual syndrome?"

He gives me a knowing look, then rests his forehead on mine. "This is your home."

My eyes start burning. That's practically a declaration of love for him and I can't handle it. The air between us is charged with emotion and his eyes soften at spotting the tears in mine. "I'm copyrighting that, you know." The words rush out of me. "DMS."

Ashtaroth pulls me in and shuts me up with a deep kiss. My toes curl and I wrap my arms around his middle, pulling him closer and sucking on his tongue like I'm checking if he does have a soul inside his body after all.

He chuckles and walks backward towards the bed, pulling me with him. Once he reaches it, he lies down on his back with me atop of him. "This is a new and interesting position," I murmur while nibbling on his gorgeous lips.

He lets his arms fall back over his head in a gesture of surrender. "Have at me." He smiles. "I am at your mercy, little lamb." The way he says it makes me think he doesn't just mean for this round of bedsports.

"Hmm," I muse, pursing my lips in contemplation. "I better start from the top then."

His eyes glow with banked embers as I lean down to gently kiss first one eyelid, then the other. I can feel his thick black lashes tickling my lips and I smile before moving down to his own, where I lick once over the seam before using both of mine to suck on his upper lip. Moving over the indent under his cheekbone to his ear, I trail soft kisses over his skin, before taking his earlobe between my teeth so I can softly bite the flesh.

His soft groan makes me release a gust of air into this ear and he twitches underneath me. Moaning, I move lower and lick a path over his neck before sucking on the protrusion of his Adam's apple at the center of it. His hiss spurs me on and I sit up so I can tear open his shirt. I trail my nails from his clavicle down toward his sides, then lean over so I can take one firm nipple into my mouth, sucking on it

278

before biting down. I can feel the pulse in the hardness pushing against me between my legs, so I repeat the process on the other side.

Scooting lower, I slowly unbuckle and open his pants as his eyes track every movement of my hands. He's breathing through his mouth in short panting breaths. He looks so hot right now, eager and impatient, that I lose what's left of my own patience, pulling his cock out and squeezing it until his head tilts back.

"Fuck," he breathes, hands lowering towards mine, until he stops himself and clenches his fists. "It's been too fucking long since I fucked you, sweetness." His voice sounds strangled from the effort it takes to hold himself back from taking over and setting the pace he wants.

"Well, you're going to wait a little bit longer, because I want that pretty dick in my mouth first," I tease, rubbing the dick in question from root to tip in slow, firm strokes.

He hisses as his cock pulses in my hand, a bead of precum gathering at the slit, tempting me to lick it off. "Damn, I need to have you on top more often. I underestimated how sinful your mouth is."

He finally wraps one of his hands around mine, making me squeeze his cock impossibly harder. I moan, both at the sight of our hands making his cockhead turn purple and at the ragged groan that comes out of his mouth.

"Let go," I whisper, then scooch lower again until I can take the glistening tip into my mouth, moaning around it as my tongue collects the salty liquid.

His fingers thread into my hair and his hips lift from the bed, making me take him in as far as the angle allows. Pumping into me a couple of times as my tongue laves as much as it can reach, he lowers back to the bed, making me release him. "Sit on my cock, pet," he pants, hands clenching the strands of my hair caught in them, making it hurt just the right amount.

I click my tongue and sit up, making him release his grip. "Bossing me around isn't letting me do what I want." He bares his teeth, the look in his eyes feral. Had he looked at me like that the first time we were in bed, I would have fainted from fright. Now it just makes me wetter, knowing he's that desperate for me. "Do you need my tight little pussy, Master?" I tease, squeezing his slick cock again.

I can feel his growl reverberate through his entire body. "I suggest you don't play with fire unless you wish to be burned."

My vision blurs as he flips us over before I can laugh. I find myself underneath my archdemon, his eyes now burning with orange flames. I gasp at the ravenous look in his eyes, and need takes control of my body, making me wrap my legs around his waist and tilting my pelvis up in demand.

He wastes no more time, placing one hand under my ass to raise my hips up further, and the other between our bodies, lining up our sexes. Still holding my gaze captive, he sheathes himself inside me with two quick thrusts. My eyes close from the uncomfortable pinch of the intrusion and his freed hand grabs hold of my chin, wordlessly commanding me to stop hiding my eyes. Once I do, he slides the hand underneath my neck, now holding both my upper and lower body steady to receive his thrusts.

When his dick is fully coated in my arousal, I tighten around him, making his breath catch. "More," I whisper, and he shakes his head. "Ash, harder," I beg, the slow and smooth slide of him not enough to satisfy the need these days of distance ignited.

"No," he murmurs, placing a soft kiss on my lips. "You will come like this." While he sounds as imperious as always, there's also a soft quality to his voice. He shifts the angle of our bodies slightly until his pelvis massages my clit with every small movement he makes.

"I can't," I practically whine, yearning for his rough touches and filthy words, the ones that never fail to push me over the edge.

Ash just rests his forehead against mine and breathes in, like a man enjoying the scent of the finest whiskey. "You will," he commands quietly, and I can feel tingles starting to build up across every inch of my skin, can smell ozone mixed in with his usual smell of warmed sugar and frosted forest.

My muscles soften and my jaw unclenches, the release of tension letting me know how strong its presence was. The sensation of his bared chest rubbing against mine, only the thin material of my nightgown between us, sends sparks from my nipples straight to my clit.

This time I tighten around his cock involuntarily and he grunts softly. "That's it," he praises, his slow and deep strokes unrelenting. "Feel me, feel us." A crack of thunder sounds outside, making me flinch with surprise.

The head of his cock is rubbing against the upper wall of my sex from the inside, and an image of how it looked in our hands, swollen and wet with his arousal, pops up in my head unbidden. I moan, the sound coming from somewhere deep inside of me.

His breathing speeds up, quick puffs of air hitting my kiss-dampened lips. "Ash," I gasp, my hands moving from around his neck to gently cradle his face.

"Mmm," he growls, the sound vibrating in his chest like a deep purr.

I feel like I'm floating on a soft cloud and the growing heat between my legs is the only thing keeping me grounded in reality. Each slide of his body over mine winds me up tighter, until I'm worried that release will feel like a rubber band snapping in my hands. I'm afraid of the sting, but unwilling to stop testing the give of the elastic.

I'm now moaning in time with his thrusts, feeling both vulnerable in my pleasure and somehow unashamed of it. Before I fully realize it's happening, my body has had enough of the teasing buildup and I scream.

"Ash!" His name on my lips sounds almost like a plea for help, and he gathers me even closer to him, tucking his head into my neck and taking the tight cords of it into his mouth.

He grunts savagely into my flesh and I can feel his cock pulsing inside me. Wetness from both of us slides out from me, dripping into the crack of my ass.

As if he feels it as well, he reaches between us again, gathers it on his fingers, and, circling the rim with the wetness once, then again, pushes one of them into my other opening. I'm so relaxed I don't even tense up, but the sensation makes me gasp, my pussy continuing to flutter over his spent cock.

Once my heartbeat starts slowing down, I sigh contentedly into Ash's hair. "You didn't let me have control for very long," I complain halfheartedly.

"Hmm," he muses, lifting his head enough to look at me. Smiling at the state I must be in, he kisses me and then whispers in my ear. "Perhaps in a few decades."

CHAPTER 46 – LANA

I'm having a very late breakfast with Puck – scrambled eggs and cherry tomatoes for me, just cherry tomatoes for him – when Ashtaroth walks in, resplendent in full-plated armor, his crown and heavy cloak on as well.

"Mmm, are you my dessert?" I give him my best lecherous look. Puck gags. I flick the tip of the wing closest to me and he squawks in outrage.

Since Ash still hasn't said anything, I turn back to him, and it's then I notice the serious expression on his face. "We are to meet with Sataniel," he says, voice tight.

I gape at him, mouth open, and sputter, "What? Where?"

"The Pits," he replies darkly, hands fisting.

"Uh, can I RSVP a 'no' to that?" Puck looks to me as I speak, then back to Ash, waiting for his reply like he's watching a tennis match. There are tomato seeds smeared all over his furry chin.

Ash gives me a slightly disdainful look. "If I infer the meaning of your words correctly, the answer is 'no'."

I sigh, my stomach fluttering with nerves. I neither want to see The Burning Pits of Hell nor meet its Crown Prince. "Should I dress in my armor, too?"

My archdemon shakes his head, looking as resigned as I've ever seen him. "It would not matter. If he wants to harm you, he will. And then our battle will bring Hell down around our ears."

Goosebumps prick my flesh at his words. "Alright," I sigh, standing up and skirting the table to reach him, leaving Puck to finish his meal and wishing I had kept an empty stomach for this.

"How are we getting there? The whole hole-in-the-ground thing seems wildly unpleasant."

Ash ignores my usual attempts of tension-relieving humor. "There is a seal we can use to open an entrance."

"Oh, I've seen that. It's on the balcony facing the sea, right?" He nods but doesn't comment further.

We're silent until we reach the balcony and the golden seal of his name. Stepping on it and facing me, he opens his arms in invitation and I wrap mine around him.

"Keep your wits about you," he warns and then everything turns orange, heat suffusing the air around us. The floor beneath us disappears and a thunderous whoosh of Ash's wings emerging sound near my ears. I briefly glance at the heated rock around us. Ignoring the fact that we're currently descending into the core of Hell accompanied by the agonized wailing of damned souls, I trust in his hold and reach out a hand to caress the silken crimson feathers at the arch of one wing. It's like fluffy down in places, the texture unexpected and comforting.

I can feel Ash's jaw clench against my cheek. "Explore those later, lamb."

"Can you feel that?" I ask, ignoring the suggestion and sliding my palm down the longer feathers within my reach.

"Very much so," he replies, voice tight.

I tilt my head back so I can grin at him. "Does it tickle?"

He gives me a stern look as if to remind me this is not the time and place for teasing. "No."

Before I can quiz him on how exactly it feels, we land softly on the dry rocky ground. It's incredibly warm down here and Ash must be broiling in his armor. He takes my hand in his gloved one, thumb caressing it once, before he pulls me toward an arched opening at the end of the cavernous tunnel we're in.

The air on the other side shimmers with heat and it feels like I'm walking into a giant hair dryer. I keep my thoughts to myself and try to fight the urge to climb Ashtaroth like he's a tree in the Savannah and I'm running from a pack of lions.

The tunnel opens into a cavern with a throne on a tiered dais. Braziers with hellfire roar around it. Ash is moving us in its direction and I flinch when something cracks loudly under my feet. The ground is littered with brittle skeletal remains. At first, I think they are the bones of children, but then I notice the deformations; bones and skulls shaped in a way that makes it clear the small creatures were once demons.

I look at the empty throne and gulp. It's the most grotesque piece of furniture a depraved mind could design. Malformed demonic wings rise behind the backrest, frozen in poses that speak of agony. A petrified snarling hellhound decorates the highest point, its mouth glowing with hellfire from within. Every jagged edge of the throne is covered in thick spiderwebs and primal fear twists my stomach.

It's empty, but Ash still addresses it as if it weren't. "You summoned us?" His voice is deep and he bows his head in deference.

A disembodied voice replies, seemingly coming from everywhere. "Ashtaroth."

A flare of brilliant white light blinds me and the throne is no longer empty. A being sits on it, vaguely shaped like a man, but any features are hidden by tendrils of light, sparkling with the glow of newborn stars. The tendrils undulate and wave in the air, as if swaying to a symphony of heavenly music only they can hear. I feel wetness on my face and instinctively move to wipe it off. My fingers come away covered in blood.

Ash swears and turns me into his arms, tucking my head to his chest. "My Prince, please," he grits out, his hand tightening on my head convulsively.

"Ah," the voice replies, sounding amused. It's somehow both as light as diamond windchimes and as deep as the farthest reaches of undiscovered sea trenches. "I forget how delicate mortals are," the creature chuckles, and the sound tightens everything within me. I really don't want to feel aroused by the Devil.

Ashtaroth's grip eases and he lets me go with a quiet warning. "Do not look directly at him."

Lucifer scoffs, the sound far prettier than it should be. "Are you afraid your mortal will prefer my visage over yours, old friend?"

Ash doesn't bother to reply and in the moment of silence, I slowly turn around. Curiosity is greater than my sense of preservation, and I glance at the Prince of Hell. I glimpse starlit silvery hair and eyes like diamonds set in a stunningly perfect face, skin glowing from within like a radiant opal. The need to drop to my knees and crawl to him in worship is overwhelming, and only Ash's grip on my hand gives me the strength to look at the foot of the dais instead. It's no wonder he was named after the brightest evening star.

"Shall I share with your master all the lovely ways you wish to worship me, Nephalem? You are quite imaginative and original, I must say." He laughs and his light tone doesn't match his hurtful words.

Ash squeezes my hand once, slowly, as if to say 'It's okay', and it spurs me to speak. "I believe he would rather hear about the reason we are here. Prince of Darkness," I add an honorific in an afterthought – maybe he'll turn me into ashes for addressing him directly.

"Mortals these days are a delight," he murmurs instead of dismembering me. "Belial paid me a visit some time ago, Ashtaroth," he says louder. "He had an interesting tale about Asmodai taking an Elioud girl by force. Normally I would not concern myself with such trivial matters, but Heaven was in a tizzy, so I had to step in."

"Why bother?" I ask, and Ash squeezes my hand again, this time in warning. "Aren't you the definition of 'I do what I want'?"

Satan chuckles again, the sound like the most glorious morning birdsong. "I am not in the habit of suffering nuisances if I gain nothing from it."

"Is Asmodai here then?" Ashtaroth asks, clearly worried for the archdemon he claimed as a little brother.

"Oh, certainly." In my peripheral vision, I see the king of demons wave a hand lazily. Suddenly, fire roars to life in front of us, widening into a circle. Within the hazy heat, a picture forms, like a hologram at an amusement park. Two cages are suspended in the air. One holds a male with short brown hair and a stunningly chiseled face. He grips the bars anxiously, his gaze unmoving from the person in the other cage.

There's Simone, looking no different than when I saw her last. Ground-shaking relief washes over me at seeing her unharmed. Except... "Is she –"

"–very much with child? Yes," Lucifer drawls. "I offered them a choice, something to appease Heaven. She refused. But seeing as she is, well, permanently tied to Lilith's progeny, I cannot let them simply leave."

"What choice?" Ash growls, eyes fixed on the caged archdemon.

"Ah, I am glad you asked, friend." Lucifer waves the fiery viewing portal off and Asmodeus and Simone disappear. "Heaven would doubtless no longer concern themselves with these unusual, messy bonds were they beyond a doubt consensual."

"I'm with Ash by my own free will," I hasten to confirm. "My mentors at Purgatory know it and I have no problem telling the entire Council myself." Ash squeezes my hand again; the only way he can communicate his gratitude.

"Not good enough," Sataniel sings, and I can hear his evil grin before I take a quick glance at his face and see it.

"What would be good enough?" Ashtaroth grits out, the tension in his voice drawing my eyes away from the most beautiful fallen angel in existence.

"You are to make a bargain with your mortal, tying you together for eternity." The literal Devil joins his hands at the fingertips, the ultimate villain mastermind.

"A soul bargain?" Ash asks, incredulous.

"Indeed," the Devil intones and I quickly look away when his gaze shifts to me. "The sacrifice must be equal, of course. Shall we say, a third of your power, *Ash?*"

"I accept," Ash replies instantly, ignoring the mockery Lucifer made of his nickname.

The latter laughs in delight. "Marvelous. Even Asmodai balked at the suggestion. And I daresay he has more at stake."

I blink up at Ash, tugging on his hand until he meets my gaze, seeming somewhat reluctant to do so. "A soul bargain? As in 'selling my soul to the Devil'?"

"Yes," he confirms softly.

I bite my lip. "So, if I get killed, my soul wouldn't end up in Purgatory, it would be here?" The wailing screams of tortured souls rise up in chorus, as if showing me what that fate would entail.

Ash uses two gloved fingers to tilt my head up by my chin. His eyes hold mine, looking both regretful and conflicted. "With a third of my power, it is unlikely you would ever be killed. Living in the Underworld already halted the aging process."

I chew on my lip, trying to picture my life if I said no. Living at Purgatory, patrolling Hell. Lucifer would make sure I never see Ashtaroth again. It's only been a couple of months, but I can no longer fit who I am into the confines of who I was before him. And he would give up a part of the most important thing he has to keep me by his side – his unfathomable strength.

"Would you be much more vulnerable without a third of your power? If another fight with an archdemon happens?"

He moves closer to me, no longer caring that we have an audience. "It would make no difference. The only creature that would have an easier time disposing of me is the one salivating over the position he put us in now."

"Careful, Ashtaroth," the Devil says softly. "You are the one who created this issue the moment you decided you wanted to play with an Elioud."

"The decision must be yours." Ashtaroth ignores Lucifer's murmured warning and places a gentle kiss on the tip of my nose.

"Do spare me."

I ignore Satan as tears roll down my cheeks and a sob catches in my throat. I don't think I really have a choice here. I don't want to spend eternity away from Ash, and a part of my soul had always already belonged to Hell. "It's a bargain," I whisper, not trusting my voice. I clear my throat and take a deep breath. "My soul for a third of Ashtaroth's power."

"Wonderful!" Lucifer claps his hands and my legs give out. I collapse in Ash's arms and he grunts just as a wave of intense heat radiates through my body. Once it passes, I right myself and look my demon over, then take stock of myself as well.

"I don't feel any different." My voice is shaky from adrenaline and I cling to Ash like a baby lemur, despite being able to stand on my own feet now. I do feel some new connection between us — maybe the power he shared with me recognizing its home within him.

"Yes, well," Ashtaroth's words stir the hair atop my head as he speaks down at me. "Do not even try to summon hellfire until there are no flammable objects within a league." I can't help the jittery laugh that emerges from me.

"This is very touching, but I am done with you now." Sataniel's voice snaps me out of the intimate bubble of the embrace and I take a step back.

"What about Belial?" I ask Lucifer, my voice getting harder as I remind myself of the duplicitous archdemon. "Ash said he's down here, too?"

"He is." The Devil now sounds angry for the first time and I can hear rocks crumbling from the stone walls in the dark corners of the cavern. "I do not appreciate being made a party to his scheming. He will remain my guest."

I shudder at the implications of the Devil's hospitality. Ashtaroth only nods, then takes my hand and turns toward the tunnel we landed in. "Until next time," he tells the ancient creature sitting on its throne.

"Ashtaroth," Sataniel acknowledges. I feel a shiver skitter down the back of my neck as he says farewell to me, voice full of promise. "Lana."

EPILOGUE – ASHTAROTH

"That was laughably pathetic."

I observe Lana's attempts to control the direction she launches her hellfire, the flames going wide every time.

"Argh, this is impossible!" Her face is red and strands of hair stick to the perspiration on her skin. She stomps her foot and uses the ether to gather a ball of water the size of a train engine. Positioning it over the smoldering shrubs that grow among the rest of the coastal flora of my domain, she releases it to douse the scorched earth.

She has been practicing ever since we made our unholy bargain – the Hell version of marriage vows, and much more permanent. The power exchange was extremely painful for me, but my pet will never know that our pact briefly turned my mortal form's insides into a crisp.

To my extreme delight, her control over the ether increased several hundredfold. She was relieved to see that also applied to her healing. Despite having sold her soul to the Devil and tying herself to an archdemon for eternity, she is still full of light.

It is unfortunate, yet also quite entertaining, that hellfire does not come as naturally to her as most other things. "You will charbroil your precious Puck if you do not learn some control, sweetness."

"Bite your tongue!" She flips me off and I chuckle at her outrage. The little imp became her constant companion. I often have to literally kick him out of our rooms before she lets me fuck her. Thankfully, her reservations only extend to the little furball. Taking her and making her scream my name in front of my court has become my new favorite pastime.

She grudgingly walks up to me, looking defeated. I tip her chin up and kiss her lips. "We will practice until you master it, lamb."

Lana groans. "I'll have to go to Purgatory soon. Liam has been chosen to assist Heaven with some top-secret issue back in the human realm. Apparently, he's partnering up with some stuffy angel for it and he wants me there for the meeting which could be at any time."

Since Lana can now easily travel using the ether, she can assist her team at Abaddon whenever she wants. I do not appreciate her disappearing for hours, but the tasks keep her feeling useful. As if feeding me and preserving my sanity is not useful enough.

"If that prick angel shows you any disrespect, call for me and I will choke him with his own intestines."

She laughs, but I'm not joking. The angel will sense our bond immediately and if he is like all the other sanctimonious pigs from Heaven, he will comment on it, likely upsetting her. I will not abide by it.

"Shall I introduce myself as a Great Duchess of Hell, then?" Her lilting voice is teasing and she pokes me in the chest with a perfect finger.

I grunt in response. "You may introduce yourself as whatever you wish, as long as they know they are all beneath you and treat you accordingly."

Still snickering, she wraps her hands around my neck and peppers my chin with little kisses. "Let's go take a bath, mighty archdemon, I'm all sticky."

"I will make you sticky with something else," I reply, pulling her lower body flush with mine.

She groans, but it's not a sound of passion. "Stop trying to be funny, Ash, you're far too hot for these stupid dad jokes."

I arch a brow. "Who says I'm joking, sweetness?"

With that, I gather the ether around us and send us to our castle, our bedchambers, and our bathtub.

Our home.

***

It will take more than a few months to dispel the millernia-old habit of being in my bed alone. Though the few hours of sleep I require have been eluding me since Lana has been sleeping here, I gather her sleep-soft body closer to mine, bury my nose into her soft auburn hair, and inhale deeply. I will take naps on my throne like a geriatric human before I give this up.

My lamb stirs and burrows closer, as if she's attempting to diminish the distance to the point where she enters my body, not knowing she has been there since the first time I touched her. Her arm stretches across my torso and curls around it until she's clinging to me like a baby koala.

"Love you," she murmurs in her sleep, her defenses down, her pride not standing in the way. The admission shatters something inside me, these jagged pieces of my being swirling in a maelstrom of emotion until the press of her body against mine is the only thing holding me together. I was not made to feel this way.

Logically, I knew how she felt about me – one does not barter their soul merely for spectacular sex. The power she gained from me is a nonfactor, she could not care less about that. What remains is love. Is it possible to be created for someone who is not born for thousands of years yet? Is it possible for creatures without a soul to have a soulmate?

The determination from the decision I made is the only thing strong enough to separate me from her embrace after her unconscious admission. I gently extricate myself from her hold, leaving her sound asleep as I use the ether to soundlessly appear at the balcony seal we used to travel to the Pits not long ago.

If he does not wish my presence, the seal will remain inert. I sense, though, that he is expecting me. As I step onto the seal, a current of power vibrates up my body through my bare feet before I find myself gliding into Sataniel's domain, wings extended.

He is not hiding behind the confines of flesh now that Lana is not here to suffer from the brilliance of his true form.

"Ashtaroth," he greets me, the voice which echoes around and within me managing to hold the slyness I cannot see. In our true form as angels, we let our thoughts and opinions emanate from us unfiltered, hiding nothing. In Hell, deception has become an art form perfected to the point where it has become completely innate.

"I have a request."

As I stop before him, he settles into his mortal form. Still brilliant, still as beautiful as a newborn star, he can now show the grin I heard in his voice. He lounges casually on his decrepit throne and lifts his hands with lazy curiosity.

"Yes?" he asks mildly, the still-present smile indicating he knows exactly why I came.

"Lana's soul –"

"Is nonnegotiable." His grin widens as he interrupts me, depraved enjoyment evident in the narrowing of his eyes.

"I did not come to beg for it."

Sataniel's eyebrow raises a minuscule amount, the only evidence of his surprise. "Oh?"

I inhale bracingly, the action not entirely necessary for my physical form, but born from uncountable years of navigating the world in it. "If Lana's mortal form should perish and her soul comes here, I would have you destroy it."

Both of his eyebrows are now raised in stupefaction, but I continue before he can speak.

"And then I would like you to destroy me."

After a beat, during which his face remained frozen, Sataniel's laughter fills the gloomy cavern, the wailing of tortured souls quieting in its wake, as if afraid to be the next source of his amusement.

"I must admit," he says, shaking his head in bemusement. 'I did not expect that to come out of your mouth." He leans back, still chuckling. "Ah... Regardless." Suddenly, he appears before me, eyes gleaming with a calculating light. "I will not let either of you perish."

Tilting my head, I observe him, trying to glean his intentions, but falling short of plausible answers. "Why?" I finally ask. "Is this not all a part of your plan to conquer Heaven? Binding your most powerful to mortals whose souls are destined for you as the ultimate leverage? Empowering those mortals with the strength of archdemons until a new generation of powerful warriors is born, until you have a superior, utterly devoted army? How does that ensure she stays out of harm's way?"

The Devil brings his face inches from mine, lips spreading into a wicked grin. "Love has not turned you into an imbecile."

By the time I open my mouth to refute his assertion, he is once again sprawled on his throne as if he had never left it. "We are not capable of love."

Sataniel looks down at his hand, where his now clawed fingers are tapping rhythmically against the armrest. He hums thoughtfully. "We learned to covet, to hate, to derive pleasure... why is learning to love so impossible?"

Meeting my eyes once more, he shrugs with dismissal. "You should return to your bride. Congratulations on your upcoming nuptials."

Narrowing my eyes, I shake my head. "I am not –"

"You are," he interrupts me again, igniting an ember of anger within me. "You just haven't thought of it yet."

I exhale with impatience. "Asmodai and the mortal?"

Lana has been asking whether there is anything I can do to help the female, and though I do not expect my question to serve any purpose, I did promise her I am not giving up on freeing my brother and, consequently, Simone.

Sataniel steeples his fingers and rests his chin on them. "Oh, not much longer, I suspect. Children have a way of building bridges between people, do they not?"

I press my lips together to hold my answer in. Asmodai has dozens of children and he forgets their names nearly as often as those of their mothers.

Tilting my chin into a nod, I turn my back to the throne. As I gather the ether to bring me back to my bedroom, I hear the most beautiful sound in existence. Sataniel singing a lullaby.

Born from light in Hell...
...this child of mortal and archdemon...
...all that is known is forgotten...
...the Lightbringer's return to Heaven.
Translation of a fragmented Sumerian cuneiform inscription, c. 3000 BC

Keep reading for a preview of book two in *The Rivers of Hell – The River of Hatred!*

THE RIVER OF HATRED

ITHURIEL

Upon arriving in Purgatory I'm greeted by a hurried murmured conversation. I lift my gaze from the grey stone floor, unchanged since I walked here last, and step towards the four figures who immediately stop talking. Maalik is flanked by two Elioud women, one with long blonde hair tied in a tight high ponytail, the other, taller one, with loose auburn hair.

Behind them, arms crossed and leaning against the wall with one foot bracing on it, leg cocked, is somebody I used to know well before his fall. My eyes widen and my jaw goes slack. I've successfully avoided Sariel all these many centuries, yet here he is, with a smirk on his face which tells me just how much he enjoys the shock I must display at seeing him. His eyes are... completely black. No white or color in them at all. They were once a clear, bright sky blue.

Maalik, likely sensing the tension in the air, clears his throat loudly. "Welcome to Purgatory, Ithuriel. It's been a long time."

Sariel snorts and his voice fills the hallway that is the designated destination for waypoint or portal travel. "Longer since I've seen him, I'm sure. It's almost like he's been avoiding me."

"I have been avoiding you," I answer coolly, though his smile only widens. For several centuries, over a millennium ago, Sariel and I were inseparable, one never to be found without the other. When Sariel began voicing his desires to interact with mankind, I thought it was a phase, merely momentary curiosity.

The emotions his fall wrought within me were powerful and perilous to my standing in Heaven. It took centuries, but I made my peace with it eventually. Or so I thought. Seeing him here now... I'm once more suffused by a feeling of unexpected longing... mixed with betrayal. It hits me like a fist in the gut.

"Ahem." The redhead clears her throat far more delicately than Maalik did. I glance at her, then back towards my once-friend, now casually rubbing his chin. My eyes, however, snap right back to the woman.

"You sold your soul," I accuse. I see now that the woman is a descendant of a Nephalem, a rare child of angels and demons. I had vaguely known the angel Ariel who defected to be with a demon decades ago, but she was destroyed soon after. No child had been made known to us. At least those of us not in the highest tiers of Elysium. My eyes narrow at her. "And you... feel like an archdemon."

She blushes then flutters the fingers of her left hand, palm facing inwards, showing a ring made out of demonic steel, the corrupted brother of angelic steel, and fitted with a large amber stone. Upon closer examination, I can see hellfire burning within it. I recognize the power output in it. "That would be my husband you feel," she says.

"Ashtaroth wed you?" My brows rise. This is unexpected.

Sariel snorts again and inserts himself into the conversation once more, making it impossible to ignore him. "Wedded and bedded, old friend."

"You are not my friend," I interject, but he ignores me and continues.

"Living with them is a nightmare, everything constantly reeks of sex – my dick is perpetually hard," he finishes, winking at me.

I somehow manage to choke on my own inhaled breath. A coughing fit follows and my face turns crimson. This mortal form can be very inconvenient. I compose myself, studiously averting my gaze from that evil smirk. He always enjoyed shocking me, though I have never heard anything even remotely as crude as his words now were.

The Nephalem who sold her soul — a mostly pure and uncorrupted soul – to an archdemon she also wed is an oddity I will ponder on later. "Are you the Nephilim I'm to work with?" I ask the shorter of the women, the leather-clad blonde with what seems to be a curved scimitar sheathed at her hip.

She flushes at my attention, her lashes fluttering with anxious blinks. Perhaps I'm the first angel she has ever seen? Yes, that is likely why I unsettle her.

"T-that's me," she stutters and somehow manages to flush a deeper shade of red. My eyes are drawn to the way her downcast eyes show off her long pale lashes. I expect Sariel to make an inappropriate remark at her bashful behavior. When he doesn't I allow myself to look at him again. A chill skitters down my spine at the intense calculating look he aims at the back of the girl's head. I frown at him and he must sense my attention – his depthless black eyes snap to mine and his face rearranges itself into an unaffected, slightly mocking mien.

"We wanted to send Liam with you, Ithuriel, but he managed to shatter his tibia just yesterday. He'll be out of commission for a few weeks. Jessica is just as skilled, however," Maalik says, making the girl's nervous smile twitch.

"I'll be there to look after them any-who," Sariel chirps enthusiastically.

"What?" I say at the same time as the tall woman with an archdemon's signature does. Jessica's eyes bounce between the four of us.

"Is this why you insisted on coming with me?" The demon's bride says through gritted teeth.

"No," Sariel replies pleasantly. "I was curious who they'd send. Besides, I wanted to fuck with Kevin a bit. Not literally, of course."

He grins at the angry woman, showing off plenty of even white teeth. I don't know what relationship they have, or who this Kevin is, but they seem to be close. Perhaps, they are as close as we once were... I send the thought off with irritation, focusing on present matters.

"We do not require your assistance," I snap at him and instantly regretting any show of emotion as his eyes widen in triumph.

"Consider me Hell's contribution to the mission." His smile slips into a look of fury I don't understand. "Also, I was the one present when those filthy humans under Belial's influence incinerated Armaros. I have the right to join."

I freeze. "Armaros is gone?" The fallen angel was another member of the younger generation of angels. He fell with the Watchers, centuries after Sariel. I did not even know they found each other here in the Underworld, let alone that he was the Fallen burned by those humans under Belial's orders. They never shared the angel's name.

Sariel's face twists with disgust. "You never even bothered to find out if it was a friend that died?"

I'm unsure if he meant the possibility of it being him or if we are still talking about Armaros. Regardless, I'm the one to flush this time. I don't answer him, having no words that wouldn't potentially inflame the situation further. Maalik, Jessica and the now confused redhead just observe us quietly.

Sariel shakes his head at my silence. "I'll be right back," he tells Maalik. To his female friend he says, "Don't get into trouble, Lana, or Ash will eviscerate me for leaving you alone."

She hisses at him. "I'm stronger than you are now, dickcheese!" But Sariel already disappeared before the crude words left her lips. I guess he's strong enough to use the ether for travel.

ACKNOWLEDGEMENTS

December 2024

Thank you, dear reader, for joining me on this hellish ride! You've made it this far, so I hope you enjoyed reading Ash and Lana's story as much as I loved writing it.♥

Next, I'd like to thank my *Dream Team* for always being my cheerleaders and helpers — Réka, Amy, Shaunie, Ivy, Ruth, Yaren, Sharon, Adelina, Necia, and Emily — as well as my Street Team *Minions* and my *Hellion* ARC readers. ♡

Thank you, Shaunie, for making my lovely covers, and Amy, for creating my marvelous maps. ♥

MK "Poppy" Stephenson helped edit The River of Fire along with S.L., and Mari checked the French. ♡

A heartfelt thanks to everyone who created beautiful TROF fan art; Shaunie, Julie, Annabelle, Kerry, Dana. ♥

Marianne, thank you for running my gorgeous website! ♡

Finally, a shoutout to my friends, family, and my fellow authors from Ivy's one-wo/man-show group chat! ♥

ABOUT THE AUTHOR

Liana Valerian

Liana Valerian is a passionate gamer, obsessed bookworm, enthusiastic sci-fi and fantasy nerd, and self-proclaimed crazy cat lady. She crafts dark fantasy romance novels filled with humor, spice, and mythology, blending gothic and romantic elements in shadowy realms where darkness reigns.

Liana's debut novel, The River of Fire, the first in The Rivers of Hell series, is a steamy romance set in the Underworld, where angels, demons, and forbidden love collide.

You can follow her adventures and connect with her on social media @liana.valerian.

Title: The River of Fire

Subtitle: The Rivers of Hell 1

Author: Liana Valerian

978-961-07-2422-3

Alternate cover edition

Self-published by Liana Valerian, Brežice, 2024

Print on Demand

Cover art and design by Shaunie Anne Schoonejans

Illustrations by Dana Kodermac and Shaunie Anne Schoonejans

Editing by MK Stephenson